NANNY TO THE MAFIA

SOPHIA RAZ

First edition March 2024

Cover design - Getcovers
Beta readers – Ruth Ellen and Eleanor T
Editors – Amy Scott and Emma Williams from Scott Editorial
Proofreader –Nicole Segro

ISBN 978-9-4649-4911-7 (paperback)
ISBN 978-9-4649-4910-0 (ebook)

www.sophiaraz.com

CONTENTS

Nanny to the Mafia
Tropes and trigger warnings

To my readers:

Nanny to the Mafia is a light-dark Mafia romance. It contains content and situations that could be triggering for some readers. This book also has explicit sexual content and is intended for readers 18+

Featuring the following tropes:

Forced marriage, age gap, possessive/jealous alpha male, forced proximity, sexual tension and steamy encounters, secret or double lives, enemies to lovers, forbidden romance, fake relationship, and "touch her and die."

Trigger warnings:

Parental death (off the page), explicit sex scenes, drug use (not by MC), gambling (not by MC), child abandonment (not by MC), murder & death (off the page), age gap, dominance, pregnancy, stalking, guns, blood, car accident (off the page), thoughts about STD, morally grey, consensual non consent, dubious consent.

Disclaimer:

This book is written in British English.

PROLOGUE

FLORINA – A RANDOM GYPSY GIRL

One moment, it was hot and humid, and the next, it wasn't. The dark and heavy clouds came out of nowhere and showed their faces to Palermo. Like the devil had mopped hell and poured out the filthy water, the clouds let go of their burden, drowning the garden in a torrent of rain.

Not that Florina had any complaints. If it wasn't for the rain, Peppe would have made her suck him off in the backyard. He didn't seem to fancy getting his dick wet, though, so he dragged her inside. At least now she could finally see the house, and it didn't disappoint. What a fancy mansion it was.

Even as her feet pitter-pattered through the house, following Peppe along the long hallway, her eyes gobbled up the wealth of its interior. The ritzy paintings and glittering chandeliers pulled at the itch in her hands. Peppe drew to a halt in front of a big brown door, making her smack into him. He pulled the door open and pushed her in. "No touch!"

She stumbled onto the marble floors, but her eyes caught on the double-height ceiling. The room was massive. It stood tall like a big wizard and looked down at her with wisdom. At least that's what all the shelves filled with books exuded.

"What this?" she asked.

"Library," Peppe huffed. "Wait there." She followed his finger to where he pointed to the dark loft up the stairs. He pushed her further into the room and pulled the door closed behind him with a soft thud.

Florina eyed the room. Even though he had put her in the dullest room, she could see that these people were wallowing in money.

Ignoring anyone's warning was second nature to her, but she didn't want to piss Peppe off and miss the opportunity of a meal. Like the obedient child she had never been, she reluctantly went up the spiral metal stairs. She moved around in the balcony of the room they called a library, filled again with shelf after shelf of books. The sofa in front of the shelves was the only other addition. She grabbed one book after another with her dirty, wet hands. Rich people and their books.

There was nothing to keep her amused here. She leaned over the balcony to glance down at the massive area surrounded by more shelves and more books. Unlike the small hidden alcove she was in, the ground floor was grand and massive for a library. A library. You must be really rich to have an entire hall for your books. This room alone was ten times bigger than her family home in Romania, she was sure.

There was a nice-looking sofa in front of the window. Some dark-coloured liquid in a fancy bottle sat on the table next to it. It tempted her to go down and have a sip.

Bet it would taste good. Rich people always have good stuff.

She flicked her glance towards the door. What was keeping Peppe? He never took long to get her something yummy to fill her belly. She liked this deal she had with him. Food for sucking him off. He was easy too. She showed him her boobs, and a few minutes of his dick in her mouth, and he came as hard as a waterfall. Extra protein for her, like her mama would say. She had, of course, neglected to inform him she was providing the same services to Alonzo next door in exchange for lodging. Men and their dicks.

Her stomach grumbled. Yesterday, the Capizzi sons had been home, and Peppe didn't dare meet her. He was terrified of the two brothers. He pretended not to be, but what he didn't know was while she roamed the back door looking for food and some extra knick-knacks to grab, she often heard the maids jabber in the kitchen. She was poor but not an idiot. She understood Italian contrary to what these people assumed of her. Idiots who didn't know they shared a Latin language. Oh yes, Peppe was terrified of the men. Then again, who wouldn't be when the Capizzi's were a part of The Mafia family? Another thing he assumed she didn't know. The man really thought with his dick. Anyone in Palermo and beyond knew that the old man Capizzi was the *consigliere* for the family.

He was even more of an idiot to think she was content with their arrangement. This was just a stepping stone in her plan. All she needed to do was capture the attention of one of the Capizzi brothers, and she was set for life.

Everyone knew how the old man Capizzi had fallen into the trap of his now wife. Fuck a man, get pregnant, and deal. If it worked for that woman, who was a two-faced bitch as good as they get, it would definitely work for her. She was known for her beauty, and seducing a man with her ample boobs and willing pussy was simple work for her.

Finally.

The door opened to reveal... fuck.

She slunk down into the dark alcove and ducked her head out of sight. The glint of a wheelchair had caught her eye. What was the old man Capizzi doing here? It was past time for him to be sealed off in his coffin. It was already a shocker that his conniving wife hadn't killed him off. She listened to the wheels rolling in, followed by... footsteps. She frowned.

"*Grazie, figlio mio.*" The old man's voice hinted at death nearby.

"*Un momento, Papà.*"

Oh, whose sexy voice was that?

Florina inched her face up and peaked down in between the iron rods. *This must be the eldest son.* She had already seen the younger one, and he was a fine specimen to fuck. She would gladly push him off the ledge for this one.

This one was hotter. She watched him walk towards the door to close it. All muscle and strength like a rich man. Not like the bodybuilder bodies of security men who she had gotten a taste of. This one looked like he got out of bed looking like one of those sculptured gods from their garden. Money and body and she was a goner, but this one's hair was so ... rich...unusual. He had very thick hair going in slight waves. Dark, dark brown mixed with a bit of silver grey, like what you would find in a nickel. She wanted to run her hands through his hair. She looked down at her hands. Well, after she washed them first. Rich men didn't do dirty.

He closed the door and walked over to join his father near the sofa.

Cristo.

If his back was yummy, his front was delicious. Like a fine piece of meat on a barbeque wrapped in thick gravy. She wanted a piece of him. The man had a beard. Not the wild ones she was used to, but one of those that rich people had. Faintly there, nicely trimmed and taken care of, barely there type of thing. Civilised. Yes, that was it. One of those civilised and fancy-looking beards the models on the bus stand advertising had.

When he sat down on the sofa, with his legs spread wide, he was almost directly below her. She snuck slightly back into the shadows reluctantly. Even the way he moved spoke of power and money as he poured himself some of that liquid and drank from it. Florina watched him swallow, his Adam's apple bobbing up and down.

Her hunger for food evaporated into the air. She was horny now, and all she wanted was right below her. She smacked her lips quietly.

"It's good to have a few minutes of peace," Old Man Capizzi spoke.

The younger Capizzi let out a laugh, although there was no humour ringing out of it. "I don't know how you stand her."

"Mistakes. You're lucky if you can learn and move forward. But some are there every day to remind you ... of a moment ... of weakness." Damn. The old man looked like he might die right now, right before her eyes. He might have been a hottie once to father such sons, but now he was all shallow skin and bones sticking out.

Hot Capizzi leaned over and grabbed the old man's hands. "Let me take care of this, Papà."

Her eyes stuck on his wristwatch. He didn't wear the normal sparkling stuff. It had a brown leather strap and a black face. It looked expensive.

Concentrate, Florina. If you go about this right, you can nick way more than a wristwatch.

"No. This is my life, and I will take my mistakes to the grave. You and Angelo need to learn from it. Besides, I didn't come here to discuss your mother."

Ha! Florina could see even from this distance that the son didn't agree with the father. There was a tick going mad at his jaw, but he kept silent, even though his eyes were wild and ready to commit murder. A cold thrill ran up her body. She suddenly understood why Peppe was petrified of him.

"What did you want to discuss, Papà?"

The old man didn't seem to notice his son's violent look. "Carlo has called in a favour."

Shit.

Florina shifted on her toes. She hoped he was not talking about Carlo Di Matteo, the boss of The Mafia.

Please don't. Please don't.

"What favour is the don calling in from a dying man?"

Shit.

She was dead. If they found her now, they would kill her. She clenched her hands tightly on her rumbling stomach.

"His cousin in Boston is having some problems. They are trying to work together with the Russian mob, but it's not working out. They need someone—"

"I don't like this direction, Papà."

"*Ascoltami, figlio mio.*" Old Man Capizzi wheeled his chair away. "Boston PD is down their throats. He is looking to turn his organisation legal. They want to embed more honour in their codes. Carlo has spoken to him about our family. Your grandfather's work. Mine. Your ambitions."

"But I—"

"Let me speak. I am trying to spare my breath."

Florina sniggered from her vantage point of view. The man was old but still good at manipulating his son. The younger Capizzi fell instantly silent and obedient. It was obvious the son would do what the father asked.

"This is what you have wanted. More diplomacy. Fewer weapons. This is what your grandfather and I have worked for. You will continue that. You have made a name here. Your diplomacy is highly valued. In Boston, apparently, they want to work with the other mobs, and they need someone who will be good at negotiating deals, including with us here. If Carlo is asking this of you, it means he trusts you and your capacity."

The old man paused to catch his breath before continuing. "I have already discussed this with him. You are to still manage your private banking business. In fact, this is what they want. More legal businesses. You will be perfect for their organisation."

No. No. If he moves to America, who am I to seduce?

The old man wheeled his chair closer to his son and took his hand in his. His hands were more a packet of bones than flesh. "This will be good for you. Go to Boston. When you are done, you can come back home. Take Angelo with you. A break from all this drama from your mother. Create some distance."

She could go with them to America. She would just have to hurry with her plans ....

"Papà—" He put his fancy drink down.

"I have little time left. It is what it is. Make no mistake *figlio mio*. I want you to take care of your mother. But never at the expense of your own happiness. Don't follow in my footsteps. Don't allow culture to dictate who you should marry. I don't care about what our culture dictates. I want you to find love."

"Love is for fucking idiots."

Old Capizzi laughed. "One day, you are going to find a woman who's going to love that foul mouth of yours. I've seen it. Love is—"

Florina's belly let out a loud rumble. She watched in horror as two pairs of eyes shot instantly in her direction.

Fuck.

Hot Capizzi shot out of the sofa and was upon her in an instant, hurling her to her feet by yanking on her arm.

She was going to die. This close, his dark brown eyes were almost black, with a never-ending depth to them. Death was upon her.

"Who the fuck are you?" The roar rolling out of him sent her eardrums trilling.

The vibration of it left a daze in its wake. Noise reduced. Movements slowed. Fear vanished. With death nearing, she found peace. Gone was her hunger. She noticed the small things cloaking them. His grip on her arm, like a metal vice. His jaw sharp, enough to kill with it. His smell, a mixture of something woody and something else. It reminded her of autumn. She just couldn't pinpoint what that other smell was. Wood and...

Her muteness worked on his patience. He shook her hard like a ragged doll. Her teeth clattered.

"Who is she?" Old Capizzi's voice floated up.

"Like fuck if I know." He turned around and dragged her down the stairs, behind him, like a cloth the maids used to mop the floor and threw her in front of his father.

"She one of the maids?"

Old Capizzi rolled closer to look at her. "No." A frown foamed in between his brows. "She's not from here. You speak Italian?"

A different smell snuck into her nostrils and pulled

her back to reality. The stink shrouding Old Capizzi was one that reeked of hospitals.

"Your name, girl?" Old Capizzi asked in Romanian.

She fought off the face of recognition. These people weren't idiots. If they knew, she would be dead.

"Is she dumb? What are you doing here?" Hot Capizzi's voice was no longer hot. It sounded mad and violent, with a rage building up that she didn't want to face.

Her stomach rumbled again loudly, drawing attention to her basic needs.

The door opened behind them. Peppe stood there, mouth open, holding a bowl of food in his trembling hands.

Hot Capizzi snapped his fingers at him. "Who the fuck is this?" he asked, indicating to her.

"I think Peppe knows the girl," Old Capizzi said, his shrewd gaze looking from him to her. "Does the girl speak our language?" he asked him in Italian.

"*No, Signor,*" Peppe answered, letting out a violent diarrhoea of streaming words. "I would never bring in someone... She was hungry... was at the back door... I just wanted to give her some food... help her out... She must have sneaked inside...somehow...."

Old Capizzi chuckled while the son looked like he might blow a fuse. "Learn to keep your fucking dick in your pants," he bellowed to Peppe, who looked like he might chop it off himself right now rather than stand here.

Hot Capizzi pulled her up again and drew her close to him. Sandalwood. That was the other smell. "If I ever see you anywhere near us again... I will deliver you as food to your family, in a fucking box."

"Get her out of here." He pushed her into Peppe, who caught on to her and started dragging her away. "One more thing, Peppe." He sauntered closer to the frozen man. "You do this again, and I will cut off your fucking dick. *Capisti*?"

"*Sì, sì, spiacente, Signor.*" Mumbling, fumbling idiot, Peppe dragged her out of the room and ditched her outside without the food bowl in the rain.

"Don't think of stepping foot here again. Fucking gipsies. Getting me into trouble as well."

He slammed the door on her face. Florina was disappointed. Not in Peppe. She had had little hope in him to begin with. Not even in her missed chance of getting some food into her. It was rather that throughout that exchange, Hot Capizzi had not once looked at her ample bosom.

CHAPTER ONE
FOUR YEARS LATER

YULIYA

R ed ants crawled up her skin and burnt her alive. The paths they burnt led to her heart, and everywhere they touched erupted into a fucking fire. A fire that reached deep inside and pounded to the beat of an elephant stampede. The outside world drowned in white noise. All she heard was the pounding of her craving. All she tasted was her craving. All she breathed was her craving. Her deep, deep craving for the next high.

She wasn't going to be choosey. She didn't care what she got into her system as long as she got something in. She needed her shot, and she needed it now. Her fists clenched on the once pristine linen sheets. Now they were crushed and tangled and soaked with her sweat. Her body trembled with an ache for something that was out of her reach. But she held onto her sheets and anchored herself to the bed. Hiding, waiting till the time was right.

Until she could escape this hell hole. Escape the fuckers in this house who watched her like hawks and blocked her way to freedom. To get fucked and to get her fix.

Fuck!

What she would do to get what she yearned for. She might even inject herself if she needed to. What was the point of hiding anyway when they all knew? But first, she had to wait. Until he left for his office. He pissed her off. Keeping her away from things she loved. Bounding her to that wailing machine. When she made it out of there, she would destroy him. Make him regret the day he decided to fucking tie her down by marrying her.

She should have known. When her father came home gushing about the young *consigliere* from Sicily. Since when did the *Bratva* gush about the fucking Italians? That should have set her red flags on alert. But he gushed, and he swooned about the thirty-year-old *consigliere* moving to Boston to make new bonds and tie clans together. If she had been of sane mind, she would have asked him how that was even possible. But she hadn't been, and she hadn't cared either. What did it have anything to do with her anyway? But he kept drooling over the man, and weeks turned into months, and months turned into a year, and suddenly she was in a fucking church, and saying yes to a man with eyes far sharper than a laser beam of a sniper. Just like that, he took away her dream of pumping her body with all the drugs she could find out of her hands.

She had to backtrack. Because of him. But she had done that. If she could hide her little secrets from her father and brothers, she could do it from him. She had to be good. She tried. She really did. She didn't mind trying for him. He was fucking hot, and impaling his cock in her gave her a different kind of high. One she rode out gladly. Over and over again.

There were no illusions between them. They were more fuck buddies than husband and wife. She didn't think he even cared for her to begin with. The coldness in his eyes only proved her right. Which made her wonder why he even tied himself to her. But he did. His lifeless eyes and controlling nature followed her everywhere, and the only time his control slipped for even a second was when he was pounding inside her like the devil himself had pushed his cock inside her. The victory in her was so much sweeter when he came, and his control slipped for that second.

Not that she liked him that much either. She liked her men willing and submissive. There wasn't an inkling of submissiveness to be found in him. He was all dominant and arrogant. Two traits she would rather live without. But still, she tried because she didn't want to piss off her daddy.

But she was who she was, and there was no changing that. It was great while it lasted, but realistically, for how long was she going to play housewife? His house was dull and reeked of boredom and sullen Italian humour. Her father may have gotten over his hatred of Italians, but that didn't mean she had to. His staff grated on her nerves like a fork on Mama's bone china. Rosa, in particular, was a fucking nuisance breathing down her neck with her fake, motherly love. If she didn't even give a fuck about her own mother, then she wasn't in need of a substitute. So, she went back to her old ways. She fucked the men she found, and she stuffed what she could find down her body. It felt brilliant. Well, till he found out. He caught on to her faster than her own family, and they were the *Bratva*.

The pounding in her head clashed with the noises outside her door. He was talking to Rosa. She tried to still her trembling body enough to listen, but they were going at it again in Italian anyway. She hated the language as much as she hated him. His deep voice whisked through the timber door and thundered into her room. She curled into a tight ball as her body shook even more.

Will he come inside?

If he saw her, he would know. Then he would be mad like the day he found out. The type of mad that made you run towards death and away from him. A dribble of sweat slid down her backbone. She wasn't sure if she could fight his fury today.

His voice pulled away and drifted down the hallway. Relief poured into her shaking bones. She shouldn't have worried. He never saw her anyway. He acted like she was a disease he didn't want to catch and avoided her at all costs. Especially today, he would lock himself up in whatever cave he hid. Oh, poor him! Today was his fucking daddy's death anniversary. The man didn't own a heart, but on his daddy's death anniversary, he acted more vile than his usual self.

Sitting up in her bed, she listened. Blessed silence. She didn't hear him anymore. She snuck her head between the drapes and watched the men file into the two black cars out front. It was raining outside like a dam unleashed. But all she felt was fucking sunshine because it was going to be a marvellous day today. He took all his men with him.

Scrabbling to her phone, she picked it up and called her man. Igor was the perfect submissive. He picked it up on the first ring like he had waited for her to call just like she had told him to.

"Sweetheart, I missed you." His voice sent warmth up her chilled bones.

"He's gone, Igor," she hissed. "He took all his men with him." Her nervous giggle filtered through the phone line and infected him, and they both combusted in a fit of giggles. Igor made her happy. Pills made her happy. She fell onto her back on the sheets and rolled around. Her body shook with the effort, and it reminded her of another ache. "I can sneak out when Rosa starts cooking."

"Yes. Yes. I have a fix, and we can fuck...." Igor stopped his rattle. "But for how long? When is he back?"

She rocked in her bed. "I don't know," she muttered as all the euphoria of a moment ago drained out of her. "I hate him, Igor," she wailed. "I want to ruin him. I want to take his heart out and squash it with my bare hands. He's blocking me off everything. He's keeping me away from you. Why won't he let me go?"

"It's because of that stupid baby."

She shook her head vigorously. He was right, of course. Igor was always right. "Stupid, stupid baby. It's what's keeping me from you."

She rocked harder as her mind went into overdrive. Wasn't it punishment enough that she was fucking tied to a bed for nine months? Now she was stuck to that wailing machine, and there was no way out. No way out. She hated her father for putting her in that contract. She hated her husband for agreeing to it. She hated him even more for putting his seed in her and destroying her life. There was no way out as long as that wailing machine was around. Unless... unless...of course, there was no more wailing. Then he would let her go. She was sure of it. No more wailing. No more bounds. The more she thought of it the more she was sure of it. "Darling, I have an idea...."

ANTONIO

LATER THAT DAY ...

I was a calm man. A patient one. Till someone fucking pissed me off. When that happened, any human brave enough to be around me was taking their life in their hands.

My footsteps leaving the elevator and stalking towards my corner office echoed throughout the top floor, resounding my anger at my Boston headquarters.

While I marched through the building, the rest of the office went quiet. Tension hung high in the air tighter than any guitar string. Calls dropped. Typing stopped. Conversations paused. A man came out of an adjoining office and immediately backtracked out of sight upon seeing me.

Coward.

I was a man to be feared on any day. Anyone who only met me for a second was a fool not to know that. Some said my all-seeing gaze was equal to being caught under a laser beam, my grip one of metal. Others would say on days like today, when my mood was as black as the devil's coat, it was much worse. It was better not to see me at all, for a second could cost your life.

If any other man made these threats, they might be taken figuratively. *Any other man*. Anyone who knew me through my multimillion-dollar, private, investment banking business feared me with a touch of jealousy. I had already achieved international success at the age of twenty-seven. After all, a man so young did not get to where he was by playing nice. I had the ability to crush anyone financially.

But for the ones who were aware of my position in *Cosa Nostra*, finances were the least of their troubles. They had everything to lose if they were to meet me under the wrong circumstances. Being appointed as *consigliere* at the young age of thirty spoke volumes. The rumours paving my path spoke of respect earned from the don, of sublime control, of master manipulation... rumours that had gained in volume over the past four years.

You take a man's *Cosa Nostra* heritage and add to it intelligence and savvy business sense, you end up with a booming business. Both in the day and in the night. A success which should have made me a satisfied man.

It didn't.

I marched into my office and slammed the door shut. Let them all hide. Sooner or later, one would have to creep out. Like a cat waiting for the mice, I waited. The urge to put a hole through someone's goddamn head weighed heavier on me today than on any other day.

I strode to the floor-to-ceiling windows with my hands taut in my pockets. The view that I paid millions for couldn't penetrate my eyes today. The frustration running inside me had no end. My troubles were dark today. I held my sharp body tight because I knew if I let go, I might do something I would regret. Like, put my fucking wife in a box. But I couldn't. My hands were bound. Besides, I never hurt a woman. That was one of my own rules. It was just that sometimes a man was tempted to break his own rules.

Was I ever actually happy with Yuliya? If I was, I couldn't pinpoint when that would have been. Was I happy when I made the deal with Vladislav to tie our clans together? His idea of forging a partnership together by marriage to his daughter had made perfect sense. What better way to seal the deal for a high-testosterone relationship between the *Bratva* and the *Cosa Nostra* than through marriage? So, of course, I went along with it. Even when the words of my dying papa floated in my mind, I paid no heed to them. Arranged marriages were nothing new in *Cosa Nostra*. I didn't care for love, anyway. My father's dreams were a fucking joke. How could I replicate something I had never seen?

Was I happy in the first days, weeks, and months of our marriage? I was sexually satisfied. I could fault Yuliya

is, at least with our clans. It took a marriage for us to realise we didn't need one to solidify our bond."

"We just needed you. In four years, you have changed so much. We are all grateful. Your father would be proud, my boy."

I sure hoped so because I was going to bring something new to our family. Disgrace with a divorce.

"We will get the paperwork arranged quietly. No need to bring our families any disgrace," Vladislav said as if he was privy to my thoughts.

"I couldn't agree more. Doubt Yuliya is going to put up a fight."

―――――――

THIS MORNING's events had left me so shaken, fucking emotions had taken over. That was a mistake. Emotions got in the way of everything. Now, it was time to get back into action. I rang in my assistant.

Isabella knocked on my door and came in. Petite, with an hourglass figure, she had been by my side for more years than I could recount. Being part of my team that came over from Sicily four years ago, she knew both sides of my business. She was professional. She never addressed me by my first name, which only a few had the privilege of using. She was also a hurricane of efficiency, which is what I needed most days, but especially today.

"Get online with the best agencies for nannies. I want a reliable person. I should have done this ages ago."

"Of course, *Signor* Capizzi. Nothing but the best for Cora." She sat down to note my requirements. "Do we have time, though? Finding someone good will take some time. Rosa is fine to look after Cora until then?"

"Rosa is incredible with her. I should have left her in charge instead of trusting Yuliya."

"How could she have done that when she is recovering from her knee replacement? Babies are tough and heavy to take care of, especially at Rosa's age."

"I never hear her complain. I need a Rosa, but younger."

"Any other requirements?"

What does one want from a nanny? I didn't know shit about this. "Young, good physical condition to run behind Cora... trustworthy..."

"Do you want a live-in nanny?"

I frowned. I didn't even want a stranger in the house, let alone at night. "No. She can go home after Cora goes to bed, or Rosa can take over the night duties."

"On it." Isabella stood up, book in hand.

Finding a younger Rosa would be like looking for an innocent man in *Cosa Nostra*. Rosa was officially my housekeeper. Unofficially? She was more of a mother to me than my own. Which reminded me...

"Isabella," I called out just as she was about to close the door.

"Yes, *Signor* Capizzi?"

"Get my mother on the phone. I need to inform her before someone else does."

"Of course."

Getting my dick shut in a door would be more enjoyable than this. Hell was about to let loose when my mother found out. She would warrant this as a necessity to visit for a few months from Italy. She wouldn't be bothered about Cora being dumped in a laundromat. But me getting divorced.... yeah, that would be a problem. A problem for which she would have a fucking solution, I was sure.

CHAPTER TWO
THREE MONTHS LATER...

DIVYA

My body screamed from exhaustion. Every day it felt like a massive rock had lodged itself in my heart, leaving the rest of my body lifeless and drained of energy. There were worse situations to be in. There must be people with bigger problems. But today, and every other day before it, felt like the weight of the entire world was crushing down on my shoulders, dragging me down.

A sigh spilt out of me as I let myself out of the bus and lugged my groceries along. Big bags of nothing filled to keep me alive. That was what food was to me these days. The bags were too heavy. But it wasn't like there was anyone around to help me out. Just when I thought Adam could be that person, he ended up showing his real colours, and they turned out to be the dark sort.

Standing still for a moment, I tried to take a deep breath, trying to get rid of that ever-present emptiness inside me, something that had permanently anchored into me since losing my parents. I hated this feeling. It felt as if someone had rammed a hand inside my chest and jerked my heart out. Try as I might, I couldn't take that deep breath. Things of the past, those deep breaths, just like my parents now.

I put my bags down on the wet footpath and fixed the strand of brown hair that had escaped. I loved my long hair. I always thought it had just the right amount of natural waves in the end. But today, just like every-thing else, it was annoying the hell out of me.

I picked up my bags again and trudged up the hill leading to my rundown apartment building.

It was over a year since they passed away. But I can remember the late afternoon call on that dreadful day like it was yesterday. I knew the moment I heard Mrs Smith's voice that something was off. My parents' neigh-bour was lovely, but I had never called her before. Or she me.

Something terrible has happened, sweetie ... your mama and papa have met with an accident... you should come home.... She didn't tell me then that they were already dead, that they actually died on impact. But I had already known that. I wish my sixth sense had shown up when I called the day before they died. I wish it had nudged me to tell them I loved them. Throughout that seven-hour flight to London, I knew they were already gone, well before I fell into the arms of my friends and Mrs Smith.

A year had passed, and I still couldn't sidestep my pain to remember the good things. Would I ever be able to do that? Remember them fondly and not miss them every single day. Would I be able to get up one morning and not have that gawking emptiness inside me? Maybe it would have been easier with a brother or a sister. Only a sibling could share this pain. The rest, no matter how close they had been to them, had moved on.

On Tuesday, when I dumped Adam, I called my mum. I hadn't disconnected their lines, and I had put all my anger and pain into that voice message. Pathetic, I knew that. But somehow comforting.

Tuesday was just a day with too much heartbreak. My universe tilted on the edge when my parents died on a Tuesday, and now bloody Adam had to show his true colours on another Tuesday. I was swearing off Tuesdays.

I had forgiven him when he had refused to fly back with me to England. I had somehow even forgiven him when he didn't turn up for the funeral. I hadn't understood why, nor had I cared. My head had been full trying to arrange the most beautiful funeral I could for two people so diverse in character and culture. When I got back, I gave him the benefit of the doubt. He couldn't handle all those emotions, all that crying. I got that. If I could, I would rather bury my head in the sand and still believe Mum and Dad were alive, waiting for my next visit or planning to visit themselves.

But on Tuesday, when I was finally ready to get along with my life, ready to make the payment for my enrolment to the university ... everything just exploded.

Anger still pooled inside my stomach. I was furious. Furious at Adam for gambling away all of my inheritance. The only thing that was left of my parents so I could do what they had dreamed I would. But more than the fury at Adam, I was livid at myself. How had I not seen this addiction of his? How had I not paid attention to my dwindling bank account? Most importantly, what a stupid dimwit I was to have put that money in a joint account. My parents had brought me up better, and this was the way I repaid them. By putting foolishness before thought.

Secretly, I admitted to myself as I tried to find the keys to my apartment in my bag that I was furious with him for too many reasons to even name. If it hadn't been for his stupid job offer, I wouldn't have moved so far away from my mum and dad. I would have been back home in London or Milan like I had originally planned. I would have been with them, maybe on that horrible stormy night. I could have prevented that accident. Or I could have just died with them. At least then, I wouldn't have this gaping hole where my heart was meant to be.

I fumbled with the key in the lock. I knew the trick. Everyone had told me this. I had to pull the door hard towards me and turn, but it wouldn't budge.

"You have to pull and turn."

I turned around to see my downstairs neighbour hovering next to me.

"I know that." I tried again. I did not desire his odious character today. He hadn't really done anything wrong, but just the way he looked at me gave me the creeps, like his eyes could see through my clothes.

"Here, let me help." He put his hand on top of mine, not waiting for me to move away, pulled the door towards us and turned the key.

He opened the door, of course.

"Thanks," I took a step back, pulling my hands from his.

I could feel his eyes on me, or rather, his eyes on my breasts. A chill ran through my veins.

"Where's that man of yours?"

"Out. He'll be back any moment." I knew why I lied. I didn't like how his glazed eyes were gliding on my body.

"You need any help with that?" He eyed the two bags standing next to me. There had been a special promotion in Aldi, and I had wanted to save up and ended up buying too much. Now I had enough for the next month or two, at least.

"No, it's okay. I can—"

"Never mind. I can help you with this. It's a piece of cake for me." The expression sounded off in his East European accent, but before I could protest, he was off with my bags. He carried them as if they were filled with air and sprinted up the stairs.

I followed at a much slower pace. I was actually happy. It saved two flights of heavy lugging up the stairs, thanks to him.

He was waiting by the door when I arrived. He was quite good-looking if you liked the type. He had a typical body of a bodybuilder and blonde hair with blue eyes. Still, I couldn't shake the predatory aura that seemed to surround him.

"Thanks," I mumbled while opening my door.

He brushed past me and carried the bags through, dumping them on my battered kitchen counter.

The muscle-man body would explain his capacity to

go at it all night long with whoever he was banging, more often recently than before. Sometimes it was an all-nighter.

Jealous much, the devil on my left shoulder whispered.

Not really. I liked sex, and sex with Adam had been good. But going about it all night or jumping at each other like wildcats had never been my thing.

He was walking around my cramped living quarters, looking around, picking up my stuff and examining it. I didn't like him in here.

He picked up the framed picture of my parents. "This your mama and papa?"

I nodded and moved further into the kitchen, standing behind the counter. Common courtesy was to give the man something to drink, but all I wanted was for him to get out of my place as soon as he could.

"What are you?"

"Ugh?"

"Papa is brown, mama is white."

"Oh." That was a weird way of putting it. Was it because English clearly wasn't his mother language? "My dad is Indian, and my mum is English." *Was.*

He came to stand in front of the counter, still holding my frame, and squinted at me. "Is that why you're so pretty?" His gaze flicked from my breasts to my eyes. "You have pretty eyes."

"I guess...." It was suffocating inside my tiny apartment, with his colossal body blocking the air to my lungs. He was standing too close to me. My tiny body was way out of proportion to his large one.

"You have green stuff in it."

He leaned over the counter and put himself closer to me. His gaze flicked from my eyes back to my cleavage.

"Prettiest eyes I've ever seen."

I knew the specks of green in my eyes were as rare as a good day in my life. When brown eyes were so dominating, I had the luxury of having brown with a sprinkle of green. Yet I had a distinct feeling he wasn't talking about my eyes. My voice was frozen in my larynx. I cleared the croak creeping up my throat. "Thank you for helping me. I'd better get started on dinner before Adam comes home."

"Okay." He put the frame down on the counter and made his way to the door. I followed him so I could lock it behind him. He stopped and twisted, making me almost bump into him.

"Everything still okay with your man? I thought I heard something last Tuesday."

I felt my brown skin going hot. Had I yelled so loud that everyone had heard? I was the epitome of politeness, but I had been so damn mad at Adam. It was a miracle that I hadn't hit him with my laptop. If he hadn't gambled my inheritance, I might have. Except now, even my old laptop was one of the only luxuries I could afford.

"I had some friends over. Sorry about that." The lie slipped out easily.

He squinted his eyes at me. I didn't think he believed me.

"If you need any help, you call me, okay?"

I nodded, hoping he would not be the person I had to go to for help.

CHAPTER THREE

DIVYA

I cleaned up after my microwave dinner. There was a time in my life when Friday night announced the beginning of the weekend to be celebrated. Now it just found me alone and sad, lacking in any kind of joy. Nothing more depressing than spending weekends alone while the rest of the world seems to enjoy theirs. Frustration whirled inside me as I busied myself with cleaning up. I was so tired of this pent-up anger, pain, and frustration that I wanted a holiday away from myself. I really wanted to go back to the person I was a year ago... but yet again, today had not been a simple day.

I needed to move on. Find a job I could manage while studying, which would hopefully pay for my studies, my apartment, food, utilities, and help me pay off the mortgage to my parents' home ... Perhaps I could even move back to my previous apartment. I loved that place, and it came with the added advantage of nicer neighbours. Another thing I had given up, to adjust to my new financial situation after their death.

A job that would solve all my problems. Easier said than done. Finding one that could cover all my expenses was nearly impossible. Leaving aside the time, I would need to follow a four-year BS degree in fashion. My eyes coasted to my Mum's sewing machine in the corner. Fashion had been my dream since the time I was in my teens. A dream I was adamant about fulfilling, especially after I started researching my Indian heritage. I loved that side of fashion even more. I wanted so much to bring about a collection that combined Indian ethnicity with the cutting edge of the Western world. Just like the beautiful couple that my parents had been, my Indian dad and my English mum. It might remain just that now. A dream.

I was up to my elbows, scrubbing away at pots when the doorbell rang. Drying my hands, I went to open it while shrugging off my annoyance. Nine was late to make a house call. But then again, I wasn't open to any house calls. At nine in the evening or morning.

Slumped in the doorway was none other than Adam. His hands in his pockets, his blond head bent and looking, probably, for his lost dignity in his scuffed shoes, or perhaps for my lost inheritance, the mean streak in me thought. He startled when the door scraped open. What did he think? That I wouldn't open the door? Come to think of it, why did I?

"What the hell are you doing here?" Did I have to see this addict today? Stealing all your girlfriend's money and gambling it away, even if it is in a posher place like the stock market, didn't make him any better than an addict.

"I live here."

My hands clutched onto the door so I could rein in my temptation to let my hands claw his face off. "You live here if you pay the rent. You haven't done that for the last six months. And now I can't pay my rent either. Because of you."

He shuffled his feet, guilt dancing on his face. There was a scuffle from downstairs, and he looked uncomfortable. "Baby, can we go inside and talk about this? Come on." He pleaded, trying to grab my arm.

I whacked his hand out of the way like the annoying fly that he was. "Don't "baby" me, Adam. You didn't think of your baby when you were gambling away my inheritance. *My* inheritance, Adam. That was the only thing left of my parents for me. What right did you have to go after that?"

"Come on, baby, it's just money. What we have together is so much more. We went through your parents' deaths together and came out strong. We have each other."

He might as well have punched me right in my heart.

"How dare you bring my parents' deaths into this!" I didn't care anymore that I was yelling. I wanted the entire building to know what he had done. "What did you go through? Huh? Were they your parents? Did you support me? Did you feel the loss? Poor you. Flying out to their funeral was an effort too much for you, you big fucking idiot."

"Come on, baby, you know that's not fair. Funerals really aren't my thing."

"Nothing is your thing, Adam," I screamed in his face, ignoring the puppy eyes he was putting on. The time that I fell for that was long gone. "You couldn't stand by me when I needed you the most. You couldn't bother to support me. Hold my hand. The only thing you could do is apparently gamble all my money away." I thought I had forgiven him for not coming with me. Turned out I hadn't.

I heard voices below. The neighbours were getting a great show tonight.

"Why are you here, anyway?"

"I miss you, baby."

A sigh left my body like the air of a burst tire. My anger ebbed away to give way to disappointment. I felt deflated.

"Do me a favour. Stay out of my life from now on. I would sue you if I could. I am sure I would have a case. But thanks to you, I have to struggle for everything now." My voice cracked. It always let me down when I was over-wrought with emotion. "I can't start my studies. I am struggling to pay my rent. I need to find a job soon. So unless you have a solution to that, get the hell out of here."

I would have loved to slam the door in his face. But of course, I had to be stuck with an old door hanging lower on the hinge, which took all of my energy just to get it to close.

Leaning against the door, I listened to his shuffling feet move away. I could faintly hear a conversation with the neighbours down. Good. He could explain all his shit to them.

Cleaning up appealed to me even less than before. Exhaustion overtook me as I dragged on Adam's stupid shirt to sleep in. I really needed to find something else, it was just that it was so comfortable. He owed me that much, at least. Switching off the lights, I crawled into bed. Tomorrow was another day and hopefully a better one.

I must have been lying in my bed for no more than ten minutes when the usual banging from downstairs started up.

The show of every night.

Covering my ears didn't block the stream of Russian being screamed out and the noise of the headboard banging onto the wall. Did they have to go at it all the time like a couple of rabbits? Did that guy not need a break? I had never seen his lady friend, but at the sound of it, she was one hot piece of sex on Red Bull.

I tossed and turned and tried covering my ears with my pillow. All I asked now was for one good night, then tomorrow, I was going to come up with a plan. Find a job, try to save something, ... or maybe I should move back home. There was nothing for me in Boston anymore.

ADAM WAS IN A CASINO. He sat in a coffin and yelled that he hated funerals. He was handing out my dollars to strangers while watching my neighbour banging a hot

Russian woman on the backgammon table in front of him. In the next minute, it was Adam with the woman, and the neighbour turned around to me. "You have the prettiest eyes I've ever seen," he whispered and touched me. I felt cold. I tried to move away, but I couldn't. All three of them were there in front of me and covered in nothing but dollar notes. There was a piece of repetitive music in the background, which got louder and louder. It sounded like a tribal song and increased in volume, taking over whatever they were yelling at me. It hurt my ears. Suddenly, it sounded like a doorbell and softened in volume. Wait.

I jerked awake. That was the doorbell being rung again and again with a repetitive tapping on the door. Half asleep, I stumbled to the door and found my neighbour had popped out of my dream to stand on my doorstep.

"Sorry, didn't realise you were sleeping." His eyes visibly licked me from top to toe, leaving me in need of a shower, badly.

I rubbed my eyes, trying to focus on him.

What was he doing here?

"We heard your argument yesterday with your man." His eyes settled on my cleavage again.

I collected my open shirt collar together, driving his eyes back to my face. No point hiding my story anymore. "We broke up."

"My woman is well connected."

Okay. And that's helpful, how?

"If you are looking for a job that pays well, she has something for you." He almost puffed out his chest when he said that. "She gave me this card to give to you." He pushed a card into my hands. It was a simple black card with *Casa Capizzi* written in embossed red letters. "They need a nanny and will pay well. Easy money." He clicks his fingers together like money would just come falling from the ceiling.

I turned the card over. There was a phone number on the back. The whole thing looked posh and out-of-place coming from him. He was already moving away when I looked up again. "Thanks!" I yelled out.

His head popped up again on top of the bannister. "No problem. Call them. Capizzi will pay well."

"Hey, what's your girlfriend's name?"

"No bother," he yelled back before shutting his door.

Ugh? That's not what I asked. I should get her name. It might help me to get in if I was referred by someone. Although I didn't know them. They had only moved in like a month before, and they knew me from my fights with Adam. Nothing good about that.

I went back inside and touched the card in my hands. It was soft to the touch like it was made of velvet. Posh and Italian? I had to google these people, and come Monday, I would call Casa Capizzi for a job.

I didn't care who gave me the card. A job was a job.

CHAPTER FOUR

DIVYA

Tuesday morning found me in front of the steps leading up to an imposing townhouse with a beautiful matte black door and brass knob. I was way out of my comfort zone in this neighbourhood, close to the waterfront and opposite a park on Beacon Street. The street was lined with perfectly manicured trees and expensive cars. I wasn't very familiar with the neighbourhoods and properties in Boston, but this had to be one of the most expensive ones, if not the most. There was no way they were going to hire me. It was also a Tuesday. I was beginning to become superstitious now.

I rubbed my trembling hands on my pencil skirt before ringing the doorbell.

One day at a time.

I adjusted the red choker around my neck.

I need to get through today.

I fiddled with my hair, which I had put into a neat bun.

I've got this.

The door was opened after a few minutes by an older Mediterranean-looking gentleman in a black suit.

"Good morning. Miss Praan, is it?" His heavy Italian accent threw me off.

"Yes. Good morning. I have an appointment with Mr Capizzi." Crap. My voice sounded croaky.

Was this Mr Capizzi? He must be in his mid-fifties with more grey in his hair than black. He could have had a child at a later stage in his life.

"I am Armando. Please do come in. *Signor* Capizzi will see you in the library." He smiled reassuringly.

So, who was Armando then?

I tried not to gawk as I looked around the entrance hall while Armando closed the door. It was massive but tastefully done. More in a European style than American. The floors were a soft, warm white marble. The curtains next to the floor-to-ceiling windows were a soft, natural kind of fabric in a cream colour. Probably linen. I could tell from how it hung and gently touched the floors. The woodwork everywhere was warm walnut, including around the bannisters leading up the stairs.

"Follow me, *Signorina.*" He led the way to a double door on the left, next to the staircase.

It was a study, beautifully decorated with a touch of modern and a whole lot of vintage. Everything in the room spoke of a story. Nothing in here was a purchase from a thrift store.

"*Signor* Capizzi will be with you in a minute. Would

you like to have something to drink? Some coffee, perhaps?"

"Just some water will be fine."

"Still or sparkling?"

"Still, please." I was about to say tap water would be fine but held back. I didn't want to embarrass myself.

"*Ecco a lei.* I will be right back." Armando left, closing the tall double doors softly behind him.

W*as Armando a butler?*

Heaving a sigh, I looked around me. A row of windows looked out to the side garden, but it was the shelves adorning the walls from floor to ceiling that grabbed my attention. Row after row filled with books of all kinds. I walked over to them and touched the massive walnut wooden shelves, running my fingers gently over the books.

I could easily live in this room. It looked like someone else did. The books were well-read, the creases on the sides giving them away. There were books in different languages. Italian, of course. But also English, French, Spanish, Russian, Japanese, ... I sighed. My dad, an avid reader, would have loved this room. The topics were broad as the languages, politics, religion, ... sex. Right next to each other.

My spine burned like a fire behind me. Startled, I flipped around.

Holy shit.

Standing in front of the double doors was an excellent specimen that could have easily popped out of one of those sex books. I swallowed the itch in my dry throat. How had I not heard the doors open *and* close? The man had sinfully beautiful hair. Thick and in shades of brown with strands of silver grey. I was a sucker for grey in men's hair, and this one had some grey sprinkled in his barely-there scruff as well. God had noted down my wish list and delivered. I wondered what gave him silver streaks because it certainly couldn't be his age. He was older than me but not enough to gain streaks.

"Miss Praan, nice of you to come in so soon." His voice had a dark edge to it like it was used only to talk of naughty things. It tugged at something inside me, wrung it out, and left me naked. When he crossed over and shook my hand with a firm handshake, I felt something pull. He tilted my nerves, and I instantly dropped his hand for the hot coals they were and took a step backwards.

Get a hold of yourself.

His chestnut brown eyes bored into mine, reading my face, taking stock, saving data before he finally moved away to sit behind his massive desk in walnut and leather.

The air cleared slightly around me, allowing me to breathe.

"Please," he indicated with his hand with long fingers to the beautiful olive-green chairs in front of his. "Have a seat."

His accent wasn't as pronounced as Armando's, but it was present. That sexy Italian vibe oozing off him flowed seamlessly with his accent.

I cleared my throat and moved to sit down. My navy-blue pencil skirt and white wide-collared shirt felt suddenly too tight on me. My large, red-beaded choker around my neck was too warm, too tight, choking me.

I needed a breather.

"Isabella gave you all the details, I presume?" His eyes had a dark glint in them as they focused on me. Like a hot cup of black coffee.

"She was quite brief on the phone."

Stupid croak. Letting me down.

I cleared my throat.

"Fair enough. There's nothing special about it. I am looking for a nanny for my daughter. She's five months old. I need someone with experience. Someone who can be there with her at all times and put her needs first." He flicked a glance at his open laptop before scorching me through my skin. "You do have the experience?"

Holy hot daddy!

"Of course. I worked for two years at a day care back in London."

"Right. You're originally from England." I couldn't read if that was positive or negative. "What brings you over to Boston?" The question seemed casual, but something told me the answer would be analysed. He was not a man who took an answer at point blank.

I wasn't going to allow idiotic Adam to ruin the possibility of me getting this job. "I came to further my studies." A nervous laugh escaped me.

"What do you plan to study?"

"Fashion."

"From day care to fashion?"

"Fashion is my dream."

He looked me over, eyeing my outfit. I couldn't tell if he approved or not. Only that there was a fire in his eyes that lit me up in flames. "So why aren't you doing that?

This is a full-time job. You can't possibly combine it with your studies."

That had occurred to me. But with the options available, this seemed to be the best one. If I could do this for a few years, I might have enough saved to start my studies after. Or I moved back home and found work there. But I wasn't ready yet to face home without my parents. All Adam's fault. I really was in the mode to throttle him again. Bitterness piled inside me.

"Wealth doesn't come easily to many people." Sometimes my mouth was better kept shut. But I didn't regret my words even if I felt my cheeks warming with embarrassment.

Armando entered after a knock. He placed the glass of water for me with lemons on the side and a soft *Prego*. For Mr Capizzi, he placed an espresso. All the time, I could feel the man across watching me with his heated eyes.

"Milan has much better schools for fashion. Why Boston?" he asked the moment Armando closed the door behind him.

"I am not a fan of Milan." I lied as Milan had been my first option, but I gave it up for Adam and moved to Boston. "Boston seemed to be a good option to me."

He raised his brows. "Milan *is* the best option."

The arrogance of this man was cringeworthy. But somehow, he left my core wet and twisty. "Boston is the best option *for* me."

His look said he didn't agree. "So why would you move here if you don't have the finances arranged yet? Can't your parents fund your studies?"

I swallowed the metal wrecking ball in my throat. I should have prepared my stories more. I had to give him the truth if there was any chance of getting this job. The problem was, I didn't want to mention Adam. For one, it would show my lack of judgment, and honestly, who would want their kid being looked after by someone with such infantile judgment? Second, a gambler, even if we had broken up, just screamed red flags. I gave him the truth I was comfortable with.

"My parents would have gladly paid for my education. Had they lived." I dropped my voice to reduce the croak. But it only got worse. "They passed away last year in an accident." I looked to a spot somewhere on his shoulder and blinked rapidly to hold back the tears.

Now I was going to mess up my mascara.

A few minutes of silence ticked away. At least it was not the customary *I am sorry for your loss charade.*

I focused on his clothes. He had an impeccable sense of style. He wore a light grey linen suit with a crisp, white shirt. No tie. The shirt was left tantalisingly open at his neck, showing a hint of dark chest hair. The only accessory on him was his watch, with a big round black head and dark brown leather bands. Something old. It wasn't one bought recently in a store.

"How do I pronounce your name?"

That was a first. Not even an I am sorry?

I looked into his eyes again. Something was whirling a war in there. "Di-v-ja"

"Divja," he repeated, but in his gruff voice, I heard my name differently, sexier. I clenched my legs. There was a warm wetness tickling down there. "Divya, may I ask what your roots are?"

I sat upright. I was proud of my roots. If he had a problem with it, he could go to hell, no matter how hot he was. "My father was Indian, and my mother was English."

He stood up and walked over to the front of the desk. I could feel his eyes on me and looked up to see him standing close, pulling at the air around me. "Interesting," he murmured, almost to himself.

ANTONIO

I was mesmerised by this beautiful creature in front of me. I had been, ever since I laid eyes on her, touching my books as if they were her lovers. She had the most beautiful, caramel-coloured skin, thanks to her mixed heritage. Her hair, in a soft hazelnut brown, bound into a bun, had my hands itching to loosen it up to find out what it would look like. Let loose. Her eyes weren't dark brown like most of the Indians I knew. No. Hers were lighter, with specks of green in them. So unusual that a man could drown in her eyes if he looked too long. Which is why I let mine drift through her body. Her skin, her eyes, her breasts in just the right size ... not too small, but not too big, either. Perfect in proportion to the rest of her body. I would say it was a B cup. They would fit nicely into my palms. I wondered what coloured nipples she was hiding under her white shirt ... dark brown? Pink?

I didn't remember anymore why I had moved closer to her. I drew my gaze away and walked back to sit behind my desk. I needed to check something on her CV and hide my hard-on.

She was young. Twenty-five. I checked her CV. Nearly ten years younger than me. Not that it was of any importance. Perfect age to look after Cora. She would be fit enough to run behind her when she started to crawl and walk. It made me imagine what else she would be fit enough to do.

But there were gaps in her story. The way she fidgeted in her tight skirt told me there was more to her than she let on. I was sure it was something petty. I would have to get my team to do a background check on her. This was a standard procedure, but this time, I was curious what they would uncover. It would take some time, of course. But I was a very patient man. I was willing to wait and find out what this gorgeous beauty was hiding from me.

Still, something jabbed at my patience. Now that she had stepped inside my home, I didn't want to let go of her. She was going to be good for Cora, and it was not like we had had so many options.

I should remember to ask Isabella from which agency Divya had come.

Divya, I rolled her name around in my head. It burned my tongue like a drip of Amaro.

The right thing to do would be to wait. To find someone within *Cosa Nostra*.

"Divya, I would like you to do a trial day. Today, if you don't mind. We can see how Cora adapts to you, and if all goes well at the end of the day, the job is yours."

NANNY TO THE MAFIA

I never did things right.

"I am free today Mr Capizzi —"

I silenced her. "Antonio, if you please. We are going to be seeing a lot of each other." An image of her naked with wild hair riding me rose in my head. I blinked to get rid of it before I continued. "As my daughter's nanny."

I rang the intercom. "Armando, can you introduce Miss Praan to Rosa and Cora? I have a few calls to make, and I will be with you shortly."

I watched her follow Armando to the door. Her butt swayed rhythmically. It was a natural walk, not a fake strut. Still, it pulled at my dick. That entire outfit screamed sex, while I was sure that was not the intention.

I should get laid fast before I jump the nanny.

I waited till the door closed before I made my call to Marco, my right-hand man.

"Are the papers ready?" I asked. The process of legalising most of *Cosa Nostra's* businesses run on this side of town was long but worthwhile. At the time, we were working on a restaurant run by a fellow Sicilian. The interaction with the Boston PD was key. I listened to Marco's report and pinpointed the details he had to work on. Before ending the call, I needed Marco to do one more thing for me.

"I need a background check on Divya Praan. Isabella should have already sent over her details. Make this a priority. She has started work today."

"You're not going to wait for the info?"

"No need. I expect nothing big to come out."

"*Certo*. Anything specific I should look for?"

"A thorough, general check, since she's going to be in

our household in close quarters to my family. Also, find out why exactly she moved to Boston from the UK."

"*Sì.* I will get on it."

"*Bene.* I am also working from home today. Inform Isabella to hold all my calls except, of course, the *Cosa Nostra*-related ones."

"We had a meeting with Massimo fixed for this afternoon."

"Massimo can wait. It's nothing urgent. Move it to tomorrow or next week. I need some time here."

I didn't pay heed to Marco's grumbles. There was an urge in me to spend the day with the beautiful nanny.

CHAPTER FIVE

DIVYA

I followed Armando out of the office. My open-toed pumps clicked loudly on the marble floor. I was relieved to be away from Antonio. He was a lot to take in. He made me feel tilted like I had too much wine. I'd even forgotten all the questions I had for him.

The crying of a baby blasted down the hall. As we neared what appeared to be an open-plan kitchen that was the size of my entire apartment, the cries became louder, sucking me in.

The scene in front of me was one of chaos. An older woman with an ample figure was moving around in the kitchen slowly. Her movements were hindered by the baby on her hip. A chubby bundle of madness screaming out her anger and making her curly, blonde hair stand upright.

I had thought Rosa was Mrs Capizzi when he had spoken of her. But it didn't appear to be the case. Unless

Antonio was into older women. Much older women. But something told me he preferred them young and active. At least so he could practice with his *Kama Sutra* book in his library.

Armando tried to make introductions. He obviously had no experience with babies. If he did, he would know that words were impossible over the sound of a wailing baby.

The woman, obviously Rosa, turned around and released a stream of Italian in his direction with a lot of hand gestures.

I noticed she was trying to get the formula ready, so I stepped into the kitchen. If I wanted this job, I was going to dive right in.

"Can I help?" I asked her.

"Ahh, grazie, Signorina. È molto difficile." Following her awkward instructions in basic English, I quickly got the formula ready and heated. I dropped a bit of milk on my pulse to check for the right temperature and handed it over to Rosa.

"No. No. You nanny, *sì?* You try. *Prego."* She pushed the baby over to me, right now a bawling, red-faced jumble of arms and legs.

The munchkin in my arms went from crying to whimpering when she caught sight of her milk to a fat sigh of relief leaving her when it landed in her mouth. The loud, sucking noises were almost music to my ears.

Rosa and Armando both heaved a sigh of relief simultaneously. Armando looked like he was allergic to babies, and Rosa looked utterly exhausted. She also seemed to have a problem with her knee, as she had difficulty walking.

"*Signorina* Praan is here to take care of our *bambina* Cora," Armando said unnecessarily.

"This is Rosa, *Signorina* Praan. She runs *Signor* Capizzi's household in Boston. If you need anything, you can ask her or me. Rosa's English is not fluent, but she tries her best. You have, of course, already met Cora," he said, looking wryly at the baby as if he expected her to suddenly kick-start her ninja moves.

"She's beautiful." I smiled down at the baby, who was now soundly whacking her milk away with her finger wrapped around mine. Her blonde curls didn't scream Italian, but she came with an overload of cuteness. She kicked her pudgy legs restlessly while looking at me with the most adorable blue eyes, her tears drying on her chubby cheeks. I had loved working with babies in England, and this was no exception. I held her close to me and inhaled that special baby smell. The closest thing to heaven.

Walking over to the nearby terracotta-coloured sofa, I sat down with her and her bottle of magic.

I looked towards Rosa and asked, "Is it okay if I remove my shoes?" I pointed at my pumps, which had been great for an interview. But they weren't ideal if I was going to be cuddling around with a baby.

"*Sì, sì, certo.*" Rosa had the kindest face, accompanied by a lot of wrinkles which showed her age. Her grey hair in a tight bun, she looked like the epitome of ideal grandmother material. Her ample bosom and simple long dress with roses only added to her vibe of comfort and home.

I wondered if my grandmothers would have been like her. My Indian grandmother, I had never met. That side of my family had chosen to never accept my dad after his marriage to my mum. He had brought disgrace to their family by choosing his own wife. Someone outside of their cast, culture, and colour. They kicked him out like a vile insect off their body and never looked me up. They didn't come for the funeral, even though I had let them know. Their message back to me read, "Vineeth died years ago to us." If there was ever a sentence to end a relationship that never was, that would be it. My English grandmother, I had vague memories of. I remembered visiting her and spending time at the beach in the summer. But she passed away when I was eight.

I kicked off my shoes and huddled on the sofa, getting comfortable with Cora in my lap.

Rosa came over, collected my shoes, and neatly placed them to the side of the sofa.

"Thank you."

"No. Grazie." She came over, lifted my chin, and looked at me through her twinkling eyes. *"Bellissima,"* she whispered.

I felt myself heating to her compliment. Not my strongest suit, taking a compliment.

Removing the now empty bottle, I burped Cora. The cutie rubbed her eyes and let out a loud burp. I put her over my shoulder and rubbed her back gently. My father used to hum the most beautiful tunes from old Indian songs. I was sure they would soothe Cora.

ANTONIO

A soft, unusual humming grabbed hold of me and drew me through the hallway, leading me to my living room. A rare sight greeted me. Not with my mother or Yuliya. I silently observed my baby girl with the nanny. *Divya.* Yuliya wouldn't have been caught dead in this situation. But this woman looked like she was born to be cuddled up on sofas with softly snoring babies in her arms.

I moved closer on silent feet. She seemed to be completely unaware of me. With her eyes closed and humming a strange tune I couldn't relate to, she looked to be in a world of her own. Her naked feet stuck out underneath her ass, as caramel as the rest of the visible her. *Would she be caramel all over, or would she have tan lines?* My hands itched to find out, even though my brain told me it wasn't my brightest idea. My brain took over.

I cleared my throat.

She jerked upright, shushing me. "You are going to wake her up!" she huffed like an angry racoon.

Her pissed-off look sparked something inside me. Make-up sex would be hot with her.

What the fuck.

My brain lost the battle.

I sat down on the armchair opposite her and ran my hand through my thick hair. Distance, that's what I needed for my brain to fucking work.

"When will your wife be available to go through the baby's routines?"

Ah! Words that can shrivel a man's dick.

"She's not."

57

"Oh." She shot me a curious look. "I can have a call with her—"

"My ex-wife is not in any way involved with my daughter's upbringing," I said tightly. Leaning back in the chair, I took a breather. No point in scaring my only option away. With effort, I softened my tone. "What routines do you want to know?"

She obviously wanted to question me more. Women and their curiosity. Divya, unlike me, had not enjoyed years of training in hiding her feelings. Conflict to indulge in her curiosity clearly played on her face before she smartly decided to ignore it. "For her milk, nap time, ..."

"Hmm... I am not sure." I glanced over at Rosa in the kitchen for help, but she just pretended she couldn't hear and went about with her tasks. I knew for a fact that Rosa had a specific set of selective hearing skills. She also only understood English when it suited her.

"Babies need routine, Mr Capizzi. Just like we do."

"Antonio," I corrected.

"Have you started her on solids?"

I didn't like her ignoring me. She moved on even after seeing my stern look.

"Does she use a dummy?"

"A dummy? What the hell is a dummy?"

"Hold on." She bent over to fiddle in her bag, giving me a glimpse of her cleavage before coming out with her phone. I catch my eyes on her boobs when she looks up from her phone. "I think you call it a pacifier?"

"*Ah, sì, ciuccio.* She has plenty of them lying around," I said.

"They do need to be sterilised."

I didn't like being chastised. No matter how hot she was. Putting my weight on my arms, I leaned forward and rested them on my thighs. "I don't know fuck about babies or dummies," I said. "I want my baby girl happy. The mother is not in the picture. So, can you look after her and make sure she has all of that? These routines. Or not?"

She looked at me with pity in her eyes and shock. At my tone or choice of words, I didn't know. "Of course, Mr Capizzi."

I didn't need her pity. I needed her to follow my rules, first by using my name. My house. My fucking rules.

"Antonio," I corrected her again. How hard was this?

She ignored me. "When would you like me to start?"

I stared a hole into her face, which was a fucking sculpture, perfectly symmetrical.

"Mr Capizzi, when do you want me to start?"

I had time today. If I had to, I was willing to wait a couple of hours...

"Mr Capizzi..." At my blank look, she gave a loud groan. "Are we going to do this?"

I bit my lip. Her loud groan was static electricity on my dick.

"If you want the job, there are rules to be followed. Rule number one, I am Antonio. Repeat after me. aa-n-t-OH-n-ee-oh,"

"Fine. Antonio." Beautiful. The sound of my name slipping off her tongue was like a sip of amaretto.

"*Sì. Antonio.* You start now. Armando will arrange for your belongings to be bought here."

"Wait." She quickly untangled her legs and slid forward on the sofa. "I have to live here? That was not part of the job description. What do I do with my apartment?"

How else was I to keep her close?

"That should have been obvious. You are the nanny. That means available to Cora," *and me,* "24/7. This is not a secretary job where you go home at five."

Her brows frowned in concentration. What was she worrying about in that pretty head of hers? A lover? Did she have one? A beautiful girl like her couldn't be single, could she?

"Is this going to be a problem?" I asked.

"No, Mr Cap...."

My gaze darkened.

"No, Antonio," she ended lamely.

"Good. A couple of things. Everything around the house, you can ask for Rosa's help. She's a godsend. She understands English better than speaking it. Armando can help if you can't communicate. Cora sleeps in the room next to me. You can sleep in the adjoining room." That thought sent joy through my veins, settling all my blood in my dick.

"Rule number two. You are not to leave the house alone. My men will be available to go out with you anytime you want. Mario and Franco are good men, and you can trust them."

She looked baffled and worried at the same time. "Is

Cora in any kind of danger?" she asked, rubbing the back of the sleeping baby in her arms.

"I don't expect every order to be questioned, Divya. If I say you are not to leave the house alone, it means just that. This goes even if you're without Cora. *Capisti?*"

I watched, satisfied with her hesitant nod of understanding.

"While we are on the topic, I hope you are single. Because no one is allowed to visit you unless thoroughly screened by the security team, and no one spends a night here."

"That won't be a problem."

"Good." I told myself the satisfaction humming in my body was simply because I had less screening to do.

CHAPTER SIX

ANTONIO

So, hot Miss Praan turned out to be a red hot liar. A spark of disappointment ran through me as I listened to Marco rattle out her history. I absent-mindedly rubbed my hand on the leather arms of my office chair. I wished it was caramel coloured.

For a week, little Miss Divya Praan had been charming the entire household. It seemed that no one was immune to her coy looks, wild hair, and sassy walks. Did she think of me each morning before she adorned another sexy-as-hell short dress? I doubted that the effort was for Cora or Rosa, and it had better not be for any of my men roaming around the house. It should have angered me. Yet it only gave me pleasure.

Of course, I liked a good fuck like any healthy man. Before and after my marriage ended, I indulged myself frequently. Sex with Yuliya had been good. Really good. I loved women, but sex was something I chose when to switch on and off. It was never an inconvenience. But ever since Miss Praan walked into my office, I seemed to be constantly walking around with a hard dick and blue balls. A distraction that wouldn't go away even after I found out that she had lied.

Divya Praan, only child of father Vineeth Praan and mother Eleanor Burns. Praan had been a software engineer, and the mother was a small-time shop owner of handmade clothing. They were a middle-class family, but that had ended when they had met with an accident, their car skidding off the roads on a stormy night and hitting a tree. Both dead on impact. That part of the story, although tragic, seemed to be true.

Interestingly, she had first applied to a fashion school in Milan and been accepted. But apparently, she had rejected it later on and moved here to Boston with her so-called lover, Adam Harris. This swine, a slimy fucker, from the look of his photos, had got himself a job in Boston, and she had followed. Second mistake. The first one was to even get involved with the mutt. Anyone who saw him could tell that he was a shitload of crap.

My connections in the financial world reaped extra benefits. Harris was also an avid gambler, and that's putting it politely. He was under the illusion of being an expert in the stock market. It turned out that Harris had freely gambled away all of his girlfriend's money and inheritance. The third and biggest mistake of all.

"It's more like omitting some details rather than an outright lie."

Marco's open-mouthed gape told me my thoughts had spilt out of my mouth.

"Shut your mouth before a fly gets in."

Marco shut his mouth. Concern played across his face.

"What?" I snapped.

"You okay?"

"Of course. Why wouldn't I be?"

"Omitting some details," Marco lets out a laugh. "I never thought I would see this day. But then again ..." Marco gives me a sneaky look. "I've seen Divya. I can understand you bending some rules. Like not waiting for the background search first."

I ignored what he was suggesting. "Divya? You're very familiar."

"She told me you are on a first-name basis."

"Exactly. *We are*. That doesn't include you."

He shrugged his shoulders. "We are friends. I like her. You, on the other hand, seem to have a one-track mind and being friends is not it."

"Don't be an idiot. She's Cora's nanny."

"Yeah, yeah. Keep repeating that, and you might actually believe it. Omitting some details, my ass." Laughing, Marco wiggled off his chair. "You may be the *consigliere,* but don't forget I've known you since we were ten."

I gave him an annoyed look. "Who wants to admit such a lack of judgment, anyway? I wouldn't. That's why she left out some stuff."

"Right." Marco looked unconvinced. "I'm out of here. I need to wrap up some details before Palermo. All right with you?"

At my nod, he took off, leaving me alone with my thoughts of Miss Praan.

I was glad of all her mistakes. That is exactly what had prompted her to show up on my doorstep, like a finely wrapped present waiting for me to unwrap. What a pleasure I will have doing this, one day, soon. Because there was no doubt, I would do this. What I wanted I always got. But not today.

Today I would have to confront her. Contrary to what I had told Marco, no one gets away with lying, not even gorgeous caramel-skinned women with breasts begging to be sucked. I left my office in search of little Miss Praan.

I moved silently along the upstairs hallway, relishing the idea of finding and confronting her. Maybe I would be happy to forget her lies in exchange for a kiss.

She must have been getting ready to put down Cora for her nap. She was crazy about routines. It seemed to be already working. Cora seemed to be a much calmer baby.

I opened the door to Cora's bedroom and found it empty. I could hear loud gurgling from her and running water from the attached bathroom. Walking over to the doorway, I stood frozen, gulping down the scene before me. Cora was seated in one of those things where she could sit upright in her Pampers, happily gurgling away. But Divya ... *che cazzo* ... the woman was standing next to the sink with her naked torso cleaning up what appeared to be vomit from her fucking gorgeous tits. Her pink blouse, which I remembered seeing on her this morning, was lying next to the sink while she dabbed at her nipple. All the blood in my body rushed to my dick.

Fuck.

I must have made a sound because she jerked up, catching my eyes on the mirror.

"Agghh! What the fuck are you doing here?" she shrieked, grabbing her blouse in front of her and clamping her mouth, looking at Cora. As if Cora understood cursing.

Merda.

Now I looked like a teenager drooling at the sight of my first naked boob. This was awkward. But for the life of me, I couldn't bring myself to regret this. "I came to check on Cora," I rasped.

"She threw up, and it was all over me."

I looked at Cora.

Good girl.

My eyes landed on the siren in front of the mirror. I caught a faint shade of crimson climbing from behind her top and tracing a path up her neck.

"I could see that." My lips quivered. What if one of my men had walked in? Although they were under strict orders not to patrol the private parts of the house, Marco totally ignored them. My breath hitched when I realised there was no bra to be seen. "Perhaps you should wear a bra? It would be less trouble to clean up, and I don't want my men to get the wrong idea."

Her head snapped up. "I will wear whatever, whenever I want, Mr *Capizzi*," she huffed. "If your men get the wrong idea, it says more about them than me."

Ouch! I hadn't expected that from little Miss Praan. She was a little firecracker.

"Fine. Don't come crying to me after with their snide remarks."

"I won't," she snapped.

I looked at her clutching her blouse, some silly pink frilly thing blocking what was mine. There was an ache building up inside me of which I had no understanding.

"You want something else?"

I lifted my gaze back to her face with effort.

You.

I had gone up there to talk to her about something, but I couldn't remember what. Instead of embarrassing myself further, I closed the door in silence and leaned against it.

So, Miss Praan ran around the whole day, in my home, without a fucking bra. My men knew better. If they took just one misstep in her direction, I would cut their balls off. I was kind, but not when they crossed the line. Looking at the nanny was already crossing the line. But not for me. I could look all I wanted.

Dark chocolate brown. The colour of her nipples. I knew what my dreams were going to be tonight.

Bloody fucking hell. I clenched my fists, listening to my team of lawyers in my downtown office. My addict, fucked-up ex-wife had found a way to get on my nerves. Again. She had gone and filed for a motion for full custody of Cora. Her sudden interest in my daughter, who she conveniently dumped at the laundromat when she couldn't be bothered to take care of her, would be laughable if it wasn't so damn terrifying. I would never allow that woman to come near Cora, let alone give her full custody.

The divorce had gone through quickly and efficiently. Yuliya hadn't cared, and the paperwork was done before the next death in *Cosa Nostra,* and I had gained full custody. But that was before she realised her father would cut her out financially, which he had cunningly only done after the divorce. Now, it seemed that she was showing her unhappiness about the situation.

I stopped my chief lawyer, Roberto Popolizio, in mid-rant. He was a man similar to my age and a raging success, spoken wildly among his peers and the media as the biggest up-and-coming lawyer in the Boston area. But I knew him long before that. We had grown up together and spent summers in Sicily. His loyalty to me and, therefore, his anger at Yuliya could excuse him from stepping out of his professionalism to rant and rave about her. But no one could be more furious than me, the father, and as far as I was concerned, the only parent to Cora.

"Does she have the finances to take this to court?"

Roberto sighed. "She won't have the means to finish a court case. But she definitely has the means to start one. You know very well this can drag on for a long time."

"Her lover seems to have some assets, plus she has her trust fund from her grandparents," a young woman with blonde hair and red lips in a too-short skirt spoke out of place.

I gave her a brief look, which was enough to put her in her place. I didn't know who she was, but I wasn't talking to her. I knew this type. Grabbing at anything and everything to get me to notice them. Hoping this would suddenly spark my attention to fuck them. Money and power. I drew women to me like bees to a honey hive.

"*Signor* Capizzi was speaking to me." Roberto glared at her. He stood up, dismissing his team. He waited until they filed out, a frown forming on his forehead as he watched the girl with the short skirt close the door behind them, giving me a sultry look.

"Just like old days," he mused. "Is there ever a girl who doesn't want to get inside your pants?"

I ignored his comment. I had bigger things to worry about than some bimbo wanting to spread her legs for me.

"What's the plan?" I wasn't interested in problems. Every problem has a solution. I wanted to know mine.

"It would help if Vladislav could cut her funds."

"He has. But Yuliya's grandparents refuse to disown their grandchild." I walked over to the bank of windows. I watched the pedestrians and cars moving about way down below, each with their shitload of problems. Confusion overwhelmed me. I didn't know how to go about this without getting the mobs into trouble.

"What are her grounds?"

"She claims you're unable to look after a child. Yuliya claims Cora would fare better with her as her mother than in the hands of your staff. She can't win this. Worst case, she will get split custody."

"Which is already too much. There is no way she will get near Cora," I said tightly.

"If we could just bring up her addiction. Plus, she

abandoned her child. This is a no-brainer in a Massachusetts court. You will get full custody. Both legal and physical."

"Roberto. You know better. We cannot disgrace her family. Vladislav might forgive us. But not his sons. We need to find another way. I need this kept away from the families. I need this resolved ASAP. Outside of the courts. *Capisti*?"

"*Certo*."

"All I have heard are problems. What are the solutions? Other than ratting her out, which We. Are. Not. Going. To. Do."

I knew Roberto had something to say by the silence that greeted me. I turned around. "What?"

"Get Vladislav to work on his parents. That's already a start and…"

"On it. What else?" I asked, annoyed at Roberto's hesitance.

"Get a woman."

"Why would I do that? I am trying to get rid of one, and I am nowhere in the mood to get involved with another," I said through clenched teeth.

"You can show the judge you are not single. The both of you can give Cora the home she deserves. Marry. A wife is more stable than a girlfriend. We can work on finding some dirt on her lover in the meantime, which we can then show as a failure to give a proper home to Cora. That is maybe not directly hitting on the family?"

"What kind of crap solution is that?" I paced the window, agitation fuelling my movements. Like hell if I was going to bind myself to another woman. Once was more than enough.

"That's the only one I have, Antonio," Roberto spoke softly. "This is a delicate matter between the families. If we can't resolve it in a direct manner, we have to go around it."

"And how do you propose I find a nice, reliable wife for this crap idea of yours? It's not like any of the women I have dated will be happy to play mummy or even capable of doing it."

Roberto shrugged. "Ask *Zia* Maria to set you up," he said, referring to my tyrant mother. "I am quite sure she will be more than happy to set you up with a good Catholic, Sicilian girl," he said with a mischievous grin. He knew very well my mother's dislike for anyone non-Sicilian and non-Catholic.

Fuck. It was already bad enough that my mother was now spending more time in Boston than in Italy. She was going to fucking ruin my life if she found me a wife.

CHAPTER SEVEN

DIVYA

I hummed to Cora while carrying her down the stairs. It was a little over a month since I met this little bundle of joy, and every day, she snatched my heart in all kinds of ways.

The little one liked me right back. She showed her attachment in ways only babies could do. By giving me dimpled smiles when she saw me or latching on to my face and holding tight.

These days, when I woke up in the morning, I had a purpose. Somehow, where all my friends had failed, little Cora succeeded. She drilled a hole through the wall of darkness that I had effortlessly put up and let a ray of light flood me. Inch by inch. One day at a time.

I put Cora down in her chair and worked on getting her solids ready. I had started her on solids a week ago, and Cora was on a mission to gobble every last bit down. Pumpkins and carrots were her favourites. I took the cutting board down and started chopping her veggies.

Rosa walked into the kitchen and gave me one of her bright smiles. I liked to think her brightest smile was reserved for me. After Cora and her daddy, but before the rest of the staff. We worked companionably together, each going about our tasks.

I loved where I was now. Except for the inability to start my studies, this was not a bad place to be. Cora was a joy. The people were kind. I loved the Italian vibe in the house. Coming from a mixed background, I had either stuck out or felt awkwardly special. In this household, I was different, but they judged my difference as just that. Different. It was neither better nor worse. Most of the staff were interested in knowing about my background and my habits. I thrived on that.

"*Ti piace questo?*" Rosa stood next to me with her big, fat, faded cookery book in hand. She pointed to a recipe. It was all in Italian, and I didn't understand anything in it. Except for the picture of another variation of a lasagne. Saliva pooled in my mouth.

"Yummy," I said with a thumbs up. The last lasagne she had made was so delicious it would have been worth killing for an extra portion. Good thing Rosa made enough every time to feed an army. This one looked like it had even more layers of meat sauce, pasta, and cheese. I loved her food, yet she asked me every time before she made something if I would like it. I never said no, and she never let me down.

I had a soft spot for her. Most times, I battled to break down her Italian into a legible amount of English.

Sometimes, she mothered me, and always, she looked out for me in her gentle but firm ways. She wasn't family. But in the absence of one, it felt like she was. It was nice to have someone looking out for me.

My feelings for my boss were more complicated. *Antonio.* He had a practised ruthlessness about him that sent chills up my nerves. His lazy eyes following me around left me pulsing between my legs. His dark gaze observed my every move, hiding his conclusions in the curtains that hid his emotions. The times I tried to confront him by staring back, I lost forlornly, standing behind a nervous and hot mess. He made me feel like the adolescent I had been a long time ago. Extremely uncomfortable and yearning for approval. As if he held the strings to my puppet and could waggle me around any way he liked.

Most of the time, he was not at home and worked from his office downtown. He travelled a lot. Other times, he would just take off in the middle of the night or arrive late. Sometimes I thought his footsteps slowed down in front of my room when he came home. But I was sure it was in my imagination. He was an enigma. One that I was not sure I wanted to resolve.

His younger brother Angelo, on the other hand, was a dream to get along with. Or, as he said later, "I am not an angel with o." Despite his arrogance when interacting with others, he always softened when we spoke. I had the feeling he had a particular fondness for me. He would often come over and hang around for breakfast with me and Cora, working on Antonio's annoyance. But really for me, some adult company who spoke a normal level of

English was a welcome break from baby talk and no talk with the boss.

A week into my stay, I met Mrs Capizzi, Antonio's mother. Although *met* might be an exaggeration. A bitter taste in my mouth lingered when I thought about that encounter. The woman had looked at me as if I was the shit under her Prada shoe. Whatever she had said about me in Italian to her son must not have been very nice, as an argument broke out straight after that. Oh, the way those two could argue. It was fascinating to watch, with the hand gestures and all. But one thing was evident. Mrs Capizzi was not a fan of mine. Then again, she didn't really seem to like anyone at all. She didn't give a second of her time to Cora, and with her son, all she did was argue. She was perhaps the most cordial towards Angelo. It was a good thing she normally spent most of her time in Italy.

I put down the food next to Cora and settled into baby mode. Oohing and ahhing with her while helping her gulp down her mashed veggies.

A cold prickle filtered through my spine. Glancing over my shoulder, I found Mrs Capizzi standing near the hallway watching me, a mocking smile on her face, which she didn't bother to hide.

What was it with the Capizzis and creeping up on me?

"Good afternoon, Mrs Capizzi." I greeted her with forced brightness, even though uneasiness crept through my body.

Rosa turned to look and then immediately went back to rolling out the dough, studiously ignoring the visitor.

Mrs Capizzi walked over to us and watched me

feeding Cora. *No greetings back*. For a small woman, she could easily cloak a room in a cloud of fear. *Did she even speak English?*

"I see my son hasn't ridden himself of you yet," she said.

Surprise washed over me. Last time, her words had been short and sharp and in Italian. So, she led me to believe she didn't speak English. Frankly, I would have preferred it if she didn't. Her words brought me no solace. Antonio was supposed to fire me? What had I done wrong? That would be crap if I lost this job just after a month.

"For how long do you plan to hang around here, anyway?"

I wasn't to be fired?

"I am not sure what you mean. I don't hang around. I am Cora's nanny. Didn't your son tell you that?" I asked.

"Don't talk back to me like that. I know damn well who you are, girl!" She spit the words out, distaste flowing off her body. "I don't like you tainting this house. When my son gets married, there will be no need for a *nanny*. I would count my days here if I were you."

He was getting married?

Why did I not know anything about it? Even though he had insisted I call him by his first name, in my mind, he had been Mr Capizzi. But somewhere along the line, things had changed. I didn't know when I went from thinking about him as Mr Capizzi to Antonio. Was it after he saw me half-naked in the bathroom? If someone saw my nipple, they were on a first-name basis. Or was it when I spotted him coming in from his morning run, all hot and sweaty? The sweat gliding off his body had got my juices running faster than Adam's nakedness. He had looked up at that exact moment. When he found me, the air sizzled. Like cold water on a hot wok pan. I suddenly felt very odd at the thought of a married Antonio.

Mrs Capizzi bristled at my silence. She looked over at Rosa and spoke to her, although the words were clearly meant for my ears.

"What is the matter with this girl? Why haven't they brought her up well? She should know to respect the elders. You should answer when someone speaks to you."

ANTONIO

I would rather dine with the Mexicans than enter my home. My mother's car parked outside spelt out too many doom scenarios to name one. Some days, I thought Papà was the lucky bastard. Death, it seemed, was the only escape from Maria Capizzi because keeping an ocean in between definitely hadn't worked out.

I followed the sound of her loud voice to the kitchen, just in time to hear her insulting Divya.

"That's enough, Mother," I said even before I walked into the room.

Divya looked upset while Rosa was bristling and holding on to her wooden spoon as if she just might clop it on my mother's head. I might help her with that. The only winner in the room seemed to be Maria Capizzi in her element again.

She turned and walked over to me. All men loved red lips, they said. Except me. The sight of red lips was enough to make my dick shrivel a silent death. "Really Antonio. You need to screen your servants more. The way this new one talks back. My, my."

"That's enough," I said tightly. Cora must have sensed the tension in the room because her cute little lips trembled before she burst out crying. Divya rushed over to carry her while her grandmother just stood and watched.

What else was new?

"Divya, I think it's better you take Cora up. I need to get rid of an intrusion."

I didn't like the way she was being talked to. I wanted her out of the room before I put a hole in my mother's head.

"An intrusion? Who is an intrusion?"

I ignored my mother's words as I let my eyes trail over Divya's body, watching her collect Cora's food and pick her up. I was sure the dress she was wearing was shorter than the one from yesterday. Was she wearing a bra underneath? I couldn't tell.

"Antonio, I was —"

"If you don't shut up now, I am going to embarrass you in front of the servants, as you put it, and it won't be in Italian," I said stonily to my mother in Italian.

She looked taken aback by my sharp words but kept quiet until Divya fled the room with Cora. If there was anyone who hated my mother as much as I did, it might be Rosa. It didn't surprise me that she followed Divya out of the room.

The kitchen smelled of tomatoes and garlic. A smell that could soothe me on any other day. Today it didn't do anything to cool the annoyance running through my veins.

"What do you want?" I got straight to the point.

"You are my son, can't I —"

"Cut the crap. Your visits to America coincide with a plan of yours. You don't visit unless you have an agenda, or you need something from me. So, which one of them is it now?"

"Is it true? Your no-good ex-wife is suing for custody?"

"Yes." No point denying it. She was going to find out anyway through someone in the family. Italians and their gossip.

I walked over to the drink's cabinet. I needed to numb my senses.

"You should never have married her. I told you, of course. But no. Antonio Capizzi thought he was too good to listen to his mama. Look where that got you, huh? A no-good, Russian whore."

"Really, Mother, you are talking about the mother of my child."

"As if you would have better words for that blonde bitch. Vladislav is a good man, but he made a huge mistake by spoiling that bitch of a daughter. He should have never proposed this connection, and you should never have accepted it. You were meant to marry one of our own kind."

79

"Should have, could have. What's the point now? Marrying for an alliance is no strange news to you. It's no secret that there was no love lost between you and Papà. Although ... why the sudden interest in Cora, anyway? I have never even known you to even hold your grand-daughter, so this sudden change is ... forgive me ... baffling."

"Oh, shut up," she snapped. "I called Roberto's office. He has become too big for his own shoes. He wouldn't discuss the case with me. What is the comeback?"

"Roberto is a professional. Obviously, he will not discuss the case with you since *you* are not his client."

"Oh, whatever. When it suits them, they are profes-sionals." She sat down on the sofa next to me. "Only we know what it is like to be in *Cosa Nostra,*" she hissed.

Typical, my mother. She didn't have the height to reach the top shelf, but she had no problem associating herself with *Cosa Nostra.*

"So, what are they proposing?" she asked.

I settled back on the sofa and ran my hands through my hair. "They suggest I marry to show that Cora has a stable support system here with me."

Watching my mother was like watching a light switch being flipped on. She brightened up immeasurably. I regretted telling her, but she was going to find out anyway. We Italians spread our gossip faster than wildfire. "That is a genius idea. Our Roberto is a genius." I watched warily, almost able to see the scheming in her head.

"*Perfetto.* I am meeting *Zia* Elena tomorrow, and I

NANNY TO THE MAFIA

will ask her to invite Viviana's daughter. She will be perfect for you. She has all the skills a good woman should have. She is young, beautiful, and unmarried, of course. Her mama has taught her to cook as well. You met her during Raffaello's wedding. That girl is such a sweet girl and —"

"Mother," I silenced her sternly, getting up. Something told me this proposal had already been in her plans long before today. She was too quick to spring her plan on me. "I will not get married because Roberto tells me to," I glared at her. "And I'm definitely not going to get married to someone you want me to."

"Antonio." She stood up. "That Yuliya woman was an obligation to the family. Carlo should have never allowed it. But this time around, you marry a girl who understands where we come from. Our values."

"And, of course, that is, according to you, only a Sicilian-Catholic girl, isn't it," I mocked her. "Because how could anyone else have good values, right?"

"You got that right. I want my Sicilian grandchildren."

"You already have a grandchild."

"She's a mistake. Just like her mother was."

"*Fanculo,*" I roared. "How are you even a mother?"

"Antonio, mark my words —"

The noise of someone barrelling down the stairs blew into the room. *Bare feet.* Divya skidded to a stop just inside the living room.

"What is it?" I hurried to her, my anger diminishing into worry for Cora.

"Oh." She bit her bottom lip, sucking it in and giving

a nervous glance to my mother. "Cora just turned over. I thought ...you would want to see..." she trailed off, her eyes coasting to my mother again.

"Don't you know better than to disturb us? Antonio is not interested in —"

"Mother," I turned around. "If you even have an ounce of respect for that word, shut up and leave now," I hissed.

I turned around and strode upstairs, but not before I heard Divya mumble, "I forgot she was here."

But I loved that she was excited enough to forget.

CHAPTER EIGHT

ANTONIO

I let myself in, silent as a burglar and softly closed the front door behind me. Moving on weightless feet was a born trait of mine. Two weeks of travelling in Europe had been more exhausting than usual. I normally enjoyed going back home. Stopping by for some business in London had been an added bonus. But I had really missed Cora.

I made my way upstairs to my room, keeping my steps mute and using my sense of awareness rather than switching on any lights. I had landed one day earlier than planned and then gone straight to the office to meet Massimo to solve issues with the acquisition we had in mind. Whitewashing the business of *Cosa Nostra* was no smooth task. In the midst of it, I had forgotten to inform my staff about my arrival. It was late. Everyone in the staff quarters would be asleep. So will Cora and Divya. *Divya*. I had missed her too, in a strange kind of way.

SOPHIA RAZ

I missed her voice, which seemed to have a slight break at the edge. Not all the time, and mostly when she spoke with me. I couldn't stop wondering if it had the same catch when she came. She was always barefoot, strolling from one room to another. Her feet left behind a trail of desire for me to follow. Yeah, I had fucking missed her sexy body.

But it had been good for me to find a distraction. Burying my cock deep in Sonia in Milan had been an excellent one. I didn't have to fucking lust after my nanny anymore.

I didn't bother switching on the lights in my room. Instead, I dumped my bag on the sofa and got undressed in the dark. When I moved over to close the curtains, a flicker of a movement caught my eye. My eyes dropped towards the pool lying beneath my bedroom window.

What the fuck.

Why would she torment me like this?

Swimming.

In my fucking pool.

I stood frozen watching her swim laps, breaking the water smoothly. I wanted to be that fucking water. If she looked up, she would see me standing naked with a hard dick eager to say hi.

Thank fuck I hadn't switched on the lights.

She got out of the water.

I shouldn't watch. I was a gentleman.

I closed my eyes.

My house. My show. Who was I kidding? I was no gentleman anyway.

My eyes flicked open.

84

Fuck if I wasn't going to watch.

She was one delicious rapture of caramel and brown from top to toe. Clad in a skimpy, white bikini, she still didn't solve my dilemma of her tan lines. Did she sunbathe nude? Like a Kinder Bueno, she appeared out of the water, one delicious piece at a time. Her long hair, wet and sleek, was tucked behind her ear, keeping it away from her shining face in the moonlight, with drops of water sliding underneath the band of white and running down to her breasts. I pictured her golden, semi-brown globes begging for my mouth. My memory showed me what I couldn't see hidden beneath the thin fabric. They would be just the right size. They would fit in my hands like a mould. Those delicious chocolate brown nipples would have beads of water clinging to them. Ideal for a thirsty man's midnight drink. My eyes trailed the water trickling past her smooth, flat belly and her curved hips down to her white slip, which I hoped hid a clean-shaven paradise. Just the way I liked it. My entire being itched with the need to be those beads of water and find out myself.

I watched her walk to the sun lounger and pick up her towel.

Fuck.

Her ass.

The urge to slam my dick in her and hear her cum while screaming my name in her broken voice overtook me. My cock jerked. I wrapped my hand around it and rubbed the pre-cum over the head, providing comfort even though it screamed for more.

I listened to her come inside the house, her feet

pitter-pattering on the wooden floors as she went to her room.

Fuck.

So, this is how she entertained herself in my absence.

It gave me immense pleasure to know that only I had access to the surveillance images of the private areas. This show was for my fucking eyes only.

DIVYA

"*Prego.*" Rosa put down the most delicious, American pancakes in front of me. Her smile was as sweet as the caramel oozing out of them. She has been making every variety of pancakes she could find ever since she found out how much I loved them.

"Thank you," I said as Rosa went back to the kitchen. I started on the delight in front of me, enjoying the sugar going inside me as much as Cora next to me in her chair, gobbling down her milk. My bliss in the sugar rush altered to a tickle of awareness floating into the room. I turned to find Antonio coming towards us.

Not only did the man look good, but he knew how to dress well. While all his men around him were in black and white, he most often was not. His soft grey shirt combined beautifully with his beige linen coat. Only an expert could combine cold and warm colours to bring out the bang.

Wait. He was back? Wasn't he supposed to only arrive tonight?

I had explicitly asked Armando last night when he was going to be back.

He bucked down to Cora's level, whispering all kinds of sweet nothings in Italian and filling her chubby face with soft kisses.

My cheeks warmed as if his kisses were laid on me. He was close enough to me to smell him. Something musky and woody with a touch of sandalwood. The urge to nuzzle my face in his neck was strong.

Leaving Cora's side, he moved past me to the bench across from me.

"*Buon giorno,* Divya." He said my name like we'd woken up together after a wild night. Soooo hot.

Hot was what I had been last night before I had indulged in some swimming. Not every day that a girl found herself in a private pool with no man in sight. Or I had thought.

"When did you arrive?"

One eyebrow rose in response to my rude question. So maybe I hadn't got my intonation quite right. Maybe I should have started with the small talk first. But I was drowning in a serious case of hives. If he had come home, he would have seen me. His room looked right into the pool. Maybe he came later ...

He watched me with his dark, intent eyes while he took his time to sit down and reach across to grab the newspaper next to me. Even his wrist spoke of strength and masculinity with a dusting of hair on olive skin.

He let his hot gaze burn me, leaving a flaming trail on my lips, my neck, my breasts, my ... there might be a table in between us, but there was no mistaking the sudden heat in my core.

Shit! Shit! Shit!

He *had* come in last night.

Embarrassment and fury crawled up my heated skin. The thought of him seeing me in nothing but my bikini threw me from hot to bothered to hot. I felt like flinging the pancake on my fork at something, preferably him.

"You came in last night."

"*Sì*," he let his wicked glance flick to my breasts. "It was an unusually hot night, no?"

Leaning forward, he took my abandoned fork from my hand and put the pancake elegantly in his mouth. The way he bit into it made me imagine him doing the same to my lips.

Rosa came over and put his espresso in front of him and swatted his hand, releasing a stream of Italian. Chuckling, he said something back. Whatever it was, it was something about me because both pairs of eyes turned in my direction.

"What did she say?" I demanded.

"She pointed out that I never have breakfast. If I want some, she can make me something."

"You should do that."

"Ah! But I told Rosa that yours is...." He licked the caramel off my fork before dropping it onto my plate again. "So much sweeter."

Bastard!

"A gentleman would at least pretend—"

"Tsk tsk, Divya. I am no gentleman."

He took a sip of his espresso, dark brown on his full

lips. When his gaze settled on my heavy breasts, my skin prickled with awareness, and I just knew. *Knew* that my nipples were standing sharp.

Couldn't he look away? Did I even want him to?

I hoped they were not visible through my silk blouse. It took all my will not to take a peek.

I had the feeling he woke up this morning with the sole intention of embarrassing me. What I needed was a distraction.

"Cora is trying to crawl," I said quickly.

"Is she?" He looked over at Cora, a smile pulling on his lips. How did he do that? With Cora, he was gentle and soft. With me, pfff, I didn't really know what he was with me. Except I felt stuffy. Hot. Bothered. Like I was about to do something in public that I wasn't supposed to.

"The other day, she almost crawled, but she went backwards." I laughed at the memory and how her chubby legs would wiggle all the time. My laugh died on my lips when his eyes fell to mine. I didn't feel like continuing with my pancakes anymore. Not with that look on his face that told me he would lick anything that came in the vicinity of my mouth.

I squirmed in my chair and looked beyond him to Rosa in the kitchen. Now would be an ideal time to have a third person in here. Someone who I could speak to.

Small talk. That was what I needed.

"So, how was your trip?"

"Interesting. I stopped by in Portsmouth."

The sudden stab of nostalgia bombarded me out of nowhere. Just like that, I was back in my childhood home, having pancakes on a Sunday morning. I could almost touch Mum's weathered hands from too much stitching and feel the warmth of Dad's smile. I tried to remember the sound of their voices, but already it was slipping away from me.

Why had he gone there?

The lump in my throat was clogging my breath. I swallowed painfully. I looked away from him to the window, trying to blink back my tears. But one silly one had already escaped and was rolling to my lips.

Dammit.

I didn't want to cry in front of this man.

"Buon giorno miei cari."

His eyes flicked to his brother, face tightening. Annoyance sparked off his shoulders. I didn't care. This was just what we needed. A third party and a second for me to recollect myself.

Angelo swooped into the chair next to him and broke out in a torrent of Italian, indicating to Antonio and his chair with his hands. *That's right.* This was very unusual for him. He never sat down in the morning. He grabbed his espresso and moved on. Whatever Antonio's long explanation was, it made his brother happy. He clapped him on his shoulder, hugged him, and looked at me, grinning. *"La mia bellissima cognata."*

"You do know I don't speak Italian, right?" Sometimes, it was like the entire household thought I had suddenly sparked up my Italian in my sleep.

Antonio whipped up, grabbing his brother by his collar. Angelo was not a small man, but somehow, he made it look so effortless.

"It's for your own good. Some of his words are not meant for your pretty ears, *signorina*," he said, pushing Angelo in front of him and walking out of the living room.

I watched them go, both of similar height. Angelo's long curly hair, next to his brother's thick brown and grey, whispering in Italian about whatever was not meant for my *pretty* ears.

I should look it up. Whatever he had said. But honestly, I wouldn't even know how to type it out, and Rosa's English was average on her best day. Beautiful something.

Crap.

I rushed to do damage control as Cora gargled out her milk all over herself. At least this time, it wasn't on me.

ANTONIO

A few weeks had passed by since I had this brilliant idea. It came to me first when I watched Divya trying to get Cora to roll over for me. Standing in the nursery, watching her on her knees bribing Cora with all kinds of silly toys and smiles. It occurred to me then that I would never find anyone on short notice who would be so good with Cora as she was. To think of it, I had rejected every other nanny who turned up on my doorstep except for this delicious one.

A few days later, when I came across her in the hallway, skipping along with Cora in her arms, barefoot as usual, I thought of it again. I felt comfortable having her around in my home, where few were welcomed.

When I was away, I thought of it again. Thoughts of her crawled all over my head. When I was fucking Sonia, I imagined I was inside Miss Praan.

I didn't have to go to Portsmouth. But when I was in London, I suddenly found myself taking the two-hour drive and walking past her childhood home. It occurred to me then why I would make the effort.

My idea evolved when I saw her in my swimming pool right beneath my bedroom window. While the water trickled to her white slip, the details began clicking.

I voiced it first to Angelo. It was already fixed the moment I spoke of it, but really it only occurred to me that my decision was made the moment I heard Angelo call her *"la mia bellissima cognata."*

Yes. She would be a beautiful sister-in-law to Angelo. Honestly, the only family I gave a fuck about. The perfect granddaughter figure to Rosa. While not her mother, she would give Cora a good upbringing. For me, she would be the perfect wife. I didn't need to marry her to fuck her. And fuck her, I must do. But this was a two birds, one stone kind of idea. It was a convenience.

This was no doubt why I had gone to Portsmouth. Why else would I go all the way there other than to check the background of the woman I was going to marry?

CHAPTER NINE

DIVYA

H e had asked that I come to his office. Antonio never asked. He demanded. Although Armando never said it like that, I knew I had no other option than to obey rather than creep into bed with my interesting novel, as I had originally planned to do. No. When the master summoned, everyone obeyed.

Now, back in that room where I first met the man, I felt as unnerved as I did that first time, under his dark look. My safe haven was too far away to reach.

He looked especially intimidating today. Standing next to me with his hip leaning on his desk and his arms casually resting on his thighs, he gave the aura of nonchalance when his razor-focused eyes on me implied the opposite. Perhaps it was because he was in black and white today. He looked like the devil himself, ready to strike a deal. I had the sudden urge to get up and run in the opposite direction. I wanted no part of this.

"There's a problem, Divya."

My head shot up from where my eyes had been. I hadn't realised it, but my eyes had somehow settled on his groin area.

"Problem?"

"My ex-wife has asked for a motion for custody of Cora."

This was the first time I had heard anything about his ex-wife. Everyone, including Rosa, was tight-lipped about the former Mrs Capizzi. Except for Rosa's "*maledetta donna malvagia*," whatever that meant, I knew nothing more about Cora's mother. How bad could the woman be? I understood Rosa's loyalty, but a child needed both parents. I couldn't imagine my life either without my mum or dad.

"Hmmm, that isn't too bad, is it? Isn't shared custody ideal for Cora?" I continued despite his deadly silence. "A child needs both parents. She needs her mother."

"Cora does not need her mother." His tight voice held a vein of anger in it. The room filled with sparks of tension till that's all it held. He moved off his table and walked towards the windows, watching the gardener mowing the lawn outside.

"Her mother doesn't even want to be a mother. She dumped her off in a laundromat for fuck's sake."

"Wait. What?"

Shit.

I remembered that story. It had been on the news but just as suddenly been taken off the media with no mention of any names. That was Cora? The security cameras had caught a woman smuggling in a baby inside one of the washers. Shortly after, a man came in and picked her up. One minute, the images were available to be released to the police, and the next, they weren't. Both the images and the baby were nowhere to be found.

He turned towards me with cold eyes. The warm swirl that I found in his eyes was nowhere in sight. "My ex-wife loves her drugs more than her own flesh and blood. I had some kind of control over her when she was pregnant, but she let go after she gave birth."

This was a first. There was always a hidden ruthlessness surrounding Antonio, but this coldness sent chills up my bones. An air of manipulation hung around him. He had a plan, and he was going to put it into action no matter what.

I shifted in my chair and gave myself a visible shake. What was the matter with me? I forced myself to mull over the news he had just dropped while he watched me. This was a lot to take in, although something didn't add up.

"So why does she want to share custody, then?"

"Not share. She wants full custody. To answer your *domanda*, money. What it always comes down to with anyone. Money."

"She will never get full custody. Or shared, for that matter. Massachusetts courts will never hand over Cora to a substance user, especially one who abandoned her."

He looked at me as if he was seeing me for the very first time. *What?*

"That may very well be, but this case needs to be wrapped up as soon as possible, preferably out of the public eye and out of the courthouse. My father-in-law is a powerful man and a good friend. I cannot discredit his family by exposing his daughter."

If I'd ever heard a shitload of crap, this would be it. How powerful was his father-in-law? Wasn't he a powerful man? It was clearly fear that outlined the behaviour of his men towards him. Fear and respect. But fear first.

What kind of man was the father-in-law if even Antonio didn't want to anger him?

"If he is a good friend, he should talk to his daughter and get her into a rehabilitation program. And get her to drop the case. She should focus on getting help first."

"Not going to happen," he said flatly, squaring his shoulders and planting his feet wide.

If it was me, my father would have dragged me kicking and screaming into some kind of program and checked in himself just to keep an eye on me. He had loved me, but he also never had a problem telling me when I was wrong.

"Then what do you want to do? Agree to share custody?"

"Of course not," he said stonily.

Annoyance tingled in my veins. "You said you have a problem, and I am trying to think of some solutions." Why was he telling me all of this, anyway? He went from muteness about his ex to clogging my brain with information.

He put his hands in his pockets and rocked back on his feet. The fabric of his pants pulled tight across his groin and thigh area. "My lawyers have come up with a solution."

Good. Because I need to get the hell out of here. The tension in here is killing me.

"What do you need me for, then?"

The fabric of his pants pulled tighter.

Stop looking.

"I am to get married."

My eyes popped up, and my mouth dropped open with a will of their own.

"What?" I croaked.

"This is the only solution for the moment. I need to present a stable front. With a wife."

A wife.

Even though I had walked in here expecting to work for a couple, I couldn't imagine him with a wife now.

That's because you've been imagining him doing other things.

I didn't like the way I felt. I didn't know why it was, but I didn't like it, anyway. I wasn't sure what I lost when there never had been anything to hold on to. Just a few stolen moments conjured up in my mind. Conjured or not, the new Mrs Capizzi wouldn't approve of them. I was sure of that.

I listened to him half-heartedly drone on about how he would no longer be single, more stability for Cora, a mother figure...

Shit.

This was why he was telling me. I was going to lose my job.

What was I to do now? I would have to say goodbye to little Cora. I would never see her walk, talk… hell, forget all that, Cora wouldn't even know me if I were to bump into her one day, ten years, twenty years down the road.

"You will, of course, have to move your things …"

That was that, then.

"To my room…"

Why would I have to do that?

"What?"

"We will apply for a marriage certificate immediately. If you want, of course, we can have a reception later on."

My head felt like it did when I had the flu. It was thickened with phlegm, and coherent thought was impossible. "I don't understand," I muttered.

What had I missed?

"Or not. If you don't want one, fine by me." He stared at me, puzzled.

This can't be happening.

"Want what?" I whispered.

"A reception, of course."

"Fuck the reception," I snapped. "Go back to what you said before."

His forehead creased. "We will need a marriage certificate soon. No point in —"

"Stop." I held my hand out. "I don't get it. Why am I involved in this?"

His eyes bored into mine. "Well, as my wife, you will have to do more than—"

"I am not Mrs Capizzi," I rushed.

He raised an eyebrow.

"Oh, you know what I mean. I am Cora's nanny."

"No one's closer to Cora than you."

I couldn't argue that point. I loved my chubby little munchkin and the light she brought into my life. Antonio, even though he tried to spend as much time with her as he could, was still a very busy man. Her mother and grandmother obviously had other things to do. That left Rosa, her uncle Angelo, and me. From those options, I was the only suitable choice. But still ...

"It doesn't mean I should marry you. You are a sexy man. I am sure you'll have plenty of damsels falling for you. Find one of those."

"No." His face darkened. "What do you think this is? I can just go out and marry some woman who I don't even know?"

"You don't know me either," I exclaimed.

"I know you enough." His tone held a finality and veiled a cold manipulation.

I didn't care for that. "Find someone else. An ex-girlfriend. You must have plenty of them, and you know them."

"None of them are options," he said tightly. "You are the only option."

"But why me?" I slumped in my chair. I had always had a wild imagination as a child and sometimes as an adult, like when I imagined his eyes following me around. But this was just beyond any vision even I could conjure up.

"Why not you?" he asked, his voice soft like smooth velvet on my hot skin.

He knelt beside me and grabbed my chin to look at him. His fingers burnt my skin as his words drilled into my mind. "You are perfect. Marvellous with Cora. Everyone loves you here. You are comfortable in my home."

He took my hand in his, his rough thumb rubbing softly on my crazy pulse point. It must have been on a private call to my core because the urge to cross my legs overtook me. His dark eyes bore into me, knowing the effect he had on me.

What is he doing to me?

"We can scratch that itch we both have. I know you want me, *mia cara*," he said in a dark and smooth voice. "Just like I want you, under me, on top of me. Any way you like. We can make this work. You, me, and Cora. Hmm."

His voice pulled me to him inside the soft cocoon of his words.

He wants me too. Those secret looks were not in my imagination. Could this work? But there was no love, not like my parents.

"I know what you are thinking in that pretty head of yours. You will be compensated, of course.... Imagine this. An end to all your financial troubles. You can keep your parents' house. You can enrol for your studies after everything cools off. Even in Milan like you wanted to —"

Wait. What?

I jerked my hand free and pushed him off, shooting off my chair.

"What the hell, Divya."

A sharp spark of fury hit me. "How did you know about my finances?" I spat the words out. "How did you know about my parents' house, about Milan?"

"Because I looked into you, of course."

"What do you mean ..." I trailed off as realisation dawned on me. "You had me investigated?"

"Of course," he said, getting back on his feet.

"What are you? The bloody mafia, to get everyone investigated?" I yelled.

He watched me with his lips in a straight, thin line with no remorse on his face. All I saw was a determination to get what he wanted.

"You seem to forget that you lied in your interview," he said tightly.

"So sue me. Fire me. You seem to forget that the job description didn't include getting investigated like I am a suspect in some murder case. Marrying the bloody boss wasn't part of the job either."

"Did you really think I wouldn't get you looked into? Find out what you were fidgeting about."

"Call me naive. I trust people are telling me the truth."

"Look where that got you," he exclaimed. "I investigate anyone who steps into my home, especially if they come near my child. This should be no surprise to you. Did you then really think I will not investigate you and your honourable Mr Harris?"

"Aren't you one to speak?" I shot back. "Didn't you investigate your wife before you married her, then?"

"Ex-wife," he said tightly. "Why are you so mad? You had to know I will look to anyone in close contact with my child."

"But you didn't just go into my social media profiles, did you? You dug deep."

What did the man not know?

"Is this why you went to Portsmouth? It wasn't for work, was it?"

He didn't have to answer. His silence was more than enough.

"I was wondering what type of business a man like you would have there. You didn't, obviously." A weak laugh spilt out. "What did you do there? Go to their house? Talked to the people there?"

I couldn't bear it. I didn't want their legacy touched. Asking questions about my parents to their neighbours, friends, strangers... The gossip that would have started. Did he even say who he was, or did he pretend to be someone... a loan shark?

"I just wanted to find out some information—"

"You could have fucking asked me," I yelled. I was so angry that I couldn't control the trembling of my body. "You could have just asked me instead of going around snooping, asking people, bringing doubt into what people thought of them. I don't want anyone to think ill of them. Don't you understand that?" My voice cracked, letting me down when I needed strength to convey my message to him. "Because they were anything but unethical." I stalked up to him and jabbed his chest. "If you had asked me, I would have told you they were fucking great people, AND it was none of your fucking business."

I stalked out of his office and slammed the door.

Then I forgot I hadn't told him, leaving my grand departure in vain. I had to retreat and open the door again. His eyes were still on the doors, still cold, still calculating.

"And the answer is NO!"

CHAPTER TEN

ANTONIO

What the fuck happened?

She acted like a ballerina, but she could summon up the strength of a super-woman. Well, a tiny one, maybe. I grimaced, watching the doors slam against the frame. She couldn't do much harm, but I was sure the entire household heard the commotion.

It had been going so well. I had her eating out of my hand when I said how perfect she was for the job. Like in any negotiation, I had to coat on the positives first. Her anger came out of nowhere faster than any blush she had had on her skin. Mad because I had her looked into? That I knew of her financial predicament? Maybe she felt embarrassed. That I could imagine. But how else was I supposed to convince her? It was no secret she was attracted to me. The coy looks and the awkwardness when I was anywhere near her could only mean one thing. Miss Praan wanted me as badly as I wanted to bury my dick inside her.

But women needed something more than sex. That's why I proposed the money. She definitely needed it. Sex and money, and you got the woman. No brainer.

So what? I had seen where she had grown up. I had spoken to people about the family. There was no better way than to find out what people thought than by asking a stranger. All I had heard was what a tragedy it had been, how kind her parents had been, what a sweet and adorable girl she was. Nothing but good about them. She should be happy about that. I would have told her everything they had said if she had asked.

It was a tad uncomfortable to see the personalised nameplate still hanging next to the front door with Vineeth, Eleanor, & Divya. Apparently, she had neither sold the house nor rented it out. It remained as it had been, with a cleaning lady taking care of it.

Which is why I knew she needed the money. She had a house to take care of in the UK, a couple of years left of a mortgage, rent here if she didn't live with me, and her studies.

She was obviously making a mountain out of a molehill.

Patience was a virtue I had acquired over the years, which was exactly why I was good in my field. I just had to wait until she came to her senses.

I WAS GETTING weary of waiting. There was a slight twinge of annoyance building up. She wouldn't even give me the opportunity to talk some sense into her. That spark of fire I had experienced faintly in the beginning was now igniting full-blown flames.

Every time I entered a room, she would leave. If I sat down for breakfast, she would get up. When the front door opened for me, almost simultaneously, I heard her bedroom door close. I swear to Jesus, it was like she was standing there waiting for me to come home so she could race to her room. Fucking adolescent. Her rage with me was so thick that Rosa, who had never faulted me before, was now giving me dirty looks. She had turned my fucking household staff against me.

Once, I was able to catch her in the hallway before she could escape. I trapped her against the wall with my hands on either side of her. I held her prisoner while trying to drill some sense into her.

"Why are you so mad? This is the best solution for us."

Looking at a very interesting spot right above my right shoulder, she had asked, "Will I still have a job ... if I say no?"

"No."

*T*hat had earned me a kick in my groin. Of course, I hadn't meant that. I wasn't letting her go. But if I said that, what was going to be my leverage? Besides, no was not an option.

So, I pursued her, and I hounded her.

The next day, I followed her and Cora to the bathroom. She couldn't block me off when she had my baby with her.

"This is getting ridiculous. This is a win-win for both of us."

"How is this a *win-win* for both of us?"

There was nothing but admiration in me for how, even when she was fuming with fury, she could handle Cora with such gentleness. She was tickling her while changing her diaper but shooting daggers at me.

"Win for me because I get custody, and of course, you aren't bad to look at ..."

"Of course," she scoffed.

"Win for you because you will get a handsome reward and me."

"Imagine that. I get you." I had a distinct feeling that she wasn't thinking of it as an advantage. "And a reward! What is this? Are you looking for your lost dog?"

Picking Cora up, she came to stand next to me, her words in stark contrast to how gently she was rubbing her tummy. "You can shove your win-win situation up your ass."

———

I was in my office with Marco when she barged in with Cora on her hips.

"Another point," she said, totally ignoring Marco and continuing our discussion as if two days had not passed by, "Your mother hates me."

I shoved my chair back to turn towards her. "What does that have to do with you marrying me?"

Marco was watching us with his mouth open, following the discussion as if he were at the Roland-Garros.

She huffed, "Everything. She is your family. You should marry a good Catholic girl like she wants you to."

Marco turned expectantly to me with a smirk on his face. He was pissing me off.

"*Mia cara,* the things I want to do to you are neither good nor Catholic and do not involve my mother. Unless you want to, of course."

"Goddammit!" She had obviously passed her not cursing in front of Cora phase. She flipped around to go, but before she left, she said sweetly to Marco, "I have the recipe you wanted. Stop by before you go. We can do coffee."

Do coffee!

My vision blurred, and I saw red. Fucking Marco gets a smile, a recipe, and coffee, and I get her shitload of attitude? I watched Marco gobbling her words down, smiling, and following her with his eyes until the door closed. Then, he turned around to smile smugly at me.

"I think she's more into me than you."

My fist hit Marco before my mind could follow. That was the first time I had ever hit him.

ON SATURDAY, I was knocking on her door.

I swear to Jesus I am this close to dragging her to city hall, voluntary or not.

"Go away!" How did she even know it was me? I didn't listen. I never listened, so I opened the door.

"What are you? Deaf?" she snapped from her bed, lying on top of her sheets in yet another short dress.

"Can we speak about this like adults?" I sat down next to her.

"Not when you are in my room," she retorted.

"Will you follow me out?"

"No."

"When are you going to be an adult, then?"

"Never."

She tested my patience like no other woman had. This felt like marriage already to me.

I stood up and looked down at her. The urge to bury my dick inside her was strong. I had half a mind to get on the bed and do it right now. But someone had to be the adult here.

"Who knew I hired a child to look after one." That had earned me a pillow on my groin. At this rate, sex was going to be off the table for a long time.

I FOLLOWED her to the kitchen on Sunday and watched her cutting the vegetables for Cora's lunch together with Rosa. The tension in the air was like the ocean before the storm. Even though I saw the dark clouds gathering, I stayed fixed. Courting danger was a birthright of mine. All I saw was progress. She hadn't left the room. Yet. Nor had she kicked me or thrown some ridiculous thing in my direction. About time.

Rosa was good with her. They silently worked beside each other, moving in coordination, ignoring me. I didn't care. Victory was close. I could feel it tickling in my skin. Persuasion always won.

She put the food in the processor and switched the on button. A soft curse flew out before she tried again. The pressure she was putting on the button was going to help break it sooner rather than later. I wisely held back. Telling her she needed to plug the damn thing in wasn't going to help me score any points. After her fourth try, she yanked the processor from its holder and slammed it across the floor. Even I didn't see that coming. Food and bits and pieces of the processor rolled around, echoing the sound of rolling plastic on a tiled floor. Rosa stood in the corner, shocked and silent.

"I am sorry." She dropped her head to the floor. "I can't do this anymore, Antonio," she said quietly, her voice breaking more than usual.

Rosa moved to comfort her immediately, like a mother hen going for her little one. I halted her in her tracks. "Give us some privacy," I said softly but firmly in Italian.

She didn't look convinced. "*Per favore, mamma Rosa,*" I pleaded. I rarely called her that anymore.

"You better fix whatever you have broken. This girl is the best thing that happened to this house!" she yelled at me in Italian.

"I know. That is why I am asking her to marry me."

"*Oh, il mio ragazzo.*" She rushed over to me, touching my shoulder to comfort me, before leaving the room, looking back over her shoulder.

I sidestepped the food spattered all over and got to her.

"It's broken," she whispered.

"Nothing is broken."

"The fucking mixer is broken!" she yelled.

I sighed. I swore the patience I had accumulated over the years was purely to handle her. Picking up the processor, I put it back together and plugged it in. "See? You just had to plug it in, *piccola mia.*"

She sighed. "I can't do this anymore. I need to leave."

My ears pricked up. Not an option. "What can't you do anymore?" I asked, gently tucking her hair behind her ear, trying to get her to look up. She didn't, but she didn't move away either. That was an improvement.

"You. You are constantly pushing me. Following me. I can't breathe."

"What do you want me to do?" I asked. Frustration fuelled inside me. This should have been so much easier.

"Take it back," she pleaded.

"I can't."

"I love Cora."

"I know that."

"I don't want to lose her."

"Neither do I. Which is why you should help me."

She sighed. "You aren't going to let go of this, are you?"

I didn't answer. As I said, no was not an option.

"I need time. I can't think with you around all the time."

"How much?"

"A month, two months..."

"Not going to happen. A week."

"That's not enough..."

"A week is all you get," I said tightly.

"Fine."

CHAPTER ELEVEN

DIVYA

Bastard. He took away my peace of mind.

I tossed and turned in my bed. It was late. A glance at the clock read half-past two. I let a groan wash through me and buried my head under the pillow.

Sleep. I want to sleep.

My sheets were all tangled around my legs, keeping me prisoner, just like my freaking mind.

I flopped back onto my back. To-do lists. That always calmed me down. I needed to email my friends back in England; saying what exactly? *Hi, my boss fake proposed?* Not really. What did I have to do tomorrow... *today* ...? I needed to ask Armando for new nappies for Cora, empty the dryer, stock up on milk powder... Crap.

I had loaded the washing machine but not switched it on because I wanted to add the underwear I was wearing. Which I was still wearing, and the washing machine, was still not switched on.

I groaned and covered my head with my duvet. I had to go down to the basement now. I didn't have a clean pair for tomorrow, and I didn't want Rosa to empty the washing machine with my dirty knickers. I didn't want to disrespect her like that.

Grumbling to no one in particular, I got out of bed. Everyone would be asleep. If they were awake, they were playing with the devil. Antonio had come home and gone straight to bed, even without dinner. I would know because I listened to his footsteps from the entrance hall to his bedroom, past mine. Always pausing before mine. It wasn't my imagination anymore.

He was giving me space. For the last five days, he had kept out of my way. I wished he would vanish forever. Out of my sight and my mind. I felt like a liar, wishing for things I didn't want.

Creaking my door open, I slowly made my way downstairs, feeling my way around till I got to the basement.

No doubt, a decision had to be made. I had wanted a marriage just like my parents.' Perhaps even with a wild love story like theirs. How beautiful it had been. Their story. When my dad sacrificed his entire family for my mum. It was maybe because of that or despite that. They ended up building their own nuclear family with me. Everything revolved around them. They treasured each other, just like they did me.

But no matter how much I wanted to replicate, I wanted to keep their house more. I never wanted to let go of the memories in that house. One day when I was strong enough, I wanted to return there. Then I could relive those days with them. Dad trying to cook a traditional Indian dish while Mum ran around, cleaning up after him, complaining about the mess but secretly enjoying it, their board game nights, or morning coffee arguments.

But it was becoming increasingly difficult to hold onto that home. My current financial situation was despicable. Living here, I didn't have the cost of my apartment, which I had sublet. But even with that and my income, I was barely paying for the final years of the mortgage of my parents' home, let alone saving for my studies. Try as I might, I couldn't replace both my parents' incomes while scrabbling to save for my studies.

It also broke my heart to leave Cora. One day I would have to. This marriage, no matter how practical he made it sound, would not last for years, like my parents' had. I just didn't want that day to be now. It would hurt less when I was stronger. I was sure of it. Just not now.

Am I really thinking of doing this?

I got out of my underwear and tried to figure out how to switch on the machine. Every time, I forgot how the damn thing worked, and the Italian words on it didn't help either.

I switched on a button and waited for it to start up. I should have changed out of Adam's shirt. Then I could have stuffed it in as well.

Why wasn't it gearing up? Was it on a timer?

"You always walk around without underwear?" I jerked around, squinting to look through the darkness beyond the dim light on top of the washing machine, even though I didn't need to look to know that dark voice.

"What are you doing here?" I whispered.

"Couldn't sleep." He stepped out of the shadows and stepped towards me. He looked tired and casual in his white t-shirt and blue jeans. Did the light just spark? The static coming out of him shot to my naked core, in between my legs.

He stopped right in front of me. A few breaths in between us. If I leaned forward, my hair would nestle in his rough scruff. My hands itched to touch. Smooth or rough was the question floating in my head.

"I couldn't sleep either," I croaked.

"I know I promised you a week...just needed to see you." His gaze fell to the open collar neck of my shirt.

The air was hot and heavy, with sex answering the call. It made me uncomfortable, and I didn't like that. "I have decided," I blurted out.

His hands landed on my waist, and he lifted me up, setting me down on the machine, putting me under the limelight of the dim bulb hanging on top.

Is that why it was burning hot?

"What have you decided?" he rasped.

When did we get so intimate? I watched as he put himself between my legs. When did it go from Mr Capizzi to this? Hardness inches from my core. Panic started settling in. It was going too fast, and he held the reins.

"Divya," he held my face, looking into my eyes, "What have you decided?"

"I always thought I would marry for love, like my parents," I mumbled.

"You are saving a child from her drug-addict mother. Your parents would be very proud of you, I am sure."

"I don't want to disappoint them," I whispered, tears collecting, ready for release.

"Why would you? You need money now more than love. You get to keep their house, save Cora, and save for your studies. Winning everywhere."

"It's not like that."

"It is," he said tightly. "What. Is. Your. Decision. Divya."

I drew a deep breath. This was it. "I will do it, but," I rushed on, "I have a few conditions."

He watched me, a muscle flicking on his jaw.

"Tell me."

"I don't want anyone to know..."

"Know we are married?" He scowled.

"No. That I am .... ugh... getting a reward," I finished, a flush sliding up my body. It was already bad enough that I was accepting money, never mind everyone else knowing.

"Not an issue. This doesn't leave this basement."

I looked to the dark corners of the basement to pick up the courage for the next one. "No sex."

"Not going to happen."

"No. Sex," I said, jabbing his chest with each word. His chest was hot, burning up with a fever we both had.

He looked down at my finger and grabbed it. Rubbing it in his hand, he asked, "Why not?"

His rough hands did things to me I didn't want to comprehend. "I need love to go with sex."

"We'll see about that. That's all?"

"No," I gulped. This was the most difficult one. Looking down, I whispered, "When this is over, when you have full custody, and everything calms down, I am free to go."

He was silent, stretching the awkwardness before he lifted my chin up. "Is that what you want?" he asked, looking into my eyes.

I nodded. Yes. There was a darkness to him I didn't want to tempt myself with. Long term was an impossibility without burning.

He drew his lips into a straight line, and displeasure slid off his face. "If that's what you want, fine. So, it's a yes?"

"Yes," I croaked.

"Good." He smiled. This must be the first time I had seen him smile. It was warm enough to melt honey. "We should celebrate."

"I am not much of a drinker," I shrugged.

"Who said anything about a drink? With a kiss."

"I just said no sex," I snapped.

"You said no sex. Kissing is not sex. A kiss to celebrate. Yes?" He was asking my permission. That was a first.

"Fine." I sighed and turned my cheek around.

He pulled me closer by putting his warm hands on my naked bum till I was at the very edge of the machine. He must have pressed a button because the machine suddenly geared up. I gasped, startled, and he zoomed in on my mouth. He nipped my lips, sending tingles up my body. He held me in place with his grip around my neck. When I made a feeble attempt to move away, he jerked me back to him. He nipped at my upper lip and made his way to my lower lip. He wasn't gentle nor soft, but a moan slipped from my mouth anyway before I could capture it, which he used to slip his warm tongue inside, exploring leisurely, like a canoe moving into a secret cave. Mixing my mintiness with the aftertaste of a drink I didn't recognise. Bittersweet with a touch of spice. It was languid and warm, and I never wanted him to stop. His hand dropped to my thigh and glided up higher. I didn't stop him. He halted on my upper thigh, bunching one side of my shirt and moving it gruffly aside.

His warm lips slid to my neck. He burned me from the inside out. When he inhaled my smell and nuzzled my neck, his soft stubble sent sparks up my body. "Will I find you wet Miss Praan?" he rasped with a wicked chuckle.

I grabbed his hand to halt his progress. I didn't want him to know. He swatted it roughly aside and inched forward. The suspense alone was building up the lava between my legs. He stopped right in front of my apex. Not moving. Neither forwards nor backwards. Just resting and feeling my clenching core. I trembled. In impatience or fear, I didn't know myself.

"No sex?" he whispered against my neck.

My heart screamed, *Yes, sex*. But my brain got my back. With the greatest effort I could gather while I sat with liquid dripping down, I whimpered the words, "No sex."

He didn't listen, anyway.

Thank god.

Two fingers moved forward. Barely touching my clit, yet just enough to feel my oh-so-obvious wetness. My breath hitched as a moan caught in my throat. He pulled them out, his weapons of pleasure, leaving me needy, wanting. Pulling my mouth, he kissed me harshly before letting me go. Letting go of my mouth, my apex, my neck. He flicked his eyes from my mouth to down below. He closed his eyes and stilled his breath. One second. Two. Three. Before he opened them and let them lick a path up to my neck.

He softly rubbed my skin around the collar. "Whose shirt are you wearing?" he asked huskily.

I gulped. Something told me he wasn't going to like the answer.

A muscle jerked in his jaw. "Whose shirt are you wearing, Divya?"

I blinked. Unwilling to answer.

Like darkness wrapping the sky before a storm, his face went dark. Latching on to my shirt by both sides of the collar, he ripped it open, buttons flying around the room.

I shrieked, clutching the fabric to hold it together.

"From now on, if you want to wear a man's shirt, you wear mine. *Capisti?*"

I trembled, the rush of cold air aiding the mixed emotions rushing through my body.

"Divya," he tilted my chin up. "*Capisti?*"

"Yes," I bit out. I was right. The darkness inside him was going to burn me up.

CHAPTER TWELVE

DIVYA

He never let go. He touched me inappropriately in places that were wet. Those two fingers snuck in and continued on a smouldering path. Dipping in my slickness. Burning me up. A groan escaped my lips, releasing with it a bit of the fire burning inside me. I wanted more. I jerked when the lights switched on. We were no longer alone, but I couldn't get myself to care. So close. I was so close to going up in flames. I urged him on. "Please." He stopped his progress. "Please," I begged him. But the lights sucked him up and became brighter, and an intruder's voice spoke up out of the darkness.

I let a frustrated wail out, squinting my eyes. Why was the sun spilling in and spoiling my dreams when I kept the curtains closed just for this reason?

"Ah ha. I see movement. Rise and shine, sunshine."

I shot up in my bed, looking at my dream who,

unlike me, looked calm and collected in a beautiful beige linen suit. The man did suits like it was nobody's business.

"What the hell. What are you doing in my room?"

His hooded gaze dropped to my breasts while his tongue crept out to lick the side of his mouth. I followed his eyes and rushed to bunch the remains of Adam's shirt together. Last night, I was too agitated to bother changing, so I went straight to bed.

This morning, I was paying the price for it.

"Well?" I tilted my face up.

"I am trying to make sure that my fiancee is ready on time for our wedding." His eyes remained on my breasts.

Fiancee.

Last night's, or rather this morning's, events came crashing in, jolting me up and down as a roller coaster ride. Then his words waded in.

"You are kidding me, right? I agreed to your stupid idea somewhere after two, and we are getting married today?"

"In two hours."

"What?" I shrieked. "Who does that?"

"We are going to. Cora is with Rosa, which gives you plenty of time to do whatever you women need to do. We leave in an hour."

The arrogance of this man left me wondering what it said about me. Because he sure left me hot and twisted. "This is not how it works. I just agreed today. I need more time to get used to the idea."

"This is exactly how it is going to work. You are testing my patience, Divya," he said, annoyance

NANNY TO THE MAFIA

reflected in his eyes when he finally moved them back to my face.

"I am testing your patience?" I snorted. Flopping back into bed, I turned around and pulled the sheets up and over my head.

There. That'll show him.

"What are you doing?"

"Sleeping. I'm not getting married today."

I heard him moving. Finally, he got the point. The bed dipped next to me, and an arm landed on my ass. What on Earth? I struggled to come out from under the sheet to be met with a pair of chestnut brown eyes staring at me.

He looked utterly comfortable on his side with his arm burning a hole in my ass.

"The thing is, Divya," he said very slowly as if he were speaking to a child. "There are only two things that interest me today. We get married, or." He moved his hand under my shirt, with his palm big and rough fingers on top of my mound. "I make your dream come true."

I skyrocketed off my bed. We weren't even married yet, and he was already messing up my mojo. He got rid of my boundaries like an eraser on a pencil line. My neck burned at the thought that I had probably been talking in my sleep. It was a good thing my brown skin covered my blushes because he shamed me enough to dig my own grave.

"Fine." I stood next to the bed clutching my shirt together. "You can leave now. I will meet you downstairs."

He made himself comfortable sinking into my duvet

with his hands behind his head, and his dark eyes whirling lava inside.

"What?" I snapped.

"Forgetting something?"

"What did I forget now, Mr Hotshot?"

A frown creased his forehead. "*Mia cara*, what did I tell you last night? That shirt needs to go."

I let out a frustrated sigh. "Not like I can wear it now, can I, since you ruined it. I'll remove it when I go in the shower."

He got up and walked over to me, standing so close that his breath warmed my skin. "Now," he said, holding out his hand.

My mouth popped open.

Was this sarcasm?

But the prolonged silence and his outstretched hand said otherwise. It was not even noon, and the man was getting on my last nerve.

What had I been thinking when I had agreed to this?

He made me mad. Mad enough to do crazy things I never would do.

"Whatever *signor* wants."

I let go of my shirt slowly and let it drop to the floor, showing off my naked body. *Let him look*. I sauntered into the bathroom. *Let him look and see what he can never have.*

MOST GIRLS DREAMED of their wedding day at some point in their lives. Who they will marry, but especially about what they will wear. It was no different with me. When I was with Adam, I had imagined that one day we would get married. I had dreamed of what I would wear. I wanted to wear a saree to pay homage to my heritage. To respect my dad. I had dreamed of finding something that my mum could work on with me. A combination of both my parents' love in that one piece I would wear.

Instead, Adam never proposed, and I was marrying a cocky bastard. So, I found myself going through my existing wardrobe. What did one replace a saree with? Nothing. But going nude wasn't an option when the few minutes of the show I had given had sucked out all my courage for a lifetime. But the urge to make him *want* remained.

I finally decided on a nude-coloured dress I had worn for a wedding last year. Who would have thought that this year I would wear it for my own? It had a beautiful wide collar with three-quarter sleeves and a pencil skirt with two side slits that enabled me to walk. I combined it with a pair of nude pumps and a pair of chunky, gold earrings, something of my mum's I had brought back with me after the funeral. It had been a gift from my dad on their wedding day, which explained the intricate Indian design. I watched the woman in the reflection of the mirror. I wasn't vain, but I looked good. A smugness overtook me as I twirled. The wide collar in the dress left my collarbone exposed, showing just the right amount of skin. The rest of the dress hugged me in the right places, enough to faintly taunt a man.

This was it. I was getting married.

Taking a deep breath, I walked out of the room to

bump into a very enthusiastic Rosa with a crying Cora in her arms.

"Oh, baby, why are you crying?" I tried to take Cora in my arms.

"*No, no, signorina. Il tuo vestito.*" Rosa pointed wildly at my dress. I got she didn't want my dress to get dirty, but it broke my heart to see my munchkin like that. Besides, it wasn't like it was a real wedding.

"Go, *signorina*. Antonio wait."

But of course, no one keeps him waiting.

I was actually getting married.

The courage I had gained dwindled into wobbling nerves as I made my way downstairs.

The warm prickle rising up my body told me he was watching me descending the stairs. The exposed parts of my skin felt too warm, my dress too tight, my breasts too heavy. When I managed to reach the last step without tripping down and making a fool of myself, he was there with his hand on the rail. Our hands collided; our gazes locked. His eyes bored into mine.

Courage bolted out of the room. His eyes glistened, and his Adam's apple bobbed up and down. Did he like what he saw? Was he nervous? Or was he just thinking about some file back in his office?

Give me a hint.

"About time. Come," he said gruffly, extending his hand and guiding me to the waiting car.

Silly me, thinking he might comfort me. Why would he when this was not an actual marriage? I bowed my head as I folded myself neatly into the car.

My mind was all over the place, while my body sat imprisoned in a fast BMW.

Cora crying didn't sit right with me. *We could have taken her.*

My stomach grumbled. I hadn't had breakfast. *Is that why I feel his eyes on me?*

What would my parents think of this ditch I had dug up myself and got into?

I hoped Adam was in a deeper ditch than me.

I let my hands run on the leather centrepiece between me and Antonio. *I should enjoy this ride more.* Other than being in taxis, this was the first time I was in a chauffeur-driven car.

His eyes are on me again. Maybe he is regretting this bloody win-win idea of his.

What time is it in England now? My mind was too tired to calculate.

I miss my friends from home. If only they could see me now. I shouldn't have blocked them off.

I should stop fidgeting. That's probably why he's still looking at me.

Did I wear both my earrings? I fingered my ears. *For a moment, I was unsure.*

What colour is my underwear? Thank god there had been a clean pair. I furrowed my eyebrows. For the life of me, I couldn't remember.

Did I get my makeup all wrong?

"What?" I snapped, looking at him.

He was leaning against the door, his body shifted sideways to inspect me under his microscopic lens.

He shrugged his shoulders, not giving an answer to

my question. "I have asked Rosa to move your things to my room."

"That's unnecessary because I will just move them out again." No way was I going to sleep with him.

Even if I dreamt of it.

"This was not the agreement ..."

"No." I held up my hands. "This was the agreement. No sex."

But it would be delightful.

I didn't give heed to the devil on my shoulder.

The car had come to a halt.

"I'm giving you the marriage you wanted. I think that's enough of me. There's nothing more left to give." I stepped out. Not bothering to wait for him or his men in black, I sped up the few stairs to city hall as fast as my tight pencil dress allowed me to.

JUST LIKE THAT. We were married. At eleven a.m. on a Tuesday. In city hall without batting an eyelid. While most people were hard at work, I arrived in a big, fat car and married Mr Hot Shot. All in a morning's work.

The traffic zooming past the windows brought no solace to my jaw being held tight with unshed tears. I just needed to get back home. Or rather, to my place of employment.

What my parents had created. That was home. Their relationship. That had been a marriage. I had just sold my soul as a form of employment. Popped into city hall for a few minutes and got hold of a piece of paper.

Ever since I lost my parents, everything I did, I had wondered what they would have thought and said. For the first time, I really didn't want to know.

I jerked my head to him when he took my hand in his. His eyes looked deeply into mine.

"What's going on in that head of yours?"

You got the paper, but not my soul. I wanted to yell in his face.

But I didn't.

The dam building up behind my eyes was too fragile for me to open my mouth and let loose my anger. All I wanted now was to creep into my bed and weep under the sheets. So, I turned my gaze back out the window, watching the passing cars.

Besides, the croak in my voice wasn't going to let any words out.

CHAPTER THIRTEEN

ANTONIO

"**N**o fucking way!"
I rocked back on my heels, blessing and cursing the day I met Divya Praan. My bedroom door flew open to reveal the object of my source of pain and pleasure. One woman and so much emotion. I gave no head to her huffs and puffs while I continued uncuffing my shirt sleeves, subtly letting my gaze glide over her through the reflection of my mirror.

She was fucking gorgeous, standing in my room. My wife. Even more so than yesterday. Probably less than tomorrow. Her hair hung loose, tangled in soft curls, still wet from her shower, her eyes blasting daggers at me. She wore that sexy white piece of a nightdress I had asked Rosa to keep ready for her. It was a pity she had covered it up with the matching robe. I frowned, noting that it had not been part of my instructions. Sometimes I wondered whose side Rosa was on.

"I see you are wearing my gift," I observed casually while pulling my shirt out of my trousers.

"Your damn payment I wore for myself, in the privacy of my room."

My mind clouded with images of her touching herself in her white negligee.

Fuck.

"What did you do? Send ten men inside while I was showering? When I left for my shower, all my stuff was there. I come out and apparently, a band of thieves had sneaked everything out and into your room."

"Something like that," I said, unbuttoning my shirt.

"Like hell. I can sleep on an empty bed."

She barged out, leaving me to charge after her. I caught her just before she entered her room, whipping her around and pinning her to the wall with my hands on either side of her. Her back slammed against the wall, her chest rising and falling rapidly.

"Why are you so angry all the time, m*ia cara*?"

"Because you..."

"Shhh." My eyes were drawn to her neck and collarbone, where an angry nerve was in danger of popping. I touched it softly to have her jerk away.

Fuck.

I wanted my wedding night.

"Why?" I muttered.

"Because you get on my nerves all the time," she hissed.

"Why do I get on your nerves all the time?"

"Because you push my buttons all the fucking time," she snapped, jabbing her fingers to my chest with every word. I grabbed her hand and held it above her head. She tried to wiggle out of it, which made me capture both her hands.

"Is that what you want? For me to push your buttons?" I suggested, a grin tugging on my lips, misunderstanding her words on purpose.

She huffed. "You know that's not what I mean, and let me go now."

I pinned her with my eyes, willing her to stay put. The greens in her eyes were hardly visible now, with her pupils enlarged. Her breathing was heavier. Every time she took a breath, her breasts would gently touch my chest. Swollen and heavy. My wife was aroused.

"Not until you agree to come back to my bed," I said gruffly, shifting to adjust my dick.

"No."

I sighed, leaning forward to press a kiss to the mad nerve popping on her neck, just below her ear. She jerked her head away, looking to the other side.

I kissed her again. "*Tesoro…*"

"Stop it. And no name-calling in Italian."

Cazzo, how was I supposed to seduce this woman?

I ignored her demands and continued to nuzzle her neck. Why stop something we both liked? "Since you seem to be fascinated by the view at the end of the hallway, why don't you lift your eyes a bit higher?" I suggested.

I knew the moment she noticed the cameras because her body went still. "Is that a camera?" Her head flipped around. "There's another one on this side as well."

"Yes, and we are being watched."

"Why do you have cameras?"

"For security, of course."

She huffed, "You rich men. What are you scared of, that someone will come and steal your paintings?"

I didn't give a damn about my paintings. I was terrified, though, that they would come after her or Cora.

She didn't wait for me to answer, anyway. "Where do you have cameras?"

"All the common areas."

"So... not in the bedrooms?"

I nodded while she watched me carefully.

"Not in the bathrooms?"

I nodded again.

"How about the... pool?"

Oh, I was enjoying this. "Don't worry m*ia cara*, those recordings come straight to me. I changed it ever since I found a brown Aphrodite in my pool." I found it amusing that even though she didn't blush, she had a slight taint of a flush around her neck accompanied by an increased heat on her skin.

She was quiet for a few minutes. Probably working out all the details, which gave me ample time to bury myself in her neck. She didn't seem to notice my kisses, but her skin under my lips burned hot as a fever.

"So, who is watching us?"

I groaned. All I wanted was to fuck my wife. Instead, we were discussing security.

"If you come back to the room, I will tell you all about it."

"You can tell me here."

"No. In my room or nothing."

"Fine," she sighed.

"That's my girl. Now kiss me."

"What?" She jerked her head away and looked at me closely.

"To give them a show, *tesoro*. Bear with me, hmm?"

She frowned, obviously reluctant to give in, her eyes suspicious.

"Here." I touched my lips with my index finger. "Just one kiss."

She moved a bit closer. "You can do it. Make it look like you mean it." At her raised eyebrows, I continued, "It will look more convincing."

I don't know what was going through my head when I decided to wait for her fucking yes, because all it did was fill me with regret.

Moving closer, she finally leaned forward to give a soft, almost intangible kiss. I wasn't having any of this. When she started to withdraw, I bit her bottom lip, making use of her yelp to slide my tongue in.

Cazzo, I had missed this.

All the heat in my body rushed to my dick. I tried to relieve the pressure by resting it between her legs, softly grinding against her. She slacked against the wall and let her body relax, her tongue thrusting out to join mine.

I gathered her closer, cradling her in my arms while running one hand roughly on her lower back and moving onto her ass.

What a fucking glorious ass.

I firmly embraced it and lifted her up to me. She wrapped her legs immediately around my hips, with my dick nestled between us. I pushed her against the wall to trail hot kisses down her neck to her collarbone and let my dick thrust against her.

I wanted her. Sooner rather than later.

I wanted a fucking release from this want she filled me with the day she walked into my office. I bit the soft skin at her collarbone, control, something I was close to losing. Her breasts peaked out and were clearly visible through her laced bodice now that her robe had slid off one shoulder. I ached to kiss those beautiful mounds, to put those nipples in my mouth, and suck.

Cazzo.

I couldn't reach them while still having her hands pinned above her. I let a frustrated groan escape me. I traced my path up to her lips, kissing, nibbling, doing my best not to leave any marks when I wanted that more than the ability to breathe. I laced her lips with my hot tongue, memorising their shapes, dipping at her cupid bow and dwelling in their depth. Moving to the bottom, I bit her swollen and plump lip. I tasted the metallic taste of blood. Hers in my mouth.

Calm the fuck down.

I invaded her mouth again and let my tongue run through her mouth. I forgot and let go of her hands, but she just used them to wrap around my neck.

About fucking time.

Slowly, I made my way to my bedroom, kicking the door shut to give us the privacy we would need. I realised too late it was the wrong move when the sound drew her out of the trance I had put her in. She was out of my arms and on the other side of the room with the bed in between us in a second. Her stance, with her hands on her hips, told me I'd better make other plans for my dick.

I sighed. I ran my hands through my hair, trying to hold back from dragging her back into my arms. This woman worked on the patience I had built over the years like nobody's business. She had to come to me.

"So ..." she drawled. "Who is watching us, exactly? Or did you make it up?" She eyed me suspiciously.

If I couldn't fuck her, then I needed alcohol in my system. Walking over to the drinks trolley, I poured myself a shot of Amaro.

Her eyes on the tent in my pants was going to make me erupt.

"We have a spy," I rasped.

"What?" Her eyes shot up to my face. Any desire she had wiped off her face.

Taking a sip of my drink, I paced the room, not looking at her. She needed to fucking pull her robe back on. "I was informed today that we might have a spy in our household."

"Informed... by whom?"

"My security team, of course," I snapped.

"Of course," she repeated tartly.

"Who are they spying for?"

"Yuliya, I think." I dropped the *obviously* since that would probably tick her off.

"That's your ex-wife?"

"Yes."

"She's Russian?"

"Yes."

"It's not like in the movies, is it? Where every

Russian is some kind of criminal?" she asked, letting out a nervous laugh.

She was so naïve it was fucking adorable.

"As I said, my father-in-law is a powerful man. Although he doesn't support his daughter's lifestyle now, his parents do."

That was a fucking nuisance I didn't need.

"And, of course, they are very powerful as well," she concluded. "What are they looking for, anyway? Nothing much interesting happening other than our daily bout of fights."

I did enjoy those, although I was happy to move past it to the making-up phase.

"That is just that. We are involved in a custody battle where she is trying to discredit me. We have to show that we have a solid marriage. If not, all this effort will go to waste."

The only effort on my part was keeping my dick in my pants.

She paced next to the bed, making me pause to take her in. I could almost hear the wheels inside her head turning.

"But you said we might?"

"What?"

"You said that your team thinks we might have a spy? So, they are not sure?"

"They are sure, Divya." I said firmly, "I misspoke. My security team won't alert me to something like that if they are not sure. We are not discussing this anymore. You are sleeping in this room."

I turned around and continued unbuttoning my

shirt. I really needed to take care of my dick, but it didn't seem to be on the receiving end of attention today. I needed a cold shower. I bit back my frustration. I was fucking married and the only gift I had got was blue balls.

"Fine."

What? I stalled with my undressing. I slowly turned around, unwilling to make any sudden movements.

"I'll sleep in your room."

Thank fuck.

My cock was elated. "Good."

"You can sleep on the sofa," she said while tugging the top sheets out of my bed.

Just like that, she let my blood run cold. This woman was going to be the death of me. "I don't think so."

"What?" she gaped. "Well, one of us has to sleep on the sofa."

"No one has to sleep on the sofa," I snapped. "You are my wife. We are both going to sleep in the bed."

"I will not sleep in your bed with you."

"If you don't want to sleep, we can play, *tesoro mio,*" I said softly.

"No! One in the bed and one on the sofa," she said, indicating them with both her hands like a damn umpire in a tennis match. "And since you are a gentleman, take the sofa." She smiled sweetly.

I removed my shirt and dropped it on the floor.

"*Ah, mia cara*, how many times do I have to tell you? I am no gentleman."

Her smile froze.

"I will sleep in my big, soft bed. Did you know the mattress has one of the best memory foams?" I let my eyes have their wicked way with her. "It imprints on your body and cradles you softly, completely adapting to all your curves and bumps. Soft when you need it, hard when you want it." I brought my eyes back to her flushed face. "You are welcome to join me if you want?"

"No fucking way," she snapped, tugging the sheet and pillow with her. "Fine. I will sleep on the sofa."

"Suit yourself." I removed my trousers.

"What are you doing?" she asked nervously, clutching the sheet in front of her.

"I am going for a cold shower, apparently." I moved past her to the bathroom before turning around. Her eyes moved from my ass back to my face.

So, she had been following me.

I smiled. "Just a warning. I sleep naked." I chuckled all the way to the bathroom, enjoying her shriek.

CHAPTER FOURTEEN

DIVYA

Sleeping in his room and waking up on a sofa felt strange. It had been a long time since I had slept next to a man, although, technically, I hadn't slept *next* to him. But for some reason, this felt more intimate.

Waking up alone, on the other hand, was nothing new to me. I sat up, looking around me. It was a beautiful room. Big, in keeping with the rest of the house. But unlike the rooms downstairs, here, all the furniture was in stained black wood, giving the room a dark and intimate vibe.

The huge, king-size bed, the focus of our argument last night, was set against the wall in textured charcoal. Intrigued, I walked over to touch it. It felt rough but warm.

Like the master of the room who got my knickers in a twist.

I let that thought slide off me just as quickly as it had entered. I couldn't be thinking thoughts like that.

I sat on the bed to feel the soft sheets. Catching a faint whiff of his smell sent me down memory lane when I was last close enough to smell his woody and sandalwood fragrance. My breath hitched, and feelings crept up on me together with those memories. That kiss. A girl could easily get used to that. Just thinking about it got my juices running.

With a sigh, I made my way to the bathroom, pausing on the way to fold my rumpled sheet on the sofa and tuck it under the pillow. I probably needed it tonight. It wasn't too bad. The sofa was surprisingly comfortable, although his interior designer probably didn't think of this scenario.

I rushed through my shower and came out wrapped in a towel. His. Black. Standing in the bedroom, I observed my surroundings again. It was lacking in two things, though. Colour was an obvious absence, together with the framed picture of my parents, which I kept in my room.

I found my clothes neatly hanging next to his. I ignored the need rushing through me to bury my head in what was his. Instead, I got dressed. I was almost out of the room when I noticed a small box and a note on the sofa. *That was not there when I went for my shower.*

Dinner at 7. Be ready.

Even his handwriting screamed arrogance and darkness.

I flipped the box to find a ring with a large ostentatious stone. Not really my style. What was this supposed to be? And dinner with whom?

A shiver of annoyance passed through my fingers, and before I knew it, I had grabbed my phone and texted him.

> What's the ring about?

He answered almost immediately. I pictured him sitting in some posh office in downtown Boston.

> Your wedding ring.

For a man who dressed with so much style, the ring was a surprise.

> Did you choose it?

> Of course not. It used to be my mother's.

That explained it. I grimaced at the thought of wearing Mrs Capizzi's ring. I wondered if his ex-wife had worn it as well, but I didn't dare ask.

> Got my note?

> Why do we have to go out?

I typed. It's not like we were married for real.

The phone ringing in my hand startled me. I picked it up cautiously.

"Divya, we are having dinner tonight at a restaurant," he said. "The judge handling the custody case is going to be there, and it's important we show our collective faces there to create a story." He broke off in a torrent of Italian to someone else. "*Capisti*?"

He obviously had other things to do than me today.

"Divya, did you understand?" he snapped at me.

"Yes. I didn't know you were speaking to me."

"Good."

"Is it posh? This restaurant?" I walked to his closet again to go through my clothes. I didn't really think I had anything that posh. Unless I wore my wedding dress again.

"I guess so. Why?" His tone implied he had better things to do than discuss the ratings of a restaurant.

I bit my lip nervously. "I don't think I have anything to wear."

Another stream of Italian followed before he seamlessly switched back to English. "Be ready at five. Remo will bring you to some shops." He hung up on me.

Well, good morning to you too.

I put the ring on. I knew him enough to know I'd better get used to it before he forced it on my finger. It weighed heavier than concrete. Problems for later.

Dropping the phone, I walked into Cora's room. A smile tugged at my lips when I saw her in between the white, wooden rails of her cot. She sat in her sleeping back rocking back and forth and gurgling with her stuffed rabbit. The moment I poked my head above the cot, she gave me the most adorable smile I'd ever seen.

Unlike her father, she knew how to greet me with a bright good morning.

———

I DRIFTED from one designer shop to another in the mall. Antonio's chauffeur, Remo, had dropped me off with the request to send a message where he had to pick me up. I loved shopping. Especially if I had the money to spend. But seeing the price tags made me uncomfortable. Antonio was a very rich man, and money was obviously of no issue for him. The credit card Remo had pressed into my hand was hopping in my handbag, eager to come out and pay. Still, I didn't feel comfortable spending it, especially when this, whatever it was, was a short-term arrangement.

I stopped in front of a dress on display. It was absolutely stunning. In a beautiful tan colour, a few shades darker than my skin, it had my name written all over it. A two-piece set with a sleeveless bodice hanging loose on the mannequin in combination with a low waist skirt with a slit in the middle. I peeked at the price. Even though I already loved it, I was only willing to admit it after I viewed the price. Finally. I almost flew into the shop, happy that I wouldn't have to pay half the price of a car to buy a dress.

Inside, I found even more creations I loved, slowly going through the collections one at a time.

"Welcome to Lakshmi's. Let me know if I can help you." I turned around to look at a petite woman in her mid-fifties with an obvious Indian heritage. She had her straight black hair in a tight bun and a *bindi* on her forehead.

"Thank you. Do you have the dress on display in my size?"

"Ah. Beautiful choice, and with your complexion even better." She took a step back to look at me shrewdly. "I think you will have the size of the mannequin. Let me get it out for you."

"Oh, I don't want to bother you too much."

"Nonsense. It's no bother at all."

Looking around, I picked up a lovely clutch in soft gold and high-heeled sandals in a cognac brown. I waited in the fitting room till the lady brought the dress for me.

"It looks like a dress, but it's actually a two-piece set." She said, handing it over to me.

The instant I put it on, relief gushed inside me. I was glad it wasn't the price of a car because I really, really loved it. The linen fabric with a touch of silk gave it a natural look with a soft shine. The colour was beautiful on me. The skirt, though tight, was less so than my usual pencil skirts, making it easier to move around, especially with the slit in the middle that came up just above my thigh.

"Everything alright?" the lady inquired from just outside the curtain. I went out to show it to her.

Her kohl-lined eyes twinkled when she saw me in the dress. "Oh, blessings to you, my child. You look beautiful in this."

Her words made me almost tear up, echoing as they did words from another time.

"I love it. Would you be able to cut the tags off? I want to wear it straight away for dinner."

"Of course."

She got her scissors out from behind the counter. "I am happy to see my design on you."

"You designed this?" I asked.

"Of course, all these designs are mine." She took the tags out of the dress. "We have shops in several places, but I mostly stay here."

I fumbled in my bag for my mother's earrings, happy I had thought to bring them with me. They would match perfectly. "I love your work."

The lady watched me wearing the earrings.

"That's an Indian design," she pointed out.

Smiling, I turned around while wearing my earrings. "It was my mother's. My father was Indian, and he gifted this to her on their wedding day."

"Oh, so romantic."

The doorbell rang, with two new customers coming in.

I walked back into the dressing room when I heard my phone beep. After typing a message out to Remo about my whereabouts, I quickly put on my new shoes and grabbed my handbag. I wanted to get down to the entrance before Antonio came. I didn't want to keep him waiting.

I was just touching up my pale pink lipstick when the curtain flew open to reveal the man himself. He wasn't in a suit today. Even in a dress shirt and pants, he edged my heartbeat to pound inside me.

The air shifted in the small space. A warm prickle

tingled up my spine. I swallowed nervously. I hadn't expected him to come up. Our eyes met in the mirror. His glinted with a dark swirl of emotion I didn't recognise. He let his gaze run the length of me, scorching a hot path through my veins. Silence vibed in the air. He twirled his finger, indicating I should do the same with my body. Like a puppet on strings, I did. When I came to a stop, he latched on to my waist and jerked me towards him, keeping me loosely entwined in his arms. There was a fever in between us.

"*Bellissima, mia cara,*" he said in a broken voice, burying his face in my neck. He inhaled me deeply like I was his oxygen. "This colour, it makes me think ... you are naked." Grabbing my hand, he put my palm flat on his thickness, pulsing, burning under me. "Taunting me with your beauty."

CHAPTER FIFTEEN

DIVYA

We arrived at a posh Italian restaurant. The classic interior with a contemporary touch spoke of the hands of an interior designer. It was warm and cosy, wrapping us in magic.

Antonio's hand slid to my lower back to guide me in, burning my skin through the soft fabric. A good-looking man in his early fifties rushed over in a torrent of Italian and led us to our table. When he pulled the chair for me, Antonio dismissed him and helped me sit down.

He tucked me under the table and leaned down, his voice a whisper on the skin behind my ear. "Fucking delicious."

The goosebumps riding up my arms had nothing to do with the music in my ears.

Instead of sitting across from me, he pulled the chair to sit next to me.

With a frown on my brows, I watched the hum of

activity surrounding my husband. The older gentleman must have been the owner of the restaurant. Despite the place brimming with customers, he hovered over us with a waiter in tow. It was strange to watch them interact with Antonio. He was treated with respect despite his younger age and, like his own men, with an obvious fear. The waiter's eyes skidded to all corners of the room except to my husband, and the trembling in his hands was strong enough to wobble the menu card. Antonio though either didn't notice or didn't care.

Antonio turned to me, putting a momentary stop in the flow of Italian. "Shall I order for you?"

An uncomfortable warmth crept up my neck, with three pairs of eyes directed at me.

I hadn't even glanced at the menu, too distracted by this man next to me.

"Yes." I cleared my throat. "Surprise me."

His lips lifted into a wicked smile. But I would have to be a fool to order at an authentic Italian restaurant when I had the specialist right at my table.

I let my gaze run through the restaurant. All tables had ample privacy. Some more than others. We were seated in a secluded corner, though not the most private. Closer to the entrance, anyone entering or leaving the restaurant would have to pass us.

He can't be that high profile if he can't get the best table in the house.

"You like the place?"

I turned to find him alone again, eyes pinned on me.

"What's not to like?"

"*Bene.*" He took my hand in his and placed a soft kiss on my pulse point. "Our first date."

I frowned. What did he have on his lips to make my skin burn so hot?

"It's not really a date." I dismissed him and his dark look, letting my glance run through the restaurant. "Is he here?"

"Yes."

"Where?"

"If you look at me, I will show you."

I turned to look at him.

"Come closer."

"I am close enough."

Leaning over, he jerked the chair with me on it closer to him, smashing the distance between us. "Not for me. In the far-right corner...." He snapped my head back to him when I tried to look. "Don't look yet. There is an older gentleman in a black suit with two men in grey." He let go of my chin. "You can look now."

I tried to flick a causal glance to the corner. I spotted the bald, heavy-weight man easily. "Is that the judge?"

I turned around to see him nod. He would not miss us when he left the restaurant.

We had the best table in the house.

"How did you know where he would be seated?"

He gave a casual shrug. "I have my contacts."

I bet he did. This man dressed today in black from top to toe looked like the devil himself, able to manipulate anyone to his will, including me. I don't know how he did it, but he wore a simple shirt and trousers like a model on a billboard. Thoughts of ripping off both crowded my mind.

Our wines arrived. Red for him and white for me. I took the chance to regain my hand, wrapped it around the stem, and took a sip.

"Tsk, tsk, Divya. Where are your manners?"

Heat kissed my cheeks as I clinked my glass to his waiting one.

"To our marriage," he murmured.

It was a good wine. I liked them sweet, but not too sweet. Somehow, he had chosen one that was the perfect blend. Another thing he was good at.

The moment I put my glass down, he caught my hand in his and rested it on his upper thigh, rubbing it softly. Just like he had on the car ride. Rough fingers on my soft skin were sending sparks up my spine.

I glanced up to find his eyes on me, visually taking me in, just like he was his red wine.

Crap.

There was a wetness in between my thighs that made me clench my legs together. I flexed my hand lying on his thigh, so close to a warmer place.

Why had I made such a big deal about the no-sex rule?

"Stop fidgeting," he murmured.

I tried to relax my hand in his, the ring heavy on my dainty finger.

He traced the stone with his finger, watching me like a hawk. "You don't like it?"

"It's not really my style of jewellery," I said bluntly.

"I can see that." He noted, glancing at my earrings.

"My mother does like to show her money around. Yuliya liked it too."

What did that have to do with me?

I didn't like it. It was loud. The damn thing was also heavy and cumbersome, hindering me in my daily tasks with Cora. "I don't want to wear it."

"You'll have to. It's just a ring. You'd get over it."

I didn't like the way he brushed it off. Like I didn't have a choice in the matter.

"It's in the way when I am busy with Cora. I don't want to break it." I really didn't want to be on the receiving end of his mother's anger. At least not more than usual.

"Don't worry about it. It's stronger than you think."

A laugh spilt out of me. "Probably more than our marriage." I regretted the words the instant they left my lips. The anger simmering in him was no good for my heart.

"I shouldn't have said that," I said hurriedly. Surprise flicked through his face. For a moment, he looked like he was about to say something but swallowed it back when they arrived with the food.

We ate and spoke of everything that Cora did or will do. Even though the conversation was light, the air between us was heavy. I was having my gelato, and he, an amber-coloured liqueur, when the owner came over and whispered something in his ear. Nodding, he let him leave. Leaning closer, inches from my face, he whispered, "He is leaving. Give me a peck."

I looked nervously at the devil in front of me. He was

in a dark mood, and I was playing with fire. But the temptation was too big for me to ignore.

I put my hands on his scruff, tilted my head, and touched his lips with mine. His hand came up to hold on to the back of my neck while his other rested on my thigh. Coaxing my lips open, he waded in like a thirsty traveller seeking a river. The mixed taste of my pistachio gelato and the spice of his drink exploded in my mouth. His other hand travelled leisurely up my skirt.

Anticipation and lust washed through me.

He groaned gruffly when his hand slid through the slit in my skirt, travelling slowly inch by inch, nearing its target. When his full palm enclosed my soaking, lace-clad core, I swear I saw sparks fly high even though my eyes were closed.

Shit.

My aching core had a mind of its own and was inching itself closer, subtly encouraging him to continue. My upper thighs trembled, thrill and dread fighting next to each other. When he slipped a finger inside my slip, I bit back a moan. My muscles clenched and dripped.

What am I doing? In a public place —

I jerked violently away and fought my way out of the daze.

What have we done?

Flushed, I tried to calm my ragged breathing. We were in a restaurant. Where anyone could and *did* pass by. I looked around me. The judge was long gone.

What was he thinking? He should have known better.

How had that been a good representation of our damn stable relationship?

"You said just a peck," I spat out.

"I lied."

The audacity of his arrogance splashed me faster than cold water on my face.

"I need the loo." I battled my way through the tables, the loud thumping of my heart overbearing above the noises of the restaurant.

I burst into the toilet. Thank god. There was a row of five, and no one around. Rushing over to the last cubicle, I tried to close the door when he marched inside, pushing me further and locking the door.

"What are you doing?" I hissed.

"Finishing off what we started," he growled, advancing towards me.

I tried to back away, but even the most elegant toilets had limited space.

"No," I pleaded, trying to swat his approaching hands away.

"Yes," he whispered, gripping me by the waist and hauling me over to him. He pushed me against the wall. His lust-induced eyes burning a fire inside me, his face a breath away from mine. "I don't know what to do," he groaned. "Should I worship you? Or fuck you?"

I whimpered. Why did he have to let loose these fucking words that turned my iron will into melted lava?

He crashed his lips to mine, kissing me harshly, nipping at my lips, growling in between.

"Tell me yes."

Yes, my body thought, jerking my hips towards his erection. But I wouldn't allow it. I wasn't mad. "Antonio," I whimpered, trying to get my treacherous body to listen.

He grabbed my hand and placed it on his hard-on. "Give me my fucking wedding night, *Tesoro.*"

He was thick in my hands. I moaned, even when I knew I shouldn't. Even when I knew he would take it as a yes.

Of course he did.

As if I wanted him to do otherwise.

Running one hand above my fabric-covered breast, he slid his other under my skirt, seeking and finding my drenching core in no time by pushing my slip aside. When his fingers snuck in, I swear I heard the chorus of a choir somewhere. When he found my clit and gave it a twist, a loud groan left my body without my knowledge.

"Shhh. Let me do this for you, m*ia cara,*" he muttered, kissing me.

The main door to the toilets opened.

I froze.

Two women talking and laughing.

I tried to still my heaving breath.

Their loud footsteps stopped in front of the vanity.

"I would dump Ben any day to fuck him."

"You'll have to pass me first. My pussy wouldn't mind some action from him."

"Did you see that body? And that fucking gorgeous hair?"

"I know. Brown and grey, brown and grey. That would look mighty dark in between my thighs."

My hand on his crotch flew to my mouth to halt my gasp. I whipped my wide eyes to him.

They were talking about him.

His wicked grin pissed me off. I tried to swat his hands away.

"Let me go," I hissed.

He did the exact opposite. Holding on to me, he jerked two fingers inside me, catching my gasp with a hard kiss. It felt so good and so bad to have his fingers inside.

I must be mad.

I was torn about what to do. But my body wasn't, my hips jerking closer to him. His rough fingers were touching places I didn't know existed. In and out they went. I was so wet there was a slickness attached to the rhythm of his fingers.

The voices outside drowned to a hum. I didn't care anymore. There was a lust riding up my body, bursting with a fever, a cure only he could give me. I ground my hips to him, rubbing my apex wantonly on his erection.

The door slammed again. They must have left. Or not. I couldn't tell anymore, and I couldn't bring myself to care. I had other things riding high on my mind.

He let go of my mouth to watch me like I was his victory. He finger fucked me like it was a damn race. In and out. In and out. I tried to bite back my moan. *Fuck.* I was going to scream. I grabbed him and kissed him hard, biting him, punishing him. Mad at him, furious at myself. I loved it. No. No. I hated it. It was soooo good. This madness had to stop.

"Don't stop."

Was that me?

My core throbbed and clenched.

There is no way I'm going to come in a toilet.

I was going to hold it in.

I tried.

Count. One to ten.

I tried to stop my muscles, tried to make my legs stand up straighter, tried to stop this impending outburst.

Fuck.

"No." Trembling and gasping, I came all over his hands.

CHAPTER SIXTEEN

ANTONIO

"How dare you do this to me!"

I swirled my chair and leaned back to eye the woman of all my childhood nightmares. It was the end of my workday. It was past nine, anyway. Although I had planned to stop, it was annoying that it now had to happen because of her.

"What did I do now?"

"As if you don't know," my mother snapped. "All I do is talk good about you to Francesca so she will want to marry you. But she saw you last night at that not-good-for-his-own-mother Piero's restaurant. She told me you were eating your nanny up in plain view of everyone."

Well, I had tried. She was more delicious than any tiramisu I had ever had. Thinking about last night made my cock jerk. The image of her all hot and rumpled in that skin-coloured, gorgeous thing she called a dress. I preferred to call it a sex invitation. That slit in the middle, directing me like a fucking arrow... She hadn't really expected me to stop, had she, when she moaned and called my name out with her whole body.

But she had. The silent car ride back home told me so.

I tried not to hang around a woman long enough to get into fights. My early experience with my mother's tantrums was enough to fill a lifetime. Once she got hold of an argument, she would not let loose. Following my father from room to room, she screamed her anger out like a dog with a bone. Yuliya had been the same but in a slightly subdued manner. Most of the time, she couldn't care less, and she took off breaking things on the way out the door. Other times she was in such a drugged daze that she let it go.

Yes. I was used to all kinds of tantrums.

But Divya's were new to me. It really depended on her anger levels. I had already been on the receiving end of some eventful yelling from her, but that had been mostly entertaining. But when she was really furious, she just withdrew. It was strange to watch and slightly painful. She vanished into her own shell right in front of my eyes.

So she thought I had done something wrong. I didn't agree. Not completely, anyway. So, I had fucked up our show with the judge. He would have definitely seen us making out like a couple of teenagers. That had not been the plan. Not good. But it had shook my self-control not to fuck her right there in that "posh restaurant," as she had called it. This was from a man who had had no issue abstaining from sex in the latter part of my marriage. But she had sat there, right next to me, like a fucking dessert I wasn't allowed to lick. I didn't really like it when I wasn't allowed things. Besides, she had been so fucking wet the whole damn restaurant could have smelled her. No one is that wet if they didn't want to fuck.

But now I was stuck with a silent, invisible wall between us. I didn't do walls and wanted it gone.

"Are you fucking her?" Ah, here she was, my mother, and people wondered where I got my foul mouth from.

"No." *Would love to.*

"Whatever you think you are doing, you need to stop it. You are fiddling with the help, Antonio." Disdain stuck to her face like a permanent mud mask.

Stalking over, she stood with her hands on my table, trying to tower over me. An impossible task given her height of four-feet-something inches over my six feet three. I had always thought that was the reason for her uncouthness. What she lacked in height, she made up for in cruelty.

Jabbing her finger at me, she ordered, "You make this right straight away. I am sure Francesca will listen to reason. Tell her whatever works. You are a man. Seduce her."

"Not going to happen," I said, my voice hard.

She narrowed her eyes at me. "What were you doing with her, anyway? Is this some kind of new bonus package for the help?" she snickered.

I waited for the guilt to rush over. But all I felt was a sheer joy that I would soon break whatever plans she had conjured up for me without my own knowledge.

"We were out celebrating... our marriage." I had to enjoy the minor pleasures in life. Like the sight of her

NANNY TO THE MAFIA

mouth gaping open and her eyes popping wide. One would think I had told her I was fucking a pig. She looked so shocked the air hung still with an imminent stroke. But of course, she recovered.

For once, I was happy that she mostly unleashed her fury in Italian. I didn't care for Divya to pass by and hear the torrent of words coming out of her lips.

"*Che cazzo.* Why would you do such a disgusting thing?"

Her pudgy figure and bloated face were red, pulsing from her frustration and fury. My mother, who always looked the epitome of perfection with her perfectly made face and bright red lips, looked ruffled, for once.

I swear my fascination with Divya has something to do with the absence of red lips.

My day might end well after all.

She dropped her expensive designer handbag on the chair and watched me shrewdly. "Francesca told me that Judge Rosso was dining there as well." She watched me closely. "You married her, of course, for the papers."

I couldn't be bothered to comment. She tapped her fingers on the table while she thought up a plan. Her fucking nails on the wood set my teeth on edge. "All is not lost, of course," she said tightly. "No one needs to know... except, of course, for the paperwork." She waved her hand dismissively. "You have a bit of time now to court Francesca, as a good Sicilian girl well deserves," she continued. "Otherwise, you might have had to rush everything. Francesca is beautiful and has, of course, high standards." She laughed nervously at me and stood up.

"You keep this quiet, resolve the custody thing, and then you can divorce this woman."

From no divorce to two?

She picked up her bag, screaming out some designer's name. "Make no mistake, Antonio, I do not want to hear otherwise. *Capisti*?" she said, sharply.

Did she really think I would listen?

I remained mute because I didn't care to speak of my plans. To her.

"I will take that as your agreement," she said, choosing to ignore my silence. She walked to open the double doors to let herself out.

I was rising from my chair when the door opened again with her head in between.

"And don't fuck her in the meantime. I do not want another one of mixed descent."

The rush of fury in my chest burst out of my very being. My vision blurred, clouding it red. When I blinked, she was gone. One day, even my respect for my father won't hold me back.

No. Non ho capito.

My mind exploded with images of a cute baby brother or sister for Cora. A combination of me and Divya, or perhaps just a mini Divya.

I seriously had to fuck my wife.

But before that, I thought, switching off my computer and closing my office doors softly to walk upstairs, I had a party to organise, to announce my wedding to the world.

This was good, I thought as I walked upstairs. I can grovel back into the good graces of my angry wife and piss off my mother at the same time. Two birds and one stone situation. I was sure she would love a party, making our marriage more real than just a piece of paper.

Did she really think I couldn't read her displeasure at city hall?

I would love to show her off to my allies and enemies alike. And maybe warm my way into her bed. I didn't know why I spent so much time trying to seduce her when I knew if I pushed through, she would relent. But I wanted her to want it as much as I did. Only then would she understand this need deep inside me to wrap around her.

A glance at my watch told me it was past ten. Just as I guessed, my pretty little wife was sleeping already. This sofa situation was pissing me off. I stood next to her, listening to her breathing. She pretended to be asleep. But she wasn't. She should have known that I could read her body better than Cora's favourite book.

I went to the bathroom to grab a quick shower. I needed to resolve this sofa situation to give my mother a grandchild, preferably more than one. This is what good Sicilian children did. Obey their parents to the letter.

I came out of the shower and sauntered over to her. She must have sensed the sexual tension in the air. If she would have just opened her eyes, she could have seen my dick, stroked it perhaps, taken it in her sweet lips. *Jesus!* Just the thought alone had all my blood pumping in one direction.

"I know you're not sleeping," I muttered.

She curled up even tighter into a ball and squinted her eyes shut.

I chuckled, running my hand over her cheeks. "How about a peck?" I didn't really expect one, but it was disappointing that she didn't even take a peek.

Frowning, I walked over to my bed. I had really thought after the restroom incident, she would come crawling to my bed. But I needed to pull out all my tricks to get my wife into mine. Like a fucking teenager.

Roberto may have been right. I'd had it easy with all these women falling for me like flies. What was the point when the siren on my sofa didn't even shoot me a glance? A wave of obscene jealousy swept over me. She lay all curled up on the sofa, her full boobs resting on it.

She had to choose. It was me or the sofa. Obviously, the sofa would have to go.

CHAPTER SEVENTEEN

DIVYA

Cora jammed her pudgy fist into her mouth, trying to gobble it down and spilling out drool in between. She wiggled her Pamper-clad buttocks on the holdup chair while trying to follow me with her twinkling eyes.

I smiled down at her while pacing the floor, the phone stuck next to my ear. Happiness was far away. I felt annoyed with myself for allowing frustration to rule me.

"Come on, baby, how long are you going to do this to me?" Adam whined on the other end, like a fork scraping on an empty plate, making me cringe.

"I am not doing anything to you."

"You are, baby. You are punishing me for my mistakes. How many times do I have to tell you I am sorry?"

"Fine. I forgive you. Happy now?"

"Of course. I want you to come home. If you tell me where you are, I can—"

"Goddammit Adam!" I exploded. "How many times do I have to tell you? I am not coming back. We. Are. Done."

"No, we are not. I miss you, baby. You know I don't gamble anymore. We can do this."

The sun would have to stop rising for me to believe him. His voice alone on these continuous calls riled my nerves.

"We are not doing anything. Ever."

"What do you want? You want to get married? Let's get married."

"I can't marry you, Adam. I am already married."

Wait. What?

Shit! That had not been my plan. Was I supposed to tell people? But this could help me out now.

"I got married a few days ago."

"To whom?" I didn't need to see him to hear his suspicion run through the line.

"A very jealous man."

A burst of laughter greeted me. "Oh baby, are you making up an imaginary husband?"

I bristled, thorns sticking out of my skin. I wished for once he was in front of me so I could jam my fist in his face.

"There is no need to play hard to get," he continued.

"I am not. I got married in city hall a few days ago."

"Yeah, and I'm Santa Claus. We broke up, and you found some guy who was willing to marry you, just like that? Please."

Willing?

My chest burned with anger, leaving acid coiling in my stomach.

What had I ever seen in this man to cross an ocean with him?

I wanted to tell him about Antonio. About his kisses which left my knickers far more twisted than his ever did. But I didn't.

"Fine. Believe whatever you want. I am married. Not married. Either way, I am not coming back. We are done." I hung up on him.

Why had I picked up the phone again when he had called? Thank god he had no idea where I was. I wouldn't put it past him to turn up at our doorstep. Somehow, I had the feeling that Antonio would not take kindly to that.

Rescuing Cora's fist from her own gobbling, I settled next to the bath and let the water run. I didn't mind a bath myself. Some relaxation would do me good. Not that Antonio could barge in. Armando told me he was away on a business trip. Which he had neglected to tell me. I guessed I wasn't wife enough for that.

The man had the strangest hours to work. Last night I had thought I was dreaming when I heard a phone go off and a hurried Italian conversation. But apparently not, because he had taken off in the middle of the night.

Cora stuffed the shampoo bottle in her mouth. I rushed over to rescue it and handed over her stuffed giraffe instead, which she promptly stuffed in her mouth.

My phone vibrating distracted me. *It better not be*

Adam again. I didn't recognise the number, although it looked familiar. I clicked open the message.

> You bitch! Who told you to go fucking tie the knot?

My breath hitched. Who was this? This wasn't Adam's number.

With shaking fingers, I tried to copy the number to find it on my contact list. Nothing. My recent call history slapped me with results. A received call. I racked my brain to remember.

> Fucking bitch!

Another message chimed in.

Heart pounding, I sat down on the edge of the bath. I knew who it was now, though his tone had been different before.

My creepy downstairs neighbour had called me once before. How he had got hold of my number was a mystery. He had been friendly in a weird sort of way. Weird, like cold and clammy, that made you want to run in the opposite direction. A phone call full of questions. His initial questions about how I was faded into weird ones at the end. Where did I sleep? Where did my boss sleep? That was downright freaky.

I had tried to throw the ball back at him. Putting aside my embarrassment, I asked his name and his girl-friend's. It was pathetic that I didn't know this, and I wanted to give it through to Antonio. He should be thankful to these people. Thanks to them, he got himself a nanny and now a wife. The man hung up on me then. It had been a strange call, and I might have told Antonio about it, had he not dumped his business proposal on my lap the next day.

Now it seemed that he was not happy I was married. How did he even know I was married? Except for the staff in the household, I didn't think many people knew. Although it was not like I kept tabs on Antonio. Maybe he was broadcasting it to the world. Maybe he got a picture published of us in the newspaper or something. Did his mother even know? Angelo knew, of course. I knew that when he came around with a bouquet of flowers and sweet words on his lips.

The phone rang in my hand, startling me out of my thoughts. It was the same number. I wasn't a fool. This time I declined the call.

A message came in with a fuck you emoji.

Yep. I needed a new number asap. I didn't get what his problem was. Did he have a thing for me and was now pissed that I was married? But he had a girlfriend, for heaven's sake. Was he mad I hadn't kept a professional relationship? That would be rich, coming from the guy whose banging kept the entire building up at night.

Men. Can't live with them. Can't live without them either. The devil on my shoulder whispered, rubbing its hands in glee at the memory of the last time I was intimate with Antonio. What was a girl supposed to do?

Later that night, I thought I would much rather live without them, staring at the place where my comfortable sofa was. Wherever Antonio currently was, he had found the time to get my sofa taken out to be replaced with a small one of half the size that looked as tempting as a bed of nails.

Good thing I wasn't a quitter. Why give up when winning would give me so much more satisfaction?

ANTONIO

I watched her floating down the stairs with Cora on her hips, both of them babbling incoherently, absorbed in their own world.

A spark of jealousy lit inside me. I was clearly the outsider in this threesome.

I had hoped getting rid of that sofa, the troublemaker in our marriage, would bring peace and relief to my cock. But Divya's determination knew no bounds, apparently.

She was a distraction I didn't care for. Stressful as it had been solving the chaos of a reported shipment, I could not stop thinking about Miss Praan. My relief was immense when we came to an agreement with the feds, fuelled faster than usual by my need to get back home.

Home. Four years in Boston and I had never thought of it as home. Palermo was home or Milan where I had my apartment. Boston was supposed to be work. But now that was where my wife and child waited for me.

I arrived two days ago from my trip in the middle of the night. That was no coincidence. I stopped off at the office for a few hours, hoping I could catch her sleeping

NANNY TO THE MAFIA

in my bed. What else could I do then other than wrap my body around hers?

But she must have been sleeping with half an ear open, because when I came in she was cuddled into the uncomfortable sofa, even though my bed felt warm, and my sheets cradled her sweet smell.

I didn't like the man she was turning me into. Some kind of pussy who juggled tricks to fuck his wife. I swear if she didn't allow me to fuck her soon, I was going to find myself a replacement.

I watched her put my little girl on the floor. Cora came crawling over to me, her chubby legs working over-time. At least I got a warm welcome from her. Which was not what I could say of my wife.

I grabbed my little girl and picked her up. I nuzzled her belly with my rough scruff, which made her burst out in a giggle. I repeated it with the same result. Over and over again. Why couldn't women be like babies?

Cradling her in my arms, I strolled around the room softly telling her all my problems in Italian. The warmth following me around spoke of Divya's gaze. When I looked, she dropped her eyes immediately, stalking over to the kitchen.

I walked over to the kitchen island to take the bottle from Divya, letting my rough fingers slide against her soft ones. Cora wasn't having any of it. Impatient as usual, she grabbed the bottle, spraying herself with half the contents before she stuffed it in her mouth.

"My mother has requested to throw a small reception for our wedding." I broke the silent battle between us.

She looked up from her cleaning, her brows

furrowed in a frown. "Your mother is *okay*... with our arrangement?"

"She doesn't know the details. But she's fine with our marriage," I lied. As if I cared what she thought of my marriage. "It would be a confirmation if we have a reception."

She looked at me, deep in thought, teeth biting into her full bottom lip.

The urge to drop her on the kitchen island and bury my dick inside was strong. I muttered a silent curse to myself. Who was I kidding? There was no replacement for this.

"If that's what you want."

"It is." *And more.*

Her face was an open display of emotions. Confusion, a bit of joy, a layer of sadness. Why did she have to be so fucking sad to be married to me?

She turned away from me, putting things away. What on earth did she have to do in the kitchen, anyway? I had people for this shit.

I wanted her focus on me.

"I will arrange for a designer to come to you. Any favourites?"

She turned around, surprised. "What do I need a designer for?"

"A wedding dress, of course."

"Oh." She stared at me blankly.

"Any favourites?"

"Actually," she cleared her throat, shuffling her feet and looking down. "I can make my dress."

Yes, and I came out of my mother's belly, hitting the

bullseye. "This is a big reception with hundreds of people. We Italians have big families."

"Your point being?"

I don't want you to make a fool out of yourself.

"Money is not an issue. Just pick a designer, and I'll make sure they personally come over."

"I don't want to pick a designer," she snapped.

"Okay, I'll pick one then and—"

"No."

I was confused. A few hundred guests would be there, and she wanted to wear a DIY dress. I was a believer in all her talents. She was amazing with Cora, and my staff adored her. I feared that Rosa had a new favourite, and it wasn't me. Of course, her ability to entertain me sexually and otherwise was noteworthy in and of itself. But she hadn't even started her schooling, and she thought she could whip up a dress to stand out among all others? Didn't she realise the bloodhounds that my family were? They'd eat her alive if she appeared in anything but perfection.

"I really think you would be better off with a good designer. You can tell them what you want," I said gently, trying to persuade her.

Adamantly she shook her head "I would like to work on my dress."

I sighed. "Fine. Suit yourself."

I made a mental note to contact designers about a backup dress. I knew what she would look good in.

"Can I invite someone?"

"Who are you going to invite?" The hurt reflected on her face told me that my words came out harsher than I intended. But really, her parents were gone, her friends were back in England, and she hadn't been here long enough to acquire new ones, or had she?

She crossed her arms in front of her, offering her breasts to my eyes. "I have a couple of friends. They may not be like your Italian family, but they are my friends."

Cora was tiring of my boring talk and wiggled her legs, trying to get to Divya. She came over and took her. A whiff of her scent snuck up my nostrils, filling me up in all kinds of places. I knew so many little things about her. She liked to shower in the morning rather than at night; she slept all curled up like a kitten. She preferred to walk around the house barefoot. The framed picture of her parents was always next to where she slept....

But some things I didn't know about her. I didn't know who these friends were of hers, who were obviously closer to her than I was. I didn't know why she had suddenly changed her phone number. I wanted to, though. I enjoyed discovering what made Divya tick. Layer by layer.

"Give their names to Marco. He will check them out."

She flipped her head around to glare at me. "Of course. Imagine the danger they might bring."

Ah! Her innocence. I hoped the darkness of my world never touched hers.

CHAPTER EIGHTEEN

ANTONIO

My chest tightened and, for a moment, the air was sucked out of my lungs.

I should never have doubted her talent. Now she was taunting me with it. This siren floating down the stairs had done the unimaginable. She had risen beyond any dress any designer could have made. Simply by setting her own rules. This was no ordinary dress.

I was familiar with the saree, the traditional attire in India for women. I've seen plenty in my travels, and it was beautiful on the right woman. Yet I had never seen it like this. Divya's was in some kind of see-through fabric with white sequins, wrapping her like a delicious second skin. Clinging onto her to hide what my eyes needed to see, yet tauntingly hanging loose to give me peeks of hot naked skin. She claimed modesty by wearing some kind of long-sleeved bodice, but the deep cleavage stopping just above her boobs made a mockery out of it. So did her entire naked midriff. This was made solely with one objective in mind. To drive a man insane.

I didn't know how I got there, but I was at the bottom of the stairs when she made it to the last one. Relief washed through my veins. For a moment, I had feared her breasts would be visible under the barely-there fabric. I wasn't sure what I would have done had that been the case. My wife's boobs on display to other men's eyes wasn't what I fucking wanted.

It was beautiful. The saree. She was beautiful. I couldn't tell if she had makeup on or not. She looked just like she did yesterday, only so much prettier today. I liked she had pulled her hair away into a low ponytail. It left her neck free to touch, to kiss, to bite. She probably wanted to come off as sweet Mother Mary, but all I wanted was to push her against the wall and fuck her.

I should fucking say something.

The display of emotions on her face was obvious. Anxious, nervous... she wanted me to say something. I knew that. But what could I possibly say to give justice to what was before my eyes? A man's wet dreams.

Should I worship her?

Or drag her up and fuck her, reception be damned.

Why did I have to be a fucking pussy and wait for her to say yes when her whole body had been screaming it for weeks?

Words abandoned me when I was considered the diplomat of *Cosa Nostra*. A fucking joke.

"*Bellissima!*" Rosa's words hit me from behind.

Rosa didn't have any such problem. It helped that she wasn't thinking of fucking her. I flicked a glance to Rosa to touch base, to recover, to clear the hot haze sizzling around my wife. Rosa's eyes glistened with a grandmother's pride as if my wife was her own creation. But no one could be prouder than I was of her. I willed my eyes to stay on Rosa so my impure thoughts could be cleared. But my eyes had a mind of their own. They rushed back to find my wife silent in front of me.

Beautiful indeed. I wanted to say so much more, but I was a man of few words on any day, and today, I was left with none, so I clung to Rosa's.

"*Bellissima, tesoro mio,*" I croaked.

Coward.

Everything in me wanted to touch her. There was a need in my body that only she could answer. If I touched her now... I didn't know how I would ever stop. I chose not to find out. I put that iron will out that I was notorious for, took a step back, and let her pass, catching the whiff that teased my nostrils of a fragrance of lotus, lilies, and amber.

I followed her, not too close for temptation, but close enough to see my fucking staff fall all over her. She left behind her a trail of ogling eyes and willing dicks.

Fucking mine!

Rosa lifted the tail end of her saree to help her get in the car. I ignored Rosa's accusing glare. I knew what I should have done. I should have helped her get in. I should have held her hand. Hell. I should have put my hand around her naked waist and pulled her in for a kiss.

I would do all that. Soon. Just not now when we had a fucking reception to get to.

I watched her fidgeting hands as the car started up. Hands that should be on me. Instead, the weight of my mother's hideous ring weighed down on the simple elegance of her style. The ache to take hold of that hand and yank her towards me was strong. I could bury my head in that cleavage of hers and never come out. She exuded innocence with her fucking doe-eyed looks. Really, she was a siren screaming for my dick.

"Why are you looking at me like that?"

Words spilling out of those fucking lips. Lips made to wrap around my cock. I shifted in my seat, the heat in my groin painful in my pants. I wanted a relief. "Like what?"

"Like I am your next meal."

"Aren't you?"

A shocked gasp spilt out of her full lips, yet she didn't shy away.

The air was sultry as I held her gaze. "Will you give me my wedding night tonight?"

She didn't answer, gulping slowly.

What would she do if I fucked her right now in the moving car?

"How many yards is this?" I gestured to her saree.

"Nine."

Leaning over, I took her hand lightly. Pinning her with my eyes, I dropped it on my dick.

"Nine yards of fucking pleasure to unwrap, *mia cara.*" My heart flared with hope. She hadn't said no.

NANNY TO THE MAFIA

"You should have told her."

"Remind me again why I invited you?"

I couldn't *not* invite the don to my wedding. I knew that. But if he wasn't here, I wouldn't have his sharp eyes nailed on me, giving me fucking advice on my marriage.

Carlo ignored me. Very few men dared to talk back to the big boss. His son and I might be the only exception. This was why Carlo liked me. Though he might regret that one day. "You should have told her."

"She wouldn't know how our world works."

"Of course not," Carlo scoffed. "Not even our women know that. That's because we keep them out of it."

"So then, *why* are you suggesting I bring her to ours?"

"I am not. She doesn't need to know the details. But she should know who we are."

And scare her away?

I think not.

"Tell her before she finds out herself. She's not going to like that."

I disagreed but kept quiet. I wasn't going to start an argument for something stupid like this. Something that was not even Carlo's business, for fuck's sake.

My eyes found her again. Dancing in the arms of my dickhead of a brother. He had his hands on her bare waist, her breast too close to his chest.

"A fine piece of ass to watch, though."

Agitation rushed through my body, filling my veins

with silent vitriol. I pinned my gaze on Carlo to find him chuckling.

"What?" I asked tightly.

"Calm down. You forget I am much older than you."

"What the fuck does that have to do with it?"

My voice must have been raised because doom hung heavy around us. Carlo's men pulled to attention. No one, not even the *consigliere,* raised their voices to the don.

Carlo brushed them off. "Fucking idiots," he muttered under his breath before he spoke to me. "I've spoken of much worse of Yuliya, and you didn't even bat an eye." He watched me shrewdly. "Maybe your father's wishes are coming true."

"What wish was that?"

"That you have a different marriage to his." Carlo let his eyes fall on my mother meaningfully.

"Unlikely," I grunted. "This is nothing more than a convenience for custody."

"Which could have been solved in so many different ways other than the one you chose. You forget, my boy, I was the first to bless you at your birth. You may be good at hiding your thoughts from the world, but not from me. *A convenience.* Don't insult me by taking me for a fool."

"I am just saying—"

"Nothing. You don't have to say anything to me. Now go dance with your woman. If you don't, I just might."

I flicked him a glance.

"Yeah. That's what I thought," Carlo said, letting a private smile fall from his fat lips.

I made my way to the dance floor. I didn't know what Carlo was thinking, but it wasn't that. I wasn't going to dance with her either. I am no masochist to put my dick anywhere near her in public. I just needed to fuck her. Then I would have the satisfaction of burying myself deep inside a woman I had been lusting after for months. *Months.* Insane. That's what I was. What I needed now was to get her home and tie her to my bed so I could get my fucking sanity back.

I jerked to a stop when my mother put herself in between me and sexual relief.

"This is too much even for you, Antonio."

Cazzo! Will my blue balls ever find relief?

I had managed to stay out of her way leading up to the reception until now. But now was not a good time for me.

"You needed to keep this affair quiet."

"It's not an affair. She's my wife," I snapped, sexual tension cutting my fuse shorter than any other day. "What better way to prove to the court that we have a stable marriage other than this?"

"If you had married Francesca, this would not have been necessary. There was no need to prove anything to the courts."

I reluctantly took my eyes off the prize to look at my mother. "And how would that have worked, then?"

Her lips formed into a thin line of disapproval. I turned my gaze back on Divya, who was much more interesting to watch. She was laughing. What was so funny now? I had a sudden urge to put my fist into Angelo's cocky expression. Take that hand that he had firmly plastered on her waist and wring the life out of it.

"I see how you look at her." My mother followed my gaze. "You better listen to me, Antonio, and keep that dick of yours in your pants."

I hoped my dick was going to have a fucking blast tonight.

"You should know better, Mother. If I am showing something, it's because I want people to see."

I could feel her unconvinced gaze on me. Sometimes I can't help dancing around her like we were inside a ring. I could easily end this with just one word, but I didn't. I turned around just in time to see her plaster a fake smile and wave someone over. "Francesca darling, come over here."

Just what I needed.

I watched the tall brunette walking over to us in a slinky green dress. She was beautiful. On another day, I would have taken her home. Perhaps even for a couple of nights. Who knows, we might have even had a brief relationship of a few months.

Except now, I had higher standards. I followed Divya on the dance floor. No one dared to dance with her, of course, other than my imbecile of a brother.

"Antonio." My mother grabbed at my attention again. "I am just telling Francesca how you are in *Roma* all the time. Maybe you two should meet up when you are there?"

I watched the two women in disgust. One who openly connived to break her son's marriage, the other so obviously ready to open her legs to another woman's man. I couldn't even be bothered to give these two my attention for a second. I let their voice drift to an annoying buzz.

My eyes drifted back to my wife. It was as if her saree hid a magnet, drawing me to her. I felt her every move even when I didn't look. Her laugh, her smile. I had seen her mingle with my family. Friendly, polite. I had watched her mingle with my allies and enemies alike. Except she didn't know she was walking among criminals. An innocent in my world. I had seen the made men ogle her, trying to hide their thoughts from me. They shouldn't have bothered. I had the same. All men thought alike, except she was only mine. She would go home with *me*.

I knew she liked my cousin Laura, who lived in London. I had stood by and watched them talking about London, reminiscing. A soft melancholy clouded her face when she spoke of her weekend travels to her parents in Portsmouth.

She had dragged a couple over, her only invitees to introduce me, a smartly dressed Indian couple in their fifties. Apparently, she had designed the saree with the lady. I didn't know whether to congratulate or curse her.

"My apartment is close to yours," Francesca's voice drifted over.

Finally.

I watched her walking off the dance floor to Rosa, holding Cora. She took Cora over, putting her on her hips, her chubby legs wrapped around her naked waist.

Leaving Francesca mid-sentence, I sauntered over to

the threesome. Leaning over, I nuzzled my baby softly, my hands on her legs, gracing my wife's waist.

"Rosa, will you take her?" I told her in Italian. Rosa carried the baby in her arms. "Oh," I winked at her, "can you keep her with you till tomorrow?" Rosa chuckled and moved away, blowing Divya a kiss.

She looked suspiciously at me. "What did you tell her, and why did she take Cora away? I could only carry her now," she accused.

I dropped down on the chair near me and spread my legs wide, indicating with my finger she should come closer.

Mistrust was written all over her face, yet she obliged, reluctantly coming to stand in front of me, just out of arm's reach.

Did she really think that would stop me?

Leaning over, I gripped her hand and jerked her closer, settling her in between my legs.

"Antonio," she hissed. "People are watching."

"*Mia cara*, do I look like I care? You have been taunting me the whole day." I wrapped one hand around her naked waist, softly rubbing my rough palm on her bare back. "The whole time you have been here, my eyes never left you." I wondered how her saree was held up. Was she wearing anything underneath? I looked up at her. "Why do you taunt me so?"

Her skin felt like velvet. She was making a poet out of me. I sighed. Leaning over, I pressed my lips to her navel. "*La mia bella moglie*, will you give me my wedding night," I muttered. "Put me out of my fucking misery."

I didn't really know what I would do if she said no.

My heated breath fell on her hot skin. I followed the rhythm of her breathing through her belly as she ran her hands through my hair. One breath, two, three. I looked up to meet her hooded eyes. "Yes."

Fucking marvellous.

These would be the sweetest words I'd ever heard. I let a wicked grin spread across my face. That's all I needed. Within five minutes, we were out of there.

CHAPTER NINETEEN

DIVYA

The drive home felt twice as long under his heavy gaze. My skin burned everywhere he touched with his eyes. When he dragged me out of that reception, I imagined he would maul me in the car. But disappointment mulled low in my belly as he kept a distance of a few feet between us.

I knew he desired me. I wasn't great at reading people. But today, there had been no doubt. His gaze had followed me everywhere, more so than my own shadow, blazing a trail from top to bottom, leaving me hot, wanting. So what if I had swayed my hips a touch too much, laughed a bit too loud, tossed my hair a bit too much?

This morning, I had missed my parents terribly. My reflection in the mirror echoed a sadness in me, one I was no longer familiar with. Sad knowing my parents weren't there to witness today, no matter how fake this marriage was. My emptiness made way to something intangible when I saw Antonio lounging at the bottom of the stairs in a soft linen suit in beige with a white shirt, open at the collar, showing off a sprinkle of hair. No black suit. No tie. He followed his own set of rules. More stylish and hot. A mix between a model and a mob boss.

I had wanted to run my hands along his collar. To trail the sprinkle of hair down. Because I was curious about what I would find under his sleek, brown leather belt.

Instead, I had stood silent watching his eyes swirl with lust, reflecting my own. That intangible feeling was desire, I realised. At that moment, I had hoped he would take me tonight.

I hadn't really known how to let him know that. He made me out to be this person I didn't recognise. Sometimes, he could get me worked up so much that I would *gladly* lead an army to his defeat and sometimes... I was silly in his presence, a flutter of confused feelings, missing words, and a lot of aches for something I didn't even understand.

Throughout the evening, I tried to figure out what to say. I had gone through the evening in a trance. I met his family; some lovely, some so vicious they acted like they killed people for a living. I had completely avoided his mother, turning in the opposite direction every time she came close, but even in the distance, I had caught those daggers flying off her eyes. I could read Mrs Capizzi's mind, and it read murder.

"Miss Praan..." Remo's words at the open door pulled me out of my thoughts. How long were we at a standstill while I was lost in my own world? Antonio was getting down on the other side. Embarrassed, I rushed to get out, jerking to a stop when the tail end of my saree wouldn't budge.

Shit!

It was entangled in the seat belt holder. I twisted and tried tugging at it, but it wouldn't let loose.

I looked to Remo for help, but he wouldn't budge from Antonio's sharp look and whatever he was saying to him in Italian, words spilling out faster than a high-speed train. Just when I thought I might have to tear my saree to get it out, Antonio came to help. Squeezing past, he worked on the fabric stuck in a small piece of metal sticking out between the seats. He was so close I could see his enlarged pupils. His warm breath fell on my face. The air in between tingled. Sandalwood and something woody drifted into my nostrils, intoxicating me. I felt heady. The fabric was released. He stepped out, and the air cleared again. I could breathe again.

I put my back to the black front door and waited while he conversed with two of his men standing outside. The man was a freak when it came to security. Seeing me waiting, he ended the conversation and came up, disarming the alarm to let me in. He had told Armando to stay on at the party, which was nice of him. He was always attentive to his staff, treating them like family. But then again, he had even married one of them.

I was halfway up the stairs when I realised he wasn't following. I turned to find him moodily watching me, hands in his pockets.

"You are not coming?" I asked bashfully.

"Go ahead."

I stood still, confused. I had thought he would be on top of me the moment we came in. Had I imagined all of this?

"What's the matter?" I asked quietly.

He walked closer to me.

"What do you mean?"

I lifted my gaze to his. "Don't you want to come?"

"*Ah, tesoro mio.*" He touched my cheeks gently, his thumb rough on my skin. "I do. So much. Preferably inside you, for many, many times. But if I follow you now, it will be over before we begin. *Sì*? Give this man a few minutes to calm down, and I'll be up." He tilted my chin. "*Capisti*?"

The man and his words. He could light a fire inside me with his foul mouth alone. Heat rose up my throat as I went up. I didn't have to look to know he was watching me until I disappeared from view.

———

AN INTENSE CASE of nerves burst in my chest. Butterflies fluttered in my lower belly. After freshening up, I didn't really know what I should do. Should I undress? His words this evening tainted my mind. I wanted him to. Except that left me with nothing to do. I felt like a virgin, though that was a long time ago, and it had been awkward and uncomfortable. I really hoped I wasn't going to go down that road again.

I removed my earrings and dropped them on the little jewellery box on the dressing table. He was taking forever. A glance at the clock on the bedside table told me it was only eight minutes ago. I removed the pin holding the saree on my shoulder.

The air shifted in the room like a loose spark in a storm. I felt his presence on the back of my spine and turned to find him filling the doorway with a glass filled with an amber liquid. He'd removed his coat and held it loosely on one shoulder. He took a few steps inside the room and threw it onto the sofa, where it landed like a blanket. His eyes draped on me like a soft cloth of velvet. The air tightened as he moved closer, sucking it out of the room, when he stopped a few breaths from me.

I felt hot and bothered. My stomach pulsed with heat. I wanted to... and I didn't. I didn't know what I wanted.

His rough hands found mine and unclenched it to reveal the pearl pin that had been on my shoulder. "So, this was what was holding up your saree the whole time?" he muttered, a whisper of frustration in his warm voice.

I nodded. The way he said saree made my insides clench. Naughty and hot. Like he might say, "fuck you."

He set the drink on the table and drew me closer in between his legs while he rested his ass on the edge of the table. The heat between his legs pulsed against my core. He coaxed my lips open and invaded my mouth, letting the warm spiced taste of his drink dip into my mouth. Whatever he was drinking was delicious. He was delicious. A sigh fell out of me as I wrapped my hands around his neck. His hands rubbed my waist, his palms rough on my soft skin, sending tingles up my body.

With a muffled groan, he hauled me closer, deepening the kiss, almost hurting me with his ferocity.

Nestled between his legs, I could feel that the drink hadn't helped much. He slid his hands up, past my breasts, past my neck, intertwining them in my hair, removing the band holding my ponytail. Letting my lips go, he watched his hands tracing my hair, a dark fascination in his eyes. He touched the strands and drew them up to my bodice, laying them on top like a cloak on a warm winter night.

"The whole day I've been dreaming about unwrapping you," he said, his voice hoarse, "and it was just this pin," he glanced over at the offending article, "holding this whole thing up," he said as amazement flickered in his eyes.

He gave me a gentle shove and walked around me, wrapping his hand around the tail end of my saree. I turned to watch him softly touch the fabric.

"I don't know if I should unwrap or not...." Anguish played on his face before he gave me a harsh twirl, folding the revealing yards of fabric to him. "I decided to unwrap," he told me darkly.

Dropping the fabric, he commanded, "The skirt needs to go." I wiggled out of my silk skirt, which enabled the saree to be tucked in.

A slow awkwardness rolled inside me, given my state of undress compared to his.

"Come here," he growled.

When I didn't move fast enough, he latched onto my ass, dragging me closer and lifting me up into his arms. I wrapped my arms and legs around him, my thin, transparent, ivory string touching his erection tauntingly.

He plunged into my mouth like I was his favourite

dessert. His hands kneaded my ass roughly, pushing me closer to his thickness. He made his way to the bed, got distracted, and drove me against the nearest wall, rubbing himself against me. I moaned, wrapping myself tighter around him, leaving no air in between. I felt warm and wet, my pulse quickening. Lust, as I've never known before, rushed through my veins. I wanted him undressed. I tried to unbutton his shirt and got two buttons down before he grabbed my hands and pinned them above my head.

"No," he grated. "I'm trying to go slow." He murmured all kinds of incomprehensible Italian words while nipping on the side of my neck, moving along to my cleavage. His rough scruff left my skin prickled and needy. Pushing me against the wall, he tried to unhook the front opening of my bodice without success.

He pulled away, breathing hard, frustration ebbing off him. "Get this thing out."

His dark, hooded eyes watched my nervous fingers slide the five invisible hooks. When my bodice popped open, his eyes jerked up to mine. "Naked? You were naked underneath this," he croaked.

"It has a built-in bra," I said timidly.

Jerking upright, he walked briskly to the bed and dumped me on it. He stood before me, his eyes hot and burning, drinking me in like he would his amber-coloured liquid.

Embarrassment clouded in from my nakedness. When I tried to scoot away, he grabbed me by my ankle and yanked me down, crawling on top of me. "What are you doing to me, *mia cara?*" he rasped, his mouth inches from one nipple. He dropped his mouth on it, sucking hard, biting it on the edges and pulling it up tight in between his teeth. It was pain mixed with pleasure that made my back arch off the bed and my toes curl. My other nipple stood out, calling out for attention, goose bumps filling in its wake. He obliged, lavishing his attention on it while pinching and soothing my over-excited nipple with his hand.

There was a wetness dripping between my legs, a need to be filled whirling inside me. I moaned out my pleasure.

Lifting his head, he gave me a heavy look and walked his hand down my belly. I watched him, my body humming with anticipation. When he slid down, I tried to flip away, but he wouldn't allow it.

Sitting up, he held onto my knees, spreading them apart.

When his gaze met mine, his pupils were dark black and simmering with lust. "Fuck slow," he muttered. Jutting his hand in between my legs, he split my beautiful lace string in two.

I gasped. I loved that piece.

"I'll get you a new one. I promise. I just can't...." He didn't finish his thoughts before levelling my knees with the bed.

I tightened my butt muscles and forced my hips back. My lips down there were swollen and thick. Heavy with all the blood in my veins. Ready to combust. Yet he taunted me. Kissing the inside of my thighs. He licked the stickiness of my juices and trailed a path that went higher. The tension was going to kill me. When he finally parted my lips and kissed me, the relief was so great I jerked wildly. He licked and nibbled, creating a path around and ending on my clit. He sucked it into his mouth, cramping my toes into a permanent clench.

Shit!

All thoughts of decency deserted me as I grabbed hold of his thick hair, pulled at it, and jerked my hips. Latching onto one breast with his hand, he pulled and tweaked my nipple. Just when I thought this was the closest thing to heaven, he slid his fingers inside me.

Goddammit!

My eyes rolled to the back of my head. His fingers inside me, deep and fast, were driving me to fill a want I didn't know I had. The hands on my nipple and tongue on my clit drove me to it faster.

Shit!

I teetered on the edge of something I couldn't fathom. The ache inside me spilt, making my thighs clench. I jumped, and I shook as I screamed out my orgasm.

My voice was cracking like fresh paint on wet plaster. I couldn't stop my shaking, but he wouldn't stop fucking me with his fingers. He sat up on his knees, watching where his finger was, still pinching my nipple.

It was so damn hot to have him still fully dressed in between my nakedness.

I wasn't going to come another time. I wasn't.

I tried to hold it back. I really did. I shook my head vigorously, trying to dislodge or distract, I didn't know, but when he let some sexy-sounding jargon in Italian flow, I came again and sputtered on his hands.

All the fire in me drained out, leaving a silent buzz inside. I watched him retreat his finger. Then he did the dirtiest thing I'd ever seen. His eyes dark and glassy, he put his fingers in his mouth and sucked it hard.

I swear I combusted silently.

"Sweet," he whispered, his voice hoarse.

I wanted him. Madly. Deep inside me. I wanted him naked. As if my thoughts had ping-ponged to him, he yanked his shirt open, sending buttons splintering all over the room, the noise loud in the silent room broken only by my heavy breathing. Skidding off the bed, he kicked his shoes and socks off and got rid of his pants and boxers in one go.

A flash of lust sparked deep inside me. The room sang with sizzling hot air. The man had an amazing body. Even though I've seen him in his briefs, this view outdid all that had passed. I followed him with my eyes as he walked to his nightstand, grabbing hold of a condom. He held my gaze as he put the rubber on him, slow and steady, watching me watch him.

"Do you like what you see, *mia cara*?" he whispered as he rubbed his erection up and down. He grew harder in front of my eyes, and I licked my lips, leaning back on my arms and spreading my legs wider.

His eyes lit up like fireworks in a dark, starless sky. With a groan, he pounced on me. Moving over me, his face inches from mine, he whispered, "Fucking mine," before he kissed me. He tasted of his drink and something new. Me.

He left my mouth, making his way down, tracing his mouth along my body as if he was drawing a path to paradise, where every halt was anxiously waiting for his arrival.

At my waist, he grabbed hold of my hands and held them in his on top of my head.

Settling on his knees, he rubbed the tip of his erection on my slit. "So long. Fucking...." He slid in, his face taut from the pressure of holding back, sliding in inch by inch. "So long." When he was completely in, he rested his head on my forehead, breathing in, giving me time to adjust.

I couldn't stand it. "Please ...."

"What do you want, *tesoro*?"

"More," I whimpered.

He let out a shaky laugh. "I am trying to go slow."

"I don't want slow."

His eyes turned black. Sliding slowly out, he plunged back in harder and deeper.

"Like this?" He gritted his teeth.

"Yes!" I yelled.

"You asked for it," he muttered.

He grabbed my ass with his free hand, hauled me closer, and kept his rhythm going. I wrapped my legs around him, the angle now deeper.

A moan escaped me. I felt heady, and a trail of fire lit my body. The pounding in my ears and the pulse beating wildly in between my legs told me I was going to come again. I wanted to hold on to this moment forever. Teeter on top of the mountain and treasure. But my body had other ideas.

"Shit," I gasped. "I'm going to come."

"That's right. Come for me, *mia cara*." His words

were like an ignition that lit my feet, sending my body flying off the cliff.

Hauling me even closer, he held on to my ass as he thrust deeper. I was going to have marks on me tomorrow. But I couldn't care less about it today as I watched him come with a groan, his face clenching as he emptied his load inside me.

CHAPTER TWENTY

ANTONIO

I was startled awake to curious, brown eyes watching me, the green around the pupils big enough to suck me in.

Che cazzo!

For most of my life, I had been sleeping with one eye open, and somehow she had gotten past that. She was dressed in my shirt, and the smell of fresh coffee told me she'd been downstairs already.

"I got you coffee," she said timidly, tugging the shirt down to cover her knees. She never failed to surprise me. One moment she was wanton and rocking her hips like a porn star, and the next, she was shy and timid, like a schoolgirl with her first boyfriend. I liked her both ways.

I swatted her hands away and snaked mine between her thighs, finding her pussy needy and wet. Warmth rushed to my groin. Tangling my hand in her hair, I pulled her down for a kiss. She was hotter than yesterday.

How that was possible, I had no clue. But she looked hot in my dress shirt. All ruffled up like she'd been fucked all night long.

Breathless, she came up for air resting her hands on my bare chest and pulling away.

"Coffee." She turned to grab my cup.

I sat up while sipping my hot espresso, just the way I liked it. I hoped she wasn't tired because, despite the discarded condoms lying around the bed, my dick was up and ready for the next run.

"Rosa should bring Cora home any minute," she points out while sipping her own coffee.

Fuck!

Had I forgotten all about my baby and the rest of the staff coming home? I couldn't remember the last time I let sex be the decision-maker.

"Can you grab my phone? I think it's on the floor next to you."

I tried not to grasp her naked ass as she leaned back to get it. Tempting as it was, I really couldn't lounge the day away in bed with my hot wife with a baby and staff running around.

I scrolled through all the messages, skipping the angry ones from my mother. Reading Rosa's message, I smiled, tossing my phone aside and placing my cup back on the nightstand. It seemed my staff understood me well.

"They'll be back tomorrow."

"Oh, did you arrange that?" A shy smile crossed her face.

"No. Rosa did."

Her skin flushed. Did she really think the staff didn't know we were fucking like rabbits?

"So," I drawled, enjoying her embarrassment. I wondered if she would ever disperse it. "What do we do today?"

"I don't know," she said coyly, even though her flushed skin and glittering eyes hinted at a few ideas.

"I have a few plans," I interjected.

"Oh." She perked up.

"We could visit my mother." She pushed her teeth onto her lower lip. "Or go out for lunch." I walked my fingers on her knee. "Or ..."

"Or ..." she croaked.

"You could ride my cock."

She gasped, spilling coffee on my shirt.

"You are filthy," she hissed, putting her coffee away and trying to clean herself.

Desire was coffee on caramel.

"*Tesoro mio,*" I muttered reaching for her waist and hauling her on top of me amidst her squeals. "Let me show you how much you like my filthy words," I whispered as coffee trickled down to her erect nipples. The sight made my groin go up in heat.

I unbuttoned my shirt and latched on to her nipple. It was incredible how responsive she was. Hearing her moans was like having her fist on my cock. Need rushed through my veins. I hadn't fucked her yet today, and that was a few hours too late. Putting on another rubber, I lifted her up and slid her effortlessly onto me. My vision blurred, and a groan escaped me. She did things to me no other woman had.

She leaned forward with her hair cradling her face. I caught my breath. What a sight. Shirt parted, perky breasts with coffee stains stopping on her chocolate nipples. I licked my lips. I had never enjoyed my *caffé* more.

Putting my hands on her thighs, I encouraged her, "Ride me, *mia cara*."

She started slowly, hesitant. Feeling her own rhythm out. Did she realise how well she tortured me?

She grabbed my hands on her thighs and moved them to her breasts. *Fucking hot!* She gained momentum riding me, hard and fast, her moans ringing loud in the room.

A desperation to fill her with my seed took over me. I dropped my harsh grip on her ass, even though I knew it would leave her bruised. I didn't care. I pumped my hips into her, harder and faster, trying to impale myself into her.

Her clenching muscles around my dick told me she was close.

Thank fuck!

I let go amid her spasms, letting my cum drain out of me.

How had I got so fucking lucky?

———

THERE WAS NEVER a prettier sight on my kitchen stool than the one on it today. Even after a shower where I had taken her hard against the tiled wall, my cock was semi-hard watching her swinging on my stool wearing a fresh shirt of mine. I wished the stool was me, except I had to give her a break. She must be sore, but it seemed my body couldn't care less.

What a moron.

I had thought fucking her would resolve this ache for her, but it seemed it only increased my need for her. Now that I had tasted her, I wanted more, much more.

I watched her swing her legs and swirl on the stool while popping some grapes and sipping a glass of white wine. I imagined her riding me on that same stool.

She missed one grape, and it slid through her cleavage. I groaned as she tried to retrieve it. Right. Time for a distraction.

"You liked the party yesterday?"

She looked up, smiling in victory, with the missing grape in her hand. "Yeah, it was beautiful." She sighed. "You have a lot of family and friends," she said, almost as an afterthought.

The control I had on my body was a fucking joke. Reaching over, I took the grape and popped it into my mouth as hers gaped open. "What can I say? We are Italian. We have big families." Especially when you were in *Cosa Nostra*.

"Must be like Indians." She smiled, hinting at something wistful, but continued on. "I like your cousin Laura."

"She's great. You can visit her in London if you want," I suggested. There was no reason why we couldn't take off for a few days with Cora. I enjoyed London as well.

She shook her head. "It's not the same."

"Why not? You haven't been here that long."

"Not the same ... without ... my parents." Her quiet words filtered to the floor and made me feel just like I should. A jerk.

"You miss your parents a lot," I stated the obvious. I am not sure what my purpose here was.

She nodded, still with her eyes fixed on the floor.

I didn't care for this awkward silence. I brought it on myself. Maybe because I really did want to know more about her, and her parents were the key to all her actions.

"What were they like?"

She shredded the bread in her hand into tiny pieces while she swirled absentmindedly on her stool. The air hung with something heavy that I didn't care for. Seconds lapped into minutes, and when I thought she wouldn't answer, she finally spoke up. "They were the best." Her voice was heavy and broken. "Strong when it was needed, soft otherwise. Real. Authentic. I was the centre of their world, and they ... mine. We were the three musketeers. We did everything together." She laughed bitterly. "Except dying, of course."

Her pain flying out of her and shooting through to my chest caught me by surprise. I didn't even want to carry the burden of emotions. But I felt it anyway. I felt suffocated and uncomfortable and didn't know what to do with it. When I tried to take her hand, she slid hers out from underneath and continued to shred the already shredded pieces of bread.

"Do you have other family?" I pushed, my insensitivity knowing no end.

"No. No more family."

There was a special place in hell for assholes like me.

"I had my mum's parents, but I lost them when I was small." She continued, laughing nervously. "My dad has a big family, like Italians, but they all dumped him when he met my mum. Every single one of them. He was no longer their son, brother, grandson..."

That sounded familiar. "We Italians can be traditional too."

She looked at me, eyes wide glistening with tears. She didn't believe me. She looked away again. I somehow pitied the bread she was shredding to soaked crumbles of sogginess.

"They made it work, though, my parents. A beautiful mix. They brought me up in England, so that wasn't difficult for my mum. But my dad made sure that I was exposed to the Indian side as well. He didn't drop his culture." She was proud. I could see that. She was proud that she was English and Indian.

"Have you visited?"

"India?" At my nod, she continued, "No," she sighed, "I would love to someday." She continued in a hurry, "Not to visit any family that might be there. If they didn't want my dad, if they couldn't even be bothered to express their grief... other than a message to say their son was long dead to them." She clenched her hands, the bread a puddle in her palm. She took a deep breath, trying to pull back tears to where they had come from, puffing her chest out to put on a strong front. "But I would love to get to know more about the culture. I think it's beautiful. My dad would put on this beautiful

NANNY TO THE MAFIA

music." She looked at me wistfully, "I never understood the words, but it sounded so beautiful and melancholic. They have so much more," she continued, "the food, the fashion ..."

She made me feel strange things. Like I had lost something precious to me, and I couldn't figure out what. She looked small and fragile and innocent seated there, and I wanted to protect her and comfort her when I was the epitome of what was bad. Still, that didn't stop me.

So, I did the only thing I knew. Reaching for her waist, I hauled her over to my lap, breadcrumbs and all. I drank her up like a man in a desert. I fucked her mouth with my tongue while ripping open my shirt. I latched on to her nipples, sucking and tugging them and left them red and wet.

I was mad. Madly, I tried to get this pain out of her the only way I knew how.

Setting her down on the counter, I felt her clit.

Thank fuck she was wet.

I reached into the back pocket of my worn jeans to get a condom, my hand almost shaking. I had to come outside her in the shower because it had slipped my mind that I didn't have a condom on. Now elation sparked inside me at my foresight because I didn't think I would last the long way back to our bedroom.

I clad myself and dived in, trying to physically drive the sadness away. I didn't really know why it bothered me so much. It made me uncomfortable, and I didn't do uncomfortable. I grabbed her face while pumping into

205

her. Passion had replaced everything else that was in her eyes. I came so hard I blew my load inside faster than any blast. I shook from the effort.

CHAPTER TWENTY-ONE

DIVYA

Passion was a strange thing. You rarely missed it when you never had it. But once you've tasted it, experienced it, and knew what it could do to you, you couldn't live without it. You ached for it. You wanted that feeling again and again. All the veins in your body hummed for it. All day and every day you spend, on your toes, waiting till you can enjoy it again. That moment when your body shot up in heat like a rocket on a launch.

It was a strange thing, this passion. It made me look at my marriage through rose-tinted glasses. It made me believe it was for real. When my husband came home and dragged me to the nearest room to bury himself inside me, it made me feel things. When he found me in between meetings, not caring if he was late for the next one, just so he could lick me like his favourite gelato, it made my heart tick just a bit faster.

Passion was not real. It was really an illusion. Hiding the sad and ugly world behind it.

I knew that. But for the last few days of my marriage, I had chosen to believe in the illusion rather than to uncover the truth.

We lived in our own story. Side characters going in and out. But our story, Antonio's and mine, together with Cora, was all that mattered. Stolen glances and discreet touches ended up in heavy thrusts in private rooms. If you asked me, this was not a bad way to live your illusion.

I watched him eat. We had an international menu in the household, mainly Italian but often French, Spanish, English... I had even cooked a curry once, not that anyone would call me a cook, but everyone had liked it or pretended to. Even Armando, who was as prim and proper as they got, had asked me a few days later if I could make it again. Today it was steak on the menu. According to Antonio it was a symbol of Florence, a city he claimed he knew well and promised to take me to in the throes of passion.

I watched him swallow the juicy steak and wash it down with some red wine. His movements rushed heat through my body. His lips chewing the meat, his Adam's apple going up and down, his wrist around the wine glass.... Heaviness landed in between my legs.

He had come home and found me immediately. It was a good thing I had already put Cora to bed because the first thing he did was drag me into the shower with him and fuck me senseless. No man had ever made me feel like him. Like I was the flame to his candle.

I hadn't liked it in the beginning, but I was now happy that the rest of the staff slept far away from us. He turned me into an animal, emitting strange sounds that even I didn't understand. Besides, his filthy words were better kept for my ears only.

He looked at me, eyebrows raised in question. "Done already?"

At my nod, he frowned. "You don't eat enough."

His arrogance should have extinguished the flame I held for him. It didn't.

"I do." I defended myself because I couldn't let this man run all over me.

He reached for my hand, softly stroking his rough thumb against the soft skin of my pulse. It was the simplest touch, but it made my insides clench. "I just want you to have enough energy, *tesoro*... for later," he murmured sending goose bumps rushing up and down my body. A touch and a word and this man made me a bundle of nerves.

I flushed, pulling my hands away before I jumped him to cool the burn in between my legs.

"How was your day?" I asked.

"Good."

I frowned. He never spoke about his work. If I asked, it was a quick retort. It was in these moments that I saw darkness creep through the cracks of my illusion and saw my marriage as it really was. Fake and on borrowed time. A facade to gain something. Speaking of which...

"How is the progress on the custody case?" I asked what I should have asked far sooner, had I not been so distracted.

He stilled, his mood turning dark. "Why do you ask?" He watched me shrewdly, his tone implying I should drop the subject.

I furrowed my brows. "Isn't it obvious? I want to know how it's going. If you will be able to hold on to full custody."

"Is it?" He continued eating, but the way he chewed his meat told me food wasn't on his mind. "Or," he took a sip of his wine and put the glass down, his hand clenched around the stem, "Is it because you are tired of our... arrangement already?" he suggested, his tone cold, his face dark.

Ugh? What happened?

The mood had shifted while I wasn't looking. One moment he was seducing me and the next ... what was he actually accusing me of?

"Don't be ridiculous, Antonio. I am only curious. As I should be, as one of the participants in this, as you called it, arrangement. I think I have the right to know what is happening. For example," I pushed through even though the anger bouncing off him told me I should do otherwise, "Did you find out who," I lowered my voice, "is spying on us?"

He continued to eat. The noise of the cutlery echoed in the silent room as tension built. There was a heaviness in the air I didn't understand. He took his time, taking a bite after another, seeming to be not bothered at all, except for the furious tick at his jaw. We shared a house and a bed, but I didn't know this man at all. Was he really not going to answer me at all?

"I suggest," he said, his voice unnaturally low, "that you drop this subject now."

"But why?" I whined.

"Because I said so," he roared, his voice loud in the otherwise empty dining room. My heart jerked, and I rushed my hand to my pounding chest.

I had never experienced this in my life. My father never yelled. He was always soft-spoken. Adam, I feared, didn't have the ability to. But Antonio did. Fear burst in my chest, and, like poison, it spread. The pounding in my ears was heavy, and the noise was drowning me. I had never seen this side of him before, and I wasn't sure I liked it. There was a ruthlessness to him that hinted at easy deaths in front of him. Mine.

He ran his hands through his hair, breathing deeply. He reached blindly for my hand again, wrapping his palm around mine. I hated that mine was trembling. "*Mi dispiace*, I scared you. We will drop this subject now. *Sì*? He looked at me, willing me to agree. Like all things he did to me, he wrapped me around his fingers, this time too. I nodded silently, swallowing the dryness in my throat.

Exhaustion hit me as unexpectedly as the fist of a friend.

"I think I better go to bed." I stood up only to be nudged down.

"Stay, huh?" he implored softly. When I didn't make a move to leave anymore, he continued his meal.

I sat down slowly. Everything that was right before

felt awkward now, the silence, my proximity to him when I wanted to move. I couldn't breathe. The need to think haunted me.

Antonio continued with his meal like any other day. Leaving me to doubt what had passed.

Am I exaggerating everything?

The sound of clip-clopping heels filtered down the marble floor and broke the stillness of a silent conversation. Antonio sighed, rubbing his eyes, looking tired for the first time.

A moment later, his mother entered the room, smartly dressed as usual in a power suit, her lips set in a firm, thin line, accentuating the lines around her mouth, her aura one of disapproval.

"Antonio."

She glanced at us seated at the table, her disdain apparent.

Neither of us greeted her, a fact she ignored.

"You can leave now," she dismissed me by waving her hand.

Gladly.

I rushed to rise to be pulled down again by Antonio.

"She's my wife, Mother. She stays here. You, on the other hand, have come here uninvited. *Again*. I really have to set some rules with Armando."

"Don't be so rude, *figlio mio*. I am your mother. I will always be in your life. Unlike your wives," she baited him unashamedly.

He didn't fall for it. "Is there a special reason for your late-night visit, or did you just drop by to goad me, as usual?"

She moved closer to drop her handbag on the table. Leaning over, she hissed inches from his face, "Roberto tells me there is no prenup. Are you that stupid?"

I paled. It had never occurred to me that there should have been a prenup. Especially given our arrangement. Antonio didn't look like someone who would mistake a detail like this. For once, I understood his mother. A man of his wealth should be careful.

We could still arrange something, couldn't we?

He continued with his meal, not bothering to glance up at his mother inches from him. "Roberto should not be divulging such information to you. I will have a talk with him. Although," he paused, putting down his cutlery and pushing his plate away, almost to his mother, forcing her to stand up straight, "It was not him who told you this, I think," he said shrewdly.

"Oh, what does it matter, who said what," she waved it off.

"I will have Roberto do a screening of his office staff. I don't want my private details divulged to *outsiders.*"

"Your own mother is now an outsider? Obviously, this woman has been poisoning your mind."

"I can still sign it," I said quietly, shifting in my seat, uncomfortable at the stern looks from both Capizzis. Sometimes mother and son did have similarities. "You could draw something out," I suggested timidly.

"Excellent idea. The girl makes sense," his mother said.

Ignoring her, he leaned forward, his face uncomfortably close to mine, he whispered, "No fucking way."

I scooted away, ignoring the fist that was clenching

mine on the bench. I didn't understand why he wanted to make me feel so uncomfortable and honestly, it was a piece of paper. I didn't want his wealth. Well, except for the money he had promised me, of course. Regret piled low in my belly and left a bitter aftertaste in my mouth.

Mrs Capizzi watched us with interest, specimens in a lab before her telescope.

"Of course not.. Why would you do that when you are obviously thinking with your dick? You are fucking her, aren't you?"

He pushed back the bench and jumped up so fast that I almost fell off it. My nerves rattled faster than nickels in a glass jar. He pushed his body forward and looked his mother straight in the eye. "Of course I am fucking my wife." A gasp hit me as my hand flew to my mouth. "And loving it. In fact, Mother, you are a hindrance." Turning to me, he plucked me off the bench and dropped me on the table. "I plan to fuck her right now." His hands fisted my skirt and hustled it up. He ignored my swatting hands like a whiff of the wind. "Unless you plan to sit down and watch," he continued darkly, grabbing hold of my ass harshly and pulling me in closer, "I suggest you get out of my house."

I didn't know whose gasp was louder. Mine or hers. The pounding in my ears was loud and heavy. All other noises buzzed around me. All movements stalled, and I watched the downfall in slow motion.

I didn't dare to look at her and find what I knew would be disgust in her eyes. So, I grabbed his shirt and pulled him closer to me. "Antonio," I whispered close to his ear, "don't do this."

"Why not?" he rasped.

"She's never going to respect me like this."

"Oh, *mia cara*, she never respects anyone." He traced his fingers along my jaw lightly, only the tremble in his finger giving any emotion away. "Besides, she needs to know you are my wife," he said roughly before jamming his lips onto mine.

Madness. This was pure madness. I heard his mother shriek and run out, like background noise to the sound of my own thundering heart.

I tried to get words out but drew only blood when he bit my lips. I was mad and horribly turned on, even as I tried to understand what was going on inside of him.

I yanked my head back, my scalp burning from the pressure he had on my hair.

"Why would you do that? Why would you disgrace me like that? She will never like me now."

He didn't bother to answer. For a man who walked the path of life in a controlled line, he was brimming with emotion, only it was the dark kind. His hands were rough as they rushed to my slip and pulled them aside. But his eyes even though they were dark called out for something I didn't know how to give. So, I let him use me or I used him.

I let him unzip his pants and pull his erection out, pushing inside me with a hard, punishing thrust. He yanked my ass closer to him and grabbed my hair, pumping harshly in and out like a madman possessed.

He took my lips angrily, tonguing and biting. It was no sweet kiss. It was one where marks would show the next day for all to see.

I hated myself. I hated myself more because I could feel my impending orgasm. How could this turn me on? But the heat inside me wasn't interested in listening. I came in his arms, followed seconds later by his harsh growl, and the flow of his cum.

He rested his head on my forehead, breathing deeply, waiting for both of us to calm down.

He traced kisses softly on my neck.

"Ahh, *tesoro mio*, what you don't understand is my mother will never like you. She only loves herself," he hissed, his voice broken when he had broken me.

CHAPTER TWENTY-TWO

ANTONIO

The pen snapped in my hands, ink flooding out, messing up my shirt sleeves and dripping onto my desk. Frustration flowed out of me faster than the red ink. I chucked it into the bin without getting up from my chair. It missed and landed on the floor.

Nothing was going according to plan.

My mother was grating on my nerves. My ex-wife was notching it up, and now it seemed as though my wife had joined the club.

Women.

Leaning over, I grabbed some tissue, roughly wiping my desk and my sleeves. The red of the ink made it look like blood, only I was familiar enough with spilling it to know this wasn't the real deal.

Sometimes, though, I wished I could spill my own. I

am not sure how far my morality rocked when I imagined a bullet through my mother's head.

As far as I could remember, I had never seen her happy. Disdain and cruelty were something she rolled into every room. One of my earliest memories was of coming home from school to find my papà pinning her against the wall with her neck between his hands. Only later did I understand what would have driven him to do such an act. Even my usually patient papà, too gentle for his kind, was constantly driven out of his mind by her. Never happy, judging, blaming, conniving. Papà didn't kill himself, but when he became ill, he gave up. Maria Capizzi might not have strangled her husband, but she did orchestrate his death.

At least now, after my crude reaction a few nights ago, there was silence. I knew better, though. When my mother was silent, she was always busy cooking up a plan.

Angelo's face popped in the doorway.

"Ever learnt to knock?" I snapped.

Angelo sauntered inside, closing the door behind him. "Why bother? I'm always welcome, anyway."

"I've had it with people dropping in and out of my house."

Angelo slouched into the chair opposite me. His legs stretched out, and his arms hung loose. He never outgrew his teenage awkwardness with his body. "I heard about that."

"What did she say?"

"Who? Mother or your wife?"

My brow furrowed. "Divya spoke to you?"

"Why wouldn't she?" Angelo looked at me shrewdly. "Oh... she's not speaking to you."

There was definitely a dent in the honeymoon phase of our marriage. Not even a month and we were already on opposite sides of the bed. Still, it pissed me off that she spoke to him.

Angelo let a loud, robust laugh overtake him.

What an idiot. I didn't have a single sensible Capizzi anymore.

"So, this is why Marco was complaining about your shitty mood. You aren't getting any."

Fuck!

That's what I wanted. To fuck my wife, but instead, it was silent war *again*. If she moved an inch further along in the bed, she would be sleeping on the floor. I should probably count on small blessings and be happy she hadn't moved onto the bloody sofa again. Except I wasn't.

"Get to the point. What did she tell you?" I growled.

"She didn't tell me much... well, except for you being a ... what did she call you now...." He pretended to think. "Ah, yes. A fucking bastard who disrespected her."

"That's all?"

"Yes. Divya's too nice to say anything else. But don't worry, I got all the gory details out of Mother. Really, brother, how was fucking your wife in front of her a good idea?"

"I don't fucking know," I snapped, pushing my chair away and standing up to pace the window. "The women in my life are intent on fucking ruining me."

So, I could have handled it better. Obviously, that

charade in front of my mother was a tad too much, except Divya got to me with her intruding questions about the case. Then my mother came and pushed me right over the edge.

"Well, that's no secret when it comes to our mother. I hope you aren't including Divya in it, though."

I wasn't, but she was not an easy woman to understand, my wife. Why, for example, was she embarrassed by the marks on her lips? I was her husband. We had sex. I was sure the staff had heard us going about it on numerous occasions. It wasn't my fault that she screamed like a porn star when she came. Unless her source of embarrassment was me.

I clenched and unclenched my hands, watching out my window distractedly. Not even a few weeks of marriage and she wanted out. She couldn't have made it more obvious. Demanding information under the pretence of being worried about the case.

"I've never seen you like this." Angelo's words cut through my thoughts.

I'd never seen myself like this either. She got to me in ways far worse than my mother ever had. The control that I prided myself on flew out the window the moment she walked in. I had actually fucked her without a condom. It had been fucking marvellous to be skin-on-skin inside her. Not even in my marriage to Yuliya had I fucked her bare. Cora had simply resulted from a burst condom.

"Have you taken a good look at her? Fucking her is bloody marvellous."

"I have."

I jerked my head towards him.

What was I thinking?

Age wise, Angelo was closer to Divya than I was. Was he fucking lusting after what was mine?

"That." He pointed at my face. "Is exactly what I mean."

"I don't know what you are talking about." I flicked my annoyed glance back out the window.

"Right. Because you've always been jealous, of course."

I didn't like the sarcasm dripping off his mouth. I wasn't jealous. I just never shared what was mine. She was also fucking pissing me off with whatever exit plan she was working on.

The poison in my veins grew a tad thicker when I glanced at the open document on my computer.

She was still talking to fucking Harris. What, I wondered, did she want to talk to him about when he had gambled away all her inheritance? Had she forgiven him already? I hadn't thought her to be an idiot, but it might be that, yet again, I would be proven wrong.

I didn't care for the way this discovery rested on my chest. I pushed it with effort to the back of my mind. Massimo would soon be here. We needed to discuss the numbers. There was a new restaurant in town, and we needed to see whose protection it was going to fall under. As far as I was concerned, it was either us or Vladislav. But it was never going to be the fucking Mexicans. It gave me peace of mind to focus on things I knew better than the back of my hand. I pushed thoughts of Harris out of the way like an ostrich burying its head underneath the sand, hoping it would go away.

FOLLOWING the soft humming of a strange song, I found her in the nursery holding a sleeping Cora over her shoulders. I walked in and settled just inside the door to watch them. Something uncomfortable ticked in my chest. My baby, chubby fists relaxed, face peaceful, clad in her sleeping bag, in the arms of my wife, softly murmuring sweet nothings in her ear.

She ignored me, of course, even though I knew she had sensed my presence. Her body was mine to read. Her shoulders had stiffened, and her back jerked upright the moment I stepped into the room. Sexual tension prickled in the air like fucking electricity in a storm.

She was wearing a hot purple dress with a tight bodice and a short flowing skirt, her hair in a ponytail. I preferred it loose, hanging around her, tangled in my hands, riding me.

Heat rushed to my groin when she bent down to put Cora in her cot, her dress riding up to show more of that caramel skin. My hands itched to follow that path. My dick twitched. A few days absent of sex left a man fucking senseless.

I watched her go around, cleaning up the soft toys quietly. Did she realise I could see her breasts from my vantage point? Bobbing up and down, calling out to my hands and mouth. I had married a temptress, going around braless all day.

I was tired after sitting in meetings the whole day and ending the day with Vladislav's team. Just because we were on talking terms didn't mean there was no tension around. More than one man in a room full of fucking egos set the room on fire like a cave of rattlesnakes. Every meeting we ended without a gun drawn out was a battle won.

All I wanted now was to bury the agitation in me between my wife's sweet thighs. This cold war at home was not what I wanted. I would much prefer a screaming fight or none at all.

How long was she going to pretend to clean a room that was already pristine and perfect?

I would have stood there all night long if I had to. It was better than a distance of a few feet in a fucking bed.

Finally, she stood still in the room, contemplating. After a slight pause, she came to move past me. I let her... almost pass before I latched onto her hand and jerked her to me.

To my surprise, she didn't put up a fight.

"Are we done fighting?" I muttered.

She shook her head, trying to pull away.

Hauling her closer, I settled her between my body. My hands slid up her naked thighs. My rough palm on her soft skin was sandpaper on velvet. It prickled my skin with need. Sexual frustration crawled all over me.

"*Mia cara*, I miss you. Can we call it a truce?" I traced my lips along her neck, already hard against her body. I meant it. I was damn sick of my nightly cold showers, and I just wanted to bury myself inside her. I wanted to forget the coldness of my world in the warmth of her body.

"Hmm?" I murmured, moving to her collarbone. There was a fever climbing up her body that had us both entrapped in it. Her breathing grew heavier, her breasts fuller. Moving my hands up, I fisted them in her hair, getting rid of the rubber holding it in, and dropping it to the floor.

Somewhere, there was a patient man inside me who wanted to give her all the time she needed. Tonight, he must have been buried six feet under. My hands rushed down and squeezed her ass. Necessity made me push her hard against me. "For fuck's sake! Say yes," I groaned against her lower lip, biting tentatively on her wounds.

A soft sigh fell out of her lips with magic words.

"Yes."

Cazzo!

My luck was turning around. I wasn't waiting around for it to flip back again.

I crushed my lips to hers, our tongues clashing, hungry after starvation. Running my hands along her ass, I pulled her up, and she instantly wrapped her legs around my waist and pushed herself against my dick, unashamedly rubbing herself on me.

A moan escaped from her mouth. I caught it and sucked it into mine.

My legs trembled from pure lust, but I refused to move away. I wasn't taking a chance on her second thoughts in the bright light of the hallway.

Fucking pussy! I wasn't terrified of the barrel end of a gun, but this had my heart pounding.

She broke away panting, "Our room."

"Soon." I grabbed her head and plunged my tongue into her mouth while making my way to the attached bathroom of the nursery.

She moaned in protest. "Shhh," I silenced her, softly closing the door in between us and dropping her on the vanity.

I flipped her bodice down and latched onto one nipple, sucking it into my mouth while fondling harshly with the other. Any protest she might have had died on her lips. I moved on to the other nipple and rewarded it with the same treatment. Another moan escaped her.

"Shhh, you have to be quiet, m*ia cara.*"

She bit her lip, concentration framing her face.

Putting her breasts together, I created a bigger cleavage and sunk my mouth in between. This must be what fucking heaven felt like.

Frustration fuelled her movements as she pulled me up and kissed me, letting loose her groan inside our mouths. With our mouths still fused, she unzipped my pants, letting them drop to the floor, and yanked my boxers down after that.

"Fuck," I hissed when she grabbed my dick, running her hand tightly on my smooth and hard flesh.

"Be quiet," she taunted, rubbing my precum over my cock.

"You're killing me," I growled into her neck as I bit into her soft skin.

Lifting her ass, I slid her dress up. The pretty little lace fabric she called a slip was in the way of what was mine. I ripped it in two, muttering, "I know, I know. I owe you another." I might as well have an open account in whatever lingerie boutique she was getting this delicious stuff from.

I opened her lips and found her drenched, her clit swollen and red.

Next time, I imagined I would take my time. Not this time. For a man known for sheer control, I found myself lacking when it came to my wife. If she were on the other end of a negotiation table, like today, she would drag me in hook, line, and sinker.

I took my dick and placed it at her entrance, slowly gliding in, enjoying that absolute feeling of arriving home, only for her to rudely pushed me out.

"Condom," she gasped.

"Right." I fought back the unexplainable disappointment flooding me. She was absolutely right, of course. That didn't mean it didn't annoy the hell out of me. Bending down, I grabbed one from my pocket, my hands trembling, trying to open the stupid thing.

She took the pack and tore it open with her teeth. Taking the rubber out, she pulled it on me, doing it so slowly, she must want me to fucking explode all over her hand.

With a groan, I gruffly pushed her hand away and pushed my rock-hard cock inside.

Fuck.

This, this was what I had missed. I wanted to enjoy this moment and settle in first, but my body had other plans. I fucked her hard and fast, my cock thickening at the sight of her bouncing breasts, wet with my saliva on her brown nipples. Goosebumps filled her like a second skin.

She was gorgeous and wild. And mine, I thought as she let another loud moan slip.

I pasted my mouth on her, swallowing her moans as I pumped in.

Fuck

I wasn't going to be able to hold it in. I groaned. I tried to hold back from coming before she did, but like a fucking teenager, I shot myself inside her, filling her up with spurt after spurt of cum. Luckily for me, she joined me soon after, milking me dry, her legs trembling.

CHAPTER TWENTY-THREE

DIVYA

"You have no idea what type of man you have married, have you?"

I bumped my head in the dishwasher, where I had my head tucked, adding salt to the machine.

I stuck my head out and looked up to find Maria Capizzi standing next to me in her high heels, her signature bright red lipstick even more striking than usual on her pale face.

Rosa had rushed out for a task assigned by Mrs Capizzi. Now the woman herself was here, no doubt for yet another of her late evening visits with impending doom. Except I had no one to hide behind now. I wished I hadn't put Cora to bed. The comfort of her innocence would have done wonders against the aggressive vibes flowing off the woman dominating the kitchen.

I stood up, swallowed a sigh, and made my way over to the sink to wash my hands. I would have preferred this confrontation another time, when I wasn't caught on my haunches, in my shorts and dirty top from Cora's last mishap with fruit juice. Because there was no doubt in my mind that this was anything but a confrontation.

Then again...

The last time she had almost seen me almost being fucked by her son. Another reason why I did not doubt that this was not going to be a pleasant tête-à-tête.

Impatient with the lack of an answer, Mrs Capizzi stomped over to me, crowding my personal space next to the sink. Even the gust around me shrank away in fear. "Short of hearing, are you?" She snapped her fingers rudely, drawing my attention to her face.

Taking a deep breath, I turned around. "I am not sure what you mean, Mrs Capizzi."

"You are not sure... You are more of an idiot than I thought. You never wonder what your so-called husband does when he leaves in the middle of the night?" She sniggered like a bully in high school. "Or are you only interested in his money?"

Mrs Capizzi had many talents if you could call them that. One of them was the ability to trigger anyone. She walked into the room and created instant carnage. Changing the mood of anyone, just like she did with the click of her long nails.

Uneasiness crept upon me. An air of imminent doom hung in the kitchen. Sheer desperation made me glance beyond her shoulders hoping Rosa would turn up. There was only a slight chance of that happening since she had just left not five minutes ago, taking Armando with her.

Don't let her see she's getting to you.

"I am sure Antonio will tell me if it's something I should know." Puffing my chest out, I put on a brave front.

He did have unusual hours, the husband of mine. Whatever it was, I much preferred to hear it from him than from this woman, who, it was quite obvious, did not have my best interest in mind. Nor his.

She, of course, contradicted me with her words. "Oh, but I think you should know. I feel a husband should be open with *his wife*, don't you?"

Holding the towel, I was drying my hands off as a shield, I made to move away. "It's really not—"

"He kills people," she cut me off.

I inhaled sharply. I stilled and struggled to make sense of her words. I came to only one conclusion. The woman was mad.

Now what? Antonio was some kind of hitman?

Maria Capizzi was obviously not done with the revelation. She came closer, breathing in my space, spreading the poison in her mouth. "In cold blood."

There was no way I was believing this crazy shit.

Even though my heart was pounding the beat of a million drums, I refused to believe the man who I ... I didn't know anymore. What was he to me? My husband. My lover...

"You have no idea who you married. How can you? Coming from your world." Disdain rolled off her tone.

"Stop!" I yelled, blocking my ears with my palms. I didn't want to listen anymore. Whatever it was, Antonio would tell me. Not this crazy bitch with some kind of vendetta against her own son.

But there was no stopping the flow of words coming off her bright red lips. She latched onto my arms painfully and jerked them away from my ears. "Listen to me. We are the mafia, *piccola ragazzina.*"

What?

My mind churned, just like the masala my dad used to make in the mixer. Anxiety rode high on my skin.

She was just trying to goad me. Wasn't she? It didn't make sense. Did it? How could it be? Just because they were Italians didn't mean they were the mafia. Right? Right?

There was a ruthlessness to my husband that cloaked him like a coat, but it didn't mean...

I couldn't think clearly ...

Is this why we had so many people going in and out of the house? Why I was never allowed to go out alone?

Why he left in the middle of the night? All that travelling? But isn't that what men with millions do? They can't all be in the mafia.

This is ridiculous. A trap set by my dear mother-in-law. Nothing else.

"For generations, we are in *Cosa Nostra*, and he has to marry someone like you." She laughs an unkind laugh at me. "An outsider. An idiot who doesn't even know what her husband does. He kills men, women and yes, *even* babies," she went on, toxin in her tone of voice. "Like you people make your bloody curries. Taking a life for Antonio is nothing but a day's work." She watched me with lips curled up in disgust. "You, my dear, have no clue. Even Yuliya was better. She was from the *Bratva*, the Russian mob if you don't know what that is and knew at least something about it, spoilt as she was."

His ex-wife was also in the mafia?

I felt sick. It was a surreal movie with hidden villains popping up left, right, and centre.

Was this why they had so much security?

Why our wedding reception had men who looked like they killed for a living? Their hushed tones and the coldness of their eyes had certainly driven shivers up my spine.

Bile clouded in my belly, ready to crawl up through my clogged throat. I clutched at my stomach.

"A true Sicilian girl in my family will know how to be a good wife for my son. Not someone like you who doesn't have the nerves to stomach this."

"Maria!" Marco roared.

I jerked around to Marco standing at the door, his face livid. I've never seen him angry. He fired off a rapid stream of Italian in our direction. But Maria Capizzi paid no heed. Ignoring him, she walked past him and out of the room, leaving behind a yelling Marco and a heaving me.

After a quick glance at me, he typed urgently on his phone, dropping it in his pocket before approaching me cautiously.

"Divya... what did Maria say to you?" he asked, testing the waters.

What did she say?

I tried to fight my body's natural reaction to curl up into a ball and violently throw up.

"Is he in the mafia?" I asked.

His eyes filtered away before focusing on me again. A

reaction of just a second that left me thinking I imagined it. But I didn't.

"He is, isn't he?" I whispered. "You all are," I exclaimed.

I had doubted Mrs Capizzi's words the whole time, except every action after that just confirmed what she had told me.

"Whatever she said, you should listen to Antonio first," Marco urged, coming closer. "He is a good man, Divya."

A good man? A good man who wanted to fuck me in front of his mother? A good man who apparently killed people for a living? *He kills men, women and, yes, even babies.* Maria's taunting words assaulted my memory. *Even babies. W*hile he had one of his own.

I drew myself straight and looked him in the eye, wanting him to tell me the truth, but my heart pleaded not to hear it out. "Does he kill people?"

His lips drew into a tight line. Of course, he wasn't going to answer. I sighed. "That's what I thought." I brushed past him to go to my room.

"Divya, let me call Antonio—"

"No!" The words came out as a shout. "Don't bother," I whispered brokenly. Damn my voice. I was tired of it breaking all because of him.

What a fucking idiot I had been. Falling for another lie by another man *again.* Different lie, different man. The same shit, yet different. Far worse. It seemed instead of learning from my mistakes, I just dug my holes deeper. I might as well bury myself now in the one I had dug. Served me right. For looking through this sham of a marriage through rose-tinted glasses.

Had he thought, given our arrangement, it was better to keep me in the dark? Good enough for a fuck, but not enough to inform me of an important detail.

Was he ever going to tell me? Or were they going to have a laugh, all of them, at my expense, about the idiot that I was?

What else could I call myself other than that, when everything had been clearly in front of my eyes, but I had refused to see it?

CHAPTER TWENTY-FOUR

ANTONIO

F*uck!*

I should have listened to Carlo.

I raced home to put out the fire that my mother had ignited. All this time I had thought I had pushed her back, but the joke was on me. She came back in full force. I was a breath away from pulling the trigger. Only my father's name held me back. Barely.

I should have fucking known. Isabella had put a call through from my mother, only to be greeted by a dead line. But in the impending chaos of a possible fed investigation, I had pushed it to the back of my mind. Now, in hindsight, I knew she had called to check I was not at home. Just like she had arranged for Rosa to be out.

Fuck! Fuck! Fuck!

The moment I got that message from Marco, I dumped all the shit in my hands to dash home.

Fucking Carlo was right. I should have told Divya

before we got married. But she was so naïve, so innocent. I hadn't wanted to bring her into my dirty world. And it was that. Dirty.

How do you even go about telling something like that? I trusted few people, and the ones I did had been around me for ages. There was no need to tell anything. The ones I didn't trust. There was no need to inform.

But with Divya, it was all so strange, so new. Our relationship was unconventional from the start. I should have, in my right mind, never even hired a stranger outside *Cosa Nostra* to look after my child. I didn't have any strict guidelines I could follow with her. Or rather, I did but chose not to follow them, anyway. I made my own rules up, and this was the fucking result.

I wanted to rewind my life back to this morning. When she didn't know. When she believed in the good in me. Because that just ended with the words of my mother.

I could argue that the current *Cosa Nostra* was not like in some absurd, Hollywood movie. We did good things too. Many good things. And my grandfather, father, and now I had put in so many more rules of strict ethics and morals.

Ah, who was I kidding?

I was what I was. A ruthless man who wouldn't think twice about putting a hole in any man's head. But it didn't stop me from landing on my feet even before the car came to a halt, racing up the steps and through the door held open by Armando. Rosa rushed over to me, guilt written all over her face, another consequence of my mother's malicious manipulation.

Cazzo! I had to calm her first before I tackled my wife.
"*Mi dispiace, Antonio.*"

"It isn't your fault. What is there to be sorry about?"

"I should have known. When your mother called and asked to do her shopping, I should have known. She never asks me. Rosa should have thought why now?"

"Nah. I haven't even figured her out yet. Then how can you? Go to bed. I will talk to her."

"She is very angry, *figlio mio*. She wouldn't listen to anything we had to say."

"Don't worry. I have my ways of calming her down." I doubted if any of my seduction techniques were going to work on her this time. It pissed me off that I was going to have to grovel. But I was going to do it, anyway.

"No doubt." Rosa chuckled, brightening up. She seemed to have more confidence in me than I did.

"Come on. It's late. Go to bed." I winked at her. "You don't want to be caught in the crossfire."

"You've got a wild one on your hands. Worse than any Sicilian girl." Chuckling, she ambled off to her room.

I didn't wait for her to leave before taking the stairs several at a time. I burst into our bedroom only to find it empty, the bed made from this morning when I had taken her on her hands and knees. That suddenly seemed ages ago now.

I checked in on Cora's room, where I found my baby sleeping soundly, her fist in her mouth, wrapped around her teddy bear, but no Divya in sight.

I skidded down again, roaming from room to room to find them all empty of her presence.

Dashing back up, I opened and closed all the room

doors one by one till I found her previous room door locked.

No fucking way! She had moved out of our room.

I rattled the doorknob. "Divya."

Silence.

I took a deep breath, resting my head on the door, trying to rein in my frustration. "*Mia cara*, open the door."

Crickets. It irked me more than I cared that she moved out of my room.

"Open the fucking door, Divya!"

Niente.

Fucking hell! I didn't have the patience to put up with this shit.

Taking a step back, I kicked the door open, sending it flying open, the noise of creaking wood echoing in the hall. It was that or show her what I did straight away by pulling the guns out. A bit too soon, perhaps.

I found her, a ball of silk pyjamas, huddled in the corner of the empty bed; the only accessory in the room was the framed picture of her smiling parents.

In contrast, she was a slobbering mess. Eyes red, she shouted, "What happened to privacy? Go away."

Like that's going to happen. Approaching her, I said tightly, "You are my wife. We. Sleep. In. The. Same. Room."

"No," she snapped, scooting further away. "I can't be with a killer."

Anger burst so hard in my chest that it left me trilling. A venom I didn't recognise crept into my veins.

"Like hell, you can't." I hissed, "Come now to our room, and we will have this discussion."

"No!"

"Yes," I said, my tone hard. I didn't bother to hide the wrath behind it.

She crept further away, trying to embed herself against the wall. What did she think she was? Fucking wallpaper?

"Fine. Don't say I didn't try."

She thought I gave up. Like I ever would. Just when she relaxed her grip around her knees, I swept in and hauled her up, carrying her upside down over my shoulder.

"Let me go." Wiggling and shrieking, she hit my back with her pounding fists.

Did she really think she was hurting me with this? I held on to her butt firmly, gritting my teeth as her fucking bare feet touched my cock.

"Shhh … you are going to wake Cora," I snapped, shutting her up immediately.

Walking to our room, I locked the door and dumped her in the middle of the bed. She scrambled away to the head of the bed, as far as she could from me.

I didn't fucking like the way she looked at me now. What did she think? That I was going to blow a hole through her?

"Don't worry. I won't kill you," I said sarcastically, watching her tits heave with her heavy breathing. "Tonight." I couldn't help myself.

Ever.

Her eyes grew as wide as the button eyes of Cora's

teddy bear.

"Is this some kind of joke to you?" she snapped.

"No, *mia cara*. This is not a fucking joke to me," I said firmly, unbuttoning my shirt and removing it. "My wife running to judgment is not a joke."

I unbuckled my belt and pulled it off. "Haven't you ever heard of an open mind?" I let my frustration out on my fucking belt, throwing it across the room, the metal clasp landing on the floor with a loud thud. "Or giving the benefit of the doubt? No? Instead, you did worse. You chose *my mother* over me."

She shrank away from me, pissing me off even more. What was she so fucking scared of? I burned a trail through her as I unzipped my trousers, getting rid of them with my shoes and socks. "It's no fucking joke, *mia cara*, my wife, moving out of our room. I swear to god ... you test my patience like no other woman has."

I got rid of my boxers and let loose my erection. Fucking siren. Even when I was mad enough to put the room on fire, she fucking taunted me with her body. I watched her ogle me, or rather my dick. I knew she was turned on. She didn't want to be because, apparently, I wasn't good enough for her now. But she was. I knew the signs. Her silk-clad pyjama top showed off her pert nipples like bullet points, her eyes glazed, the green gone, her pupils big, her breathing heavier and deeper, her smell... I could smell her a mile away, especially when she was so turned on. And she was all of that now.

I got onto the bed on my hands and knees and latched onto her ankles, dragging her down.

She gave out a shriek, trying to scurry away, but

relented easily under my touch.

"Shut up," I hissed, freezing her movements immediately.

Grabbing her hands, I pinned them above her head with one hand and yanked her silk pyjama bottoms down. Our breaths mingled as our eyes fought each other. There was a steam hanging around us, hotter than any boiling kettle.

"Did it ever occur to you, my wife of mine, to talk to me first, before you condemn me and squash me beneath your pretty little toes?"

I dragged her further down and spread her legs, pushing two fingers in to find her sticky and dripping. Lust washed through me like nobody's business.

Taking my fingers out, I put them in my mouth and licked them dry, watching her shocked eyes.

"So wet for me," I groaned.

I found her clit and gave it a hard tweak, watching her jerk.

"You are no different from my mother." I hissed, "You condemn me so easily m*ia cara*, from your high horse, never good enough for you."

Spreading her legs wide, I pushed myself in, her gasp loud in the room.

"Fucking not enough," I muttered, pumping in and out, hard and fast, sweat collecting on my forehead.

"Are you too good for me, m*ia cara*?" I rasped before taking one nipple between my teeth. A yelp was the only response. It pissed me off. I wanted a fucking no.

"Not good enough for you to stay?" I abandoned the left nipple to move on to the right. My teeth on her nipples should have hurt her. I only wanted to punish her, but all I saw was desire in her eyes. For some reason, that pissed me off even more. I wanted her to hurt. Just like I was now.

"*Si*, I am a killer," I pinned her with my eyes, watching hers glaze, fighting her orgasm. I pumped harder, like a man possessed, eager to throw her over, prove her wrong.

She will never be able to live without me.

Leaning down, I bit her lip hard. Let her try to explain that tomorrow.

She was always wanting to leave. *When was the case resolved? Was the spy found?* Now my mother had given her another excuse.

I thrust as deep as I could. I wanted to imprint myself on her. She was mine. I was a killer. But she was a killer's wife.

I watched her face contort, trying to fight her orgasm. Another deep thrust and I watched her spiral out, clenching around me, body shuddering, grabbing hold of me, and milking me dry.

A guttural groan escaped me as I pumped harder. This woman was the death of me. My dick jerked inside her as my seed emptied inside her.

I dropped my weight on her, heavy and sweaty, but I couldn't bring myself to care. At least this way, she couldn't move. I bit her neck, leaving bite marks on her skin. The energy in my body was drained right out of me, but the anger boiling inside remained like smouldering coal.

"For you, I will kill anyone," I whispered in Italian.

CHAPTER TWENTY-FIVE

DIVYA

I woke up to an empty bed, the sheets ruffled, the smell of sex heavy in the silent room.

Running my hands on the sheets, I found them cold, telling me he had left bed early or I had overslept.

The clock on the bedside table told me it could be both.

The picture frame on the dressing table caught my eye. My throat tightened. He had probably put it there. I didn't know how to read that.

Swinging my legs to the side of the bed, I sat up, ashamed to look at my body. Treacherous but satisfied. Marks on it told a story of a possessive lover. He had taken me like he was on death row, and *I* had *allowed* him to.

My thighs clenched at the memory of him between my legs.

The respect I had for myself, which I had gained over years of self-love, slowly slid off me like a second skin. I didn't know who I was anymore. Not the woman who was brought up by proud and ethical parents, for sure.

The smell of him on me should have disgusted me. Yet all it did was leave me longing. For more.

I didn't recognise the woman that I was with him. There was a static vibe between us, cracking with invisible sparks that pulled me constantly to him. The more he turned dark, the more I yearned for him. I wanted it gone.

Getting up, I walked to the bathroom. I had to wash him off me, first with water, then in real life. Only then would I be able to survive.

Cora lit up when I picked her up from her cot. There were no dark days around her, yet I had a hard time banishing it entirely from my thoughts. She whimpered in my arms as if she could feel my sadness. The last thing I wanted was for it to soak into her, so I made an effort at fake playfulness while I washed and dressed her.

The house greeted me quietly like the aftermath of war when I came down with Cora in my arms. Rosa's smile lacked the warmth radiating off her on any other day. After a too-polite *buon giorno*, she rushed out of the room.

When Maria Capizzi said they were the family or something along that line, she really meant that. It seemed I was no longer in the good books of the household.

"Looks like it's just us, *Kutti*," I told Cora, fondly

calling her by one of the nicknames my dad used to call me.

I put some breakfast together for her as I continued our jabbering conversation, trying not to think what Antonio was up to because then I might think he was killing someone's child right at the moment that I was feeding his.

I blinked back my tears. The heaviness in my heart did nothing to fill that gaping wound deep inside me. A wound, which had been healing nicely ever since I arrived in this home, was now bigger. One step forward and ten backward. Just when I thought life was giving me a good deal.

Some days, I missed my parents more than others. Today it seemed to be a "more" day.

Pulling Cora's chair closer to the table, I buckled her in and sat down to feed her. Lucky baby. No problem for this one other than grabbing hold of the flying plane of food in her mouth.

While flying my third plane to Cora's open mouth, Rosa came in, bringing with her an embarrassed Armando.

A cloud of activity followed both of them. An agitated Rosa, Italian flying out of her mouth, to a nervous Armando muttering back.

I was tired of not understanding the language, especially Antonio's mutterings in my ears.

Apprehension filled my stomach. "What's going on?"

"*Signora*," Armando cleared his throat to rid of the break in his voice, "Rosa would like me to translate something for her."

I nodded slowly, concentrating hard, trying to pick up words coming off Rosa, but my Duolingo step one was no match for the flow out of her mouth.

Armando held up his hand to silence her so he could translate.

"Rosa was married off very young by her family. Her husband was older. A violent man. He would assault her every night and..." he continued after a nod from Rosa, "abuse her."

"Oh, Rosa..." I shot up in my chair to comfort her, but Armando held up his hand, signalling to wait. Rosa encouraged him to continue.

"She knew no one in *Cosa Nostra,* and they didn't know her. But someone got to know of this and brought it to *Signor* Capizzi's grandfather's attention."

I sat down again, not liking where the story was going.

"At first, they sent some men to speak to her husband, warning him in no uncertain terms to stop harming his wife. But he wouldn't listen. Then, one day, *Signor* Capizzi's grandfather visited her in her home. He asked her if she was happy in her marriage. When she said no, he asked if she would be happy if her husband was no longer in her life. She knew what he was asking. Yet, she said yes. That night, her husband didn't return home. They found him with a bullet in his head and," Armando looked down, gazing at his shoes, "And some missing body parts."

I tried to swallow the lump in my dry throat. I had never known that this sweet lady with a smile on her face every day had had such a tragic past.

Rosa rattled off more details to Armando, and with a nod, he looked up at me.

"Rosa wants to know if you think she's a bad person?"

"Of course not," I exclaimed.

"Then why..." Armando rushed on, "Do you think so badly of *Signor* Capizzi?"

I put down the fork, Cora's food forgotten on her plate. Luckily, she seemed to be happy playing with the buttons on her chair, making the occasional nursery rhyme ring out.

"That is different," I answered softly.

"It is the same," Armando said firmly. "No one is perfect. Everyone has good and bad in them. She," he said, pointing to Rosa, "could have let her husband walk, sent off somewhere. But she chose to have him killed. *Signor* Capizzi didn't have to get involved over a matter that didn't involve his family. But he chose to help out a young girl who had no way out."

Cora dropped one of her rattles on the floor and Armando came immediately to pick it up and laid it back on the chair. He looked at me sternly but with a glimpse of kindness in the depths of his dark brown eyes.

"Perhaps it is not my place *Signora*..." he said as he frowned his thick grey eyebrows, "but I feel I have to defend *Signor* Capizzi. Rosa's is not the only story in this house. *Signor* Capizzi's father and grandfather have done a lot for many people and so has *Signor* Capizzi. Are they bad men? Yes. Especially if you anger them. But there is also good in them. You should not believe everything *Signora* Capizzi tells you."

He turned to Rosa to listen to her before turning back to me with a soft smile. "Rosa says she should never have been a wife, let alone a mother. Rosa can be, how do you put it... dramatic sometimes. But this time, I will have to agree. Neither her sons nor her husband could ever be good enough for her."

He watched me stir Cora's food absentmindedly.

"We..." he gestured to Rosa and the house, "all of us would appreciate it if you would think about this. *Sì?*"

The cacophony of my thoughts in my head wore down on me. I felt an impending headache and rubbed my forehead.

He backed away at my silence. "I think we have taken enough of your time, *Signora*," he said, quietly leaving the room with Rosa in tow.

I WENT OVER and over the words uttered by Armando the next day like one would a song on a recorder, trying to understand the lyrics of it.

Under the pretence of reading a book, I had dragged myself to the back terrace, but my book remained open on page one, the story unread.

I didn't know if Antonio came home or not last night. I had gone to bed early, exhausted in mind and body, to wake up just as tired but to the faint smell of an absent man. He had been in the room, I was sure. But I didn't dare ask the staff after yesterday.

What I didn't fail to notice was my previous

bedroom, with the open doorway, was now completely bare. Even the lonely bed had been taken out.

The sound of footsteps drifted to my ears, and I turned my head to find Angelo walking towards me with a glass of amber liquid in his hands. The glass and the smell of it instantly brought me back to Antonio and our first night together. So much had happened after that amazing "wedding night," as he called it.

"*Buona sera, Cognata,*" he greeted me, giving me a peck on the cheek and settling down on the chair next to mine.

"What does it mean?"

"What?" He raised his eyebrows.

"Whatever you said now?"

"Oh." His tone implied he had expected me to ask something else. "It means good evening, sister-in-law."

I nodded. "Where's your brother?"

"Your husband is in his office, nursing his broken heart," he quipped, watching my reaction.

I sneered, "I didn't think he had one."

"Wow... claws out much today?"

"Well, if he has one, he wouldn't be going around murdering ... women and children, while he has one of his own," I retorted.

He was sitting upright and turned towards me before I was done speaking.

"Is that what my mother told you?" he inquired.

"Isn't it the truth?" I asked.

"Why don't you ask your husband?"

"I am asking you."

He watched me for a minute, his Adam's apple visible when he swallowed slowly.

"There are many shades of black, the darkest being to kill women and children, which we are not."

"Black is black."

I wished I could talk back like this with Antonio. It was so much easier with Angelo. With Antonio, I was a dimwit without a thought process and a throbbing between my legs.

"Black is black," Angelo repeated after me. "*Sì*, except it's not. We don't harm women, we don't trade women, we don't harm children. We don't even harm men... unless there is no other option."

"Your mother..."

"My mother was giving word to her dreams," he snapped, startling me. He sighed at my shock and took a sip of his drink before looking back at me.

"My mother is not the best of women, and that's putting it kindly. You know this, right?"

He shook the drink in his glass, swirling it softly around, his eyes following the movement. "Why don't you have some faith in your husband? He is not all that bad as he would like people to believe in. Without him in my life, I would be a different person."

"Probably not killing people," I muttered.

He took another gulp of his drink. "Believe it or not, *Cosa Nostra* is not like it has been pictured in the movies. Especially not with the involvement of my family. We don't just go around killing innocent men. If they get killed, they ask for it. That doesn't mean he doesn't have a heart. Is he innocent? If you ask me, who is? Although if you ask him, he will tell you that you and Cora are."

I swallowed the lump in my throat.

Does my husband really think so highly of me?

He finished his drink and put down his glass, looking at me. "We have very strict moral codes to follow, just like any good company. Some of these rules were brought in by my grandfather, and then my father. Antonio has followed in the tradition. Do you know this is the exact reason they asked him to come to Boston?"

"What?"

"Boston wanted to legalise parts of their business, and our family has been strongly advising for this very step. That is why Antonio came here. To get it set up."

He picked up his glass. "You know he could have easily killed off Yuliya..." I squeaked, hands flying to my mouth. "No need to panic, *cognata*. He didn't, because that's not what he is. Although many other men would have gladly done that in his place, *Cosa Nostra* or not."

"What you two should do is..." he pointed with his finger to my chest and in the direction of Antonio's office, "talk. Communicate. With each other. Did you even ask what he does?"

He let a frustrated sigh slip out at my silence and got up. "*Amore!* A couple of idiots." Muttering further, he walked back inside.

CHAPTER TWENTY-SIX

DIVYA

My stomach dipped at the sight of father and daughter huddled in the armchair. Both fast asleep, one more comfortable than the other.

With his eyes closed, the air in the room was lighter. It was a relief for once not to have those razor-sharp eyes follow me around like a warm breath down my neck.

He had this habit of reading to Cora before bedtime when he was home. Even though the baby didn't have the attention span to even last a page, it made for a great bonding moment between father and daughter. Moments like this made me wish for my rose-tinted glasses so I could forget. Forget that this man, holding this baby so gently, is a killer, a member of a crime organisation.

Trying to wrap my head around all that had

happened the past few days made me come up empty and confused. There was a cacophony in my head that would make even the most eccentric take a side step. I needed time. Time to process everything.

What, then, was I doing here, seeking him out?

An inkling of doubt had crept into my steadfast convictions. Maybe I had been quick to judge which was what my parents had always taught me not to be.

So many times, my dad had spoken about his family, who had been quick to judge his relationship with a white woman. Not willing to open up to a different way of living.

Had I done the same now and run to my own conclusions?

But how could it be the same when this was far worse?

The only information I had of the mafia was from some random Hollywood movies. I hadn't even bothered to google the organisation. I never needed to.

Now I knew more. Even though it was biased, Rosa and Armando's view seemed genuine to me.

Everyone has good and bad in them. Armando's words whirled in my mind.

Did I really have the right to judge others?

Angelo's words, spoken and unspoken, showed a different side of Antonio. One of a brother and of the burden of a firstborn son. One of a different mafia.

But it was still a crime organisation. One where illegal deals were happening every day.

On the other hand, illegal deals were happening every-where, every day, not only in The Mafia.

Was I really trying to talk myself into staying married to this man?

Why not? At least until the case is done and I have the finances to start my new life.

Mad, that's what I was. Going mad.

I let my eyes feast on my husband, trailing him from head to toe. His grey dress pants and white shirt looked dishevelled. He looked tired, sleep deprived, almost as if he, too, had spent some sleepless nights just like me. I didn't know why, but I liked that idea.

Cora snuggled deeper into his arms, kicking her legs and rubbing her nose free of snot on his chest. The book on his lap slid off and landed on the floor with a thud. Not loud enough to wake the baby, but plenty to wake the man. His eyes shot awake and straight to mine, his relaxed posture dropping for one of alertness as if he expected danger to stab him any minute.

And those eyes are back on me.

I pushed off the wall and closed the distance between us. Every step I took made the air between us tingle. Tension rode high. By the time I lifted Cora from his arms, the air was as tight as the cables on the Zakim bridge.

His hand landed on my arm, holding me tightly in place. Heat penetrated my skin.

This close, I could drown in his eyes. Killer or not.

"Just going to put her in her cot." The croak in my voice was going to be my downfall.

"You'll come back to me?" His was hoarse, sleep still residing.

I nodded, and he let me go.

Why did I do that?

I put Cora in her cot and carefully covered her up. She rolled her plump thighs on top of her teddy bear. I imagined the breath leaving the bear in a whoosh.

How could this little angel be the product of two killers? Was this training with the bear?

I shook my head roughly, ridding myself of these ridiculous thoughts. Besides, I didn't care to imagine Antonio with another woman.

One day, though, he will be... after this arrangement is over.

I turned around to find him watching me. He looked casual sitting in that chair but there was a hardness to his eyes that screamed Mafia. Funny how I was seeing it only now. He gestured with his finger to come closer. Like the metal to his magnet, I went. I was defenceless and under his power.

He looped his arms around my waist, pulled me closer, and rested his head on my belly. Giving in to the urge to rub his hair would be too easy. Which is exactly why I fought it. But my body had other plans and relaxed into his arms, wallowing in comfort.

"Everyone's been telling me good things about you," I whispered.

He tilted his head and pinned me with his hard eyes. "They lied."

His direct words shot a sharp arrow into my mind. When I was trying to hold on to the ledge, he kicked me off. I pushed him away, whirled around, and rushed out of the room into ours. I paced the length of the bed, agitation drilling through my body.

When he strode in, I threw his words back at him. "They lied? Did you tell them to?"

"No."

"What part of it was a lie?"

"I've no idea what they told you."

I stood in the middle of the room, my mouth open. "You just told me they lied."

"I don't need to know what they said to know that." He stepped closer to me, his hands in his pockets. With his sleeves rolled up he eluded casualness. "What did they say? That I am a good man?" He let a thin laugh slip out at my surprise. "Don't need to be a rocket scientist to know that."

He walked over to the dresser and poured himself a glass of his liquid. Cool, controlled movements. He must truly not care to be this calm. Turning around, he watched me as he sipped his drink. "Well, I am not."

"Well then, this arrangement is done," I snapped and strode to the door.

He was on me in a second, spinning me around and pinning me to the wall.

"What do you want me to say, then?" he hissed.

"Let me go!" I screamed.

"No." He sighed, trying to rein in his anger and failing miserably. "I do horrible things. I am involved in all kinds of illegal businesses. Do you know what my position is? I am the *consigliere*. Do you know what that is? I advise the don about anything and everything. So, there is no activity I know nothing about. I kill people. I don't get any pleasure from it. But if I have to, I will kill and I have. That is how you become a fucking made man. So, you see..." he slammed his fist onto the wall right next to me, jerking my nerves and splintering the plaster on the wall, "There is nothing fucking good about me."

"You should have told me—"

"Yes. I should have fucking not hired you, and I should have fucking told you. So shoot me. I'll give you the gun." He laughed at my startled face. "You were so innocent. You *are* so innocent and good... I didn't want to bring the darkness of my life into yours."

"But you did anyway," I wailed. "You are bringing all your darkness when I was already drowning. I can't handle this. I can't. You kill babies—"

"For fuck's sake. We don't fucking kill babies or women."

"Tell me what you do, then."

"I can't."

"What?"

"I can't tell you what we do. Then I put you in danger. The women in our family are on a need-to-know basis only..."

"'Need-to-know basis'", I repeated his words. "So what... I know you do a shit load of illegal things, just not what they are?"

"Something like that."

"Fucking bullshit."

"That's how it has been for ages, and I am not about to change that so you can go and get yourself killed. Just accept the fact of who I really am, Divya, and move along. Not everything in life is black and white. This is a grey zone. Embrace it."

"I—"

"Fuck's sake!" He banged his head against the wall. The sound of a skull on a wall gave me a headache. "Why do you have to be fucking difficult?"

"*I am* being difficult?" I barked.

"Fine. I should have told you. I don't just go around killing people, m*ia cara,*" he muttered, his fists clenching and unclenching next to me on the wall. "Can't you just believe that?"

"No." I shook my head vigorously. "Tell me what you do. Otherwise this ends right now."

"I can't." He rested his forehead on mine, his words broken. "Don't push me to break a rule of conduct I have inherited. We do so much. There's some good in them. They sent me here to legalise more aspects of the business because the Capo wants it. Because my father, grandfather... I stand behind it. But it doesn't mean we don't do ugly things, m*ia cara*. We do plenty."

He let out a sigh, a whiff on my forehead. "We have morals and ethics that we stand up to. Which is very important to us."

He lifted my chin up to his. "Can't you believe that the man you married will not just go around killing women and children?"

"It's not only killing," I hissed.

"All this time, you were screaming murderer at me, and now it's more?" he bit out. "Every day, you find something new to pin on me. But yes, there are so many ugly things in the world," he said resoundingly. "I am what I am. Nothing good in that."

He looked dissolute. It rocked my boat because I'd never seen him like this. But I was lost too and angry ... at the world, at his mother, at him.

"I don't know how to move past this. I don't know if I can do this... no matter how short-term this is for." The moment the words slipped out, I called myself a liar.

But he believed me. Even though he dropped his head onto my shoulder to hide his gaze, the arm that wrapped like a fist around my waist told another story. It was as if he thought I might walk out right now.

But I wouldn't.

I couldn't.

Who is the fucking liar now?

For Cora, I will stay.

For him too.

Yes. For him too. Somehow, I had come to care for this life he had created for us.

"Is it so difficult to be with me, m*ia cara*?" His voice vibrated on my skin. It sent goosebumps into my heart.

No. It wasn't difficult at all.

I let my eyes slide close. I had too many thoughts in my head to see through the mist. What would my parents have said?

"Run! They would have said run!" said the angel on my shoulder.

"Stay! Keep an open mind. Soul-scorching love doesn't happen every day," the devil on my shoulder whispered.

His head tilted to look at me. The whisper of his

voice was strained. "Talk to me... tell me what you are thinking."

"It's not easy with you," I sighed, trying to draw away.

He held me tighter. His front pressed to mine. "Why not?"

"Because... you make me feel so..." I stopped the flow of my words, the thoughts moving further in my head. Uncomfortable, out of depth, like I was in the middle of a sandstorm but one I didn't want to live without.

Dread infiltrated my body, taking over my vital organs, and squeezed hard.

Soul-scorching love?

Is this it? I have never felt like this before. With Adam, it was different. Lighter. Weightless. Easier to let go. Which is exactly what I should do with this man.

Who willingly stayed in a marriage with the mafia?

But he was holding the strings to my body, moving me to his will like the puppet I was. If he let go, I was scared I might simply collapse to the ground and cease to exist.

I jerked away, ducking under his arms, and allowed distance to come between us.

He turned, reaching for me.

"No!" My voice came as a shout, breaking the static air in the room.

He ran frustrated hands through his hair. "Tell me what to do."

"Nothing." I jerked away. "You've done enough." I bit my lip, ignoring his agitation. "I need time to process this. I can't think clearly. I need space. Please." Time would help. Even I didn't really believe that as I scurried out of the room. But I let the illusion be. I needed time to figure out how I ended up falling for my husband. Time to figure out how I would survive the end because the end would come to this scam of a marriage we had. It was time to figure out if I would end it or wait for him to end it.

CHAPTER TWENTY-SEVEN

DIVYA

An uncomfortable vibe settled into the house for the next few days. I embraced it. It tickled inside my veins and filled me up till I was full of unease. I couldn't pinpoint that exact moment when I fell in love with my husband. Because even if I buried my head in the sand in the desert, I couldn't deny it. The Divya before would have high-tailed it out of here the moment I heard "Mafia" or "killer." But the Divya now was still lounging around, sipping coffee, coming up with excuses to stick with a scam of a marriage. Only a madwoman would do that. A madwoman in love.

When did it go from desire to love, or was it always love? The signs had been there, but keeping with my idiotic streak, I hadn't seen it. I had never had sex without an emotional attachment, and the number of times I had been wildly busy wrapped around him should have been a big, red flag.

Imbecile.

It explained everything. It explained why I turned into thick honey whenever he was around.

I didn't recognise myself with him. Sometimes, I was a better person, but sometimes I was worse, orbiting out of control, as if I needed him to pull me back to balance. Was he my damn gravity?

Moron!

I had always so badly wanted what my parents had had. A love that consumed me. Where my soul connects with someone, and I am a part of him, no matter what. Where I didn't know where I ended, and he began. They say be careful what you wish for. I got exactly what I wanted, except with a man who used me as a fuck machine, would surely dump me the moment the case was settled, and was part of The Mafia.

Did I need any more reasons to run? Except my heart was adamant, blatantly refused to listen, and was too busy anchoring metal chains to stay.

Talk about a bunch of bad choices I had made: this must be the worst of them all. This was beyond moron Adam and his gambling addiction and selfish love. That one felt immature now.

What an idiot.

All that money my parents spent on my education was down the drain because there wasn't a shred of intelligence left in me.

Exhaustion hit me from the cannonball of emotions inside me. This was now. One day, when he came around asking for that divorce, I would have to put a shitload of pieces of myself back together.

Rosa came over from the kitchen, worry lining her forehead. She sat on the sofa next to me and touched my shoulder gently. She murmured something in Italian, but I didn't understand any of it. All her efforts to soothe me had all gone in vain, and I felt even more terrible for it. "Call friend?" she asked.

It was a good idea. I needed a breather. I needed a friend who would talk some sense into me. But drowning in my sorrow after my parents' death, I had isolated myself, and one by one, they had flown off the radar. I knew if I picked up the phone and called a few, they would be back on track. But really, something in me, probably my big ego, didn't want to reveal my mishaps.

So I did the next best thing. I invited my new friend Lakshmi over for a coffee.

———

THIS WAS EXACTLY what I needed.

Curled up on the sofa, my hands wrapped around the chai tea Lakshmi had made with me, I listened to her stories of India. The smell of cardamon and cinnamon hung heavy in the air, making Rosa wrinkle her nose. Maybe she regretted her idea, but her smile from the kitchen told me she didn't.

My mind wandered occasionally to the words uttered by Armando and Angelo right before I would jump back to some new story of Lakshmi's family, and she had a lot of them back in India. Her uncle with four wives, her cousin who was trying out for a Bollywood film, her grandmother's family who refused to have toilets inside the house. But there were also stories of a cousin starting a small business, another one not only looking after her elderly parents but also her elderly in-laws.

"You see, *beti*, there is nothing good or bad in this world. It is just different. That is very important to understand when you are associating with different cultures. No?"

I nodded, enthralled by her words. *Nothing good or bad, just different.*

"What does *beti* mean?"

"Daughter. You feel like a daughter to me. Do you mind if I call you that?" she asked sweetly.

"No, of course not."

"So, where is this husband of yours?"

"At work." D*oing lots of illegal stuff.*

She nodded. "Ramesh said your husband has quite the reputation."

My heart screeched to a stop like I'd not seen that bus before me.

"Apparently, he has some big accounts in his company," she paused, confusion crossing her face at my open-mouthed shock. "You know men. Ramesh thinks he knows a thing or two about private investment banking. He did some digging into your husband's company, and now he thinks he knows everything."

Oh!

I heard my heart beating in my ears, *Lab-dab lab-dab.* It wasn't a bus, after all.

"I told him I don't care about his business. The way

that man looks at you, one has to be blind not to know his heart is beating for you."

I thought it a pity that my new friend turned out to be blind. I hoped Antonio was shortsighted as well. What was worse than falling for the man? Him finding out.

"So, when are you off for your honeymoon?"

The daze around me cleared for a minute.

"Ugh... honeymoon." I wouldn't mind that. Just the two of us with Cora... except it wasn't an actual marriage. "He doesn't have much time... you know... with work and all." My words trailed off. How did The Mafia work? Did he get, like, a three-week, paid holiday?

"Oh, *beti*, you have to take the time to enjoy. Life could end just like that, you know. Might as well enjoy it while you can."

Just like that, I was back to that phone call from Mrs Smith, listening to the voice on the other end telling me to come home. Grief dropped to the pit of my stomach like a heavy stone. I blinked a few times.

If this was my last day today, what would I want to do?

Be with him.

Both the angel and the devil on my shoulders seemed to agree.

I was so sick of not being with him. I deserved him. I deserved to enjoy life too.

I picked up my phone next to me, Lakshmi's words fading to a buzz.

> I was thinking …

Armando interrupted me by showing Ramesh in.

"I finished work early and thought I'd pick you up from Divya's," he said sweetly.

Dropping my phone, I went to welcome him, asking them both to stay longer.

Lakshmi was a talker, while her husband was quiet and hung more in the background. His wife handled the conversations and he the intonations by popping in a remark once in a while. They made an odd but interesting pair. I imagined that Antonio and I might be the same.

Lakshmi's description of India wrapped me in a warm blanket while I enjoyed my second cup of chai. I could almost believe I was already there.

"You see, *beti*, you should visit India. You can then see it through your own eyes and understand what your father's experience was living there."

"Divya." I was startled, nearly spilling my tea on me, at the sound of Antonio's warm voice floating down the hallway.

He marched into the room a second later, coming to an abrupt stop when he saw I wasn't alone. His brows drew into a frown, displeasure flowing off him at the unexpected visitors.

Idiot. What was I doing, acting like this was my house and inviting people over?

Should I have warned him they were visiting? But he wasn't home, and we were in the midst of a fight.... What was he doing here in the middle of the day then? I felt heady, like the first few weeks of our marriage, when he would just pop home to plant himself inside me.

Heat crawled up my neck even as I shrugged that memory away. I sprang up and nervously laced my fingers. "Antonio, you remember Lakshmi. She made my wedding dress..." Shit. I wanted to sound nonchalant. Instead, my voice was breaking on the edges like water on the dunes. Grabbing onto his arm, I directed him towards the couple. "And this is her husband, Ramesh. I invited them over for a coffee." *But ended up making chai and making your whole house reek.*

His arm flexed below my hand, sending need through my veins. When I tried to withdraw mine, he held onto it with one hand while greeting the couple with his other, all fake-friendly politeness now.

"Sorry for the interruption. I just had to discuss something urgent with my wife." His eyes held a fire when they trained on me. "Can you excuse us for a minute?" he asked but didn't wait for their response before he pulled me out of the room.

"What did you —"

"Not yet...." He pushed me into his office and slammed the door shut behind us.

All the air in there must have snuck out because the room was hot. Unease sent goosebumps up my arms. Was he so mad that I had invited people over without informing him? But he didn't look mad.

I didn't like the way he was looking at me, though. I moved away to his table. An agitation pulsed in him as he stood with his hands in his pockets, rocking on his feet.

"Well...?" he encouraged me.

"I should have obviously let you know I was having

visitors. It's your house, of course. I thought you wouldn't mind. That's why I—"

"*Mia Cara*, I don't give a damn who you invite. You are my wife. You can invite whoever you want as long as they're screened, and they have been."

Tilting my head up to meet his gaze, I watched him, confused. "Then what are you talking about?"

"Your message?" he rasped.

"My mess... oh!" Realisation dawned on me. "I didn't realise I had sent that," I said guiltily.

"Doesn't matter." He closed the distance between us, and I suddenly found myself between the desk and a hard place. "What were you thinking?"

The day I first met him here flooded through my mind. All his books. His *sex* books.

"I was just..." I sighed, trying to save my eyes from the fire in his. "I am tired of all of this..." I waved my hands to include the space, "I thought..." I stopped short as his face darkened, a muscle in his jaw ticking. Anyone with half a mind wouldn't complete my thought.

"You thought what? Spit it out, whatever it is you are mincing in your head," he hissed.

I clutched the desk with both my hands. Warm walnut and leather. "I thought... maybe...." His hands came up to grip my chin. "We can call a truce?" I finished weakly, my eyes fixed on his.

He released a puff of air as if he had expected me to say something else.

A hint of a smile tugged at his lips as he rested his forehead on mine. "A truce, huh?"

"Well, yes, unless you don't—"

"I do," he silenced me. He gave me a warm kiss on my forehead. Heat slid up to the back of my neck. "Does this truce involve sex?"

Of course. Isn't that why the man was into me? His fuck machine. A shiver of bitterness ran up my spine. "If you want."

"I do. I do want." He eyed me like I was his addiction. I was the spiced-up Amaro he liked to drink. His eyes glinted with something I couldn't pinpoint, and he moved his hand to unbutton my shirt.

I jerked away, swatting his hands off. "Not now," I hissed. "We have visitors."

"I don't give a fuck." I swear his words set off a fire in between my legs. He shoved me against the desk, unbuttoning my shirt to reveal my breasts. "Jesus, you can torture me. Do you ever wear a bra?" He didn't bother to wait for an answer before he took a nipple into his mouth, tugging harshly.

Horny as I was, I had to think of the two people I had left behind in the living room. "Antonio, please," I pleaded as I tried to tug his head. *Half-heartedly.*

He grabbed my hands and pinned them on the desk behind me. "We haven't fucked for ages, *tesoro mio,*" he mumbled against my breasts. "I'll be quick, I promise. *Sì?*"

"Fine," I muttered. I would do this for him— *not entirely.*

"You just have to stay quiet."

I bristled at his order but forgot about it when he crushed his mouth to mine. Our kiss turned wild instantly. Like wildfire on a dry summer. Our lips infused together, sucking the life out of each other. It was like he was trying to make me combust with just a kiss.

He grabbed my ass harshly and pulled me closer to his thickness. Letting my arms go, he grabbed a handful of my skirt and jerked it up.

A frustrated sigh escaped him. "Fuck! I don't have time for this shit." He ripped my underwear open, muttering to himself more than me he would buy me a whole damn shop.

His movements were jerky as he unbuckled himself and pushed his trousers down, together with his boxers. His erection sprang free, head angry, pulsing for release.

His eyes closed for a second, and a groan spilt out as he rubbed himself against me, precum oozing.

I wiggled closer and aligned him with my slit, my knees spread wide. A whimper escaped me when he pushed inside. My muscles clenched.

"You never...can...keep quiet," he rasped. Heat pulsed inside me. He made it sound more like a compliment than an insult.

He pulled out completely and thrust back in, pulling my head up to plunge his tongue into my mouth. My gasp got sucked into his.

He was so deep inside me that there wasn't any emptiness anymore. Wrapping my legs around him, I kept him tight against me.

He read my mind when he muttered just below my ear, "No more fights. Promise. Me. No. More. Fights." His warm voice on my skin sent sparks up the back of my neck.

"No. More. Fights," I groaned.

Pushing my torso flat on the desk, he thrust in and out of me. Hard and deep, just the way I liked it. The dark swirl of his eyes rested on my breasts. He let his hands follow the path. His hands captured them. "Fucking missed these."

He hadn't missed me. Just my body. It was better than nothing. Still, I couldn't hold his gaze. My jaw trembled. I let my eyes drop to where our bodies joined.

Shit. So hot.

The room was heavy with sound. Our breaths and groans filled every nook, every shelf, and filtered into every book. Maybe my friends heard us. Maybe they didn't. Maybe the gardener passed by the window. Maybe he didn't. I didn't care anymore. I loved having him go in and out of me. The heat I felt outside spread inside, making my muscles clench inside. I bit my lip, trying to hold back the imminent scream. It was beautiful how perfectly tuned he was to my body. Sweat spilt under my breasts, and a flush heated my body. Leaning over, he took my mouth just in time to swallow my scream.

I held on tight to him as he jerked inside me, emptying his cum in me. I loved him the most when he was like this. As much a victim to his body as me.

CHAPTER TWENTY-EIGHT

DIVYA

I *love this life you and I are creating.*

I watched the man sauntering over to us with a glass of Amaro in his hand.

Cora and I, lounging on the sun lounger, got excited. It was clear he was the highlight of our lives. The baby, jiggling her buttocks on my belly, launched into action. Bubbling enthusiastically, saliva dripping, she took to the floor, like an alligator taking to the water on a lazy, sunny afternoon and crawled to her father.

Antonio was sweet and gentle with her. Scooting down, he waited patiently for her, setting his glass on the table nearby.

"Marry a man who will be a good father." My mum's words echo in my mind.

I did, Mum, I did. Except one day, this life will come to vanish like smoke in the air.

With a heavy heart, I watched the pair. The baby

putting one pudgy thigh in front of the other, occasionally distracted by the choas of scattered toys. The man, ruthless to most, hunched down, keeping his eyes on the baby, encouraging the approach in sweet words of a language I didn't understand.

Days flew by in a flash, like a synopsis of a movie. A glimpse and it was another day again. Filled with moments of true happiness and desolate sadness.

I loved the way he reached for me blindly first thing in the morning, snuggling his scruff on the crane of my neck, inhaling me like I was the best fragrance he'd ever smelt. It made me feel precious.

I loved his insatiable appetite for me when he found me at all times of the day, ever ready to bury himself deep inside me. It made me feel sexy.

I loved how he gave strict orders to his men for his mother not to be allowed inside the house without his permission. It made me feel protected.

But I hated his complete shutdown, his invisible wall when talking about his work. Even though I wanted nothing to do with it, I still wanted him to want to tell me, anyway. It made me feel lost.

I hated his dark anger and his exploding rage when I dared to question anything regarding the custody case or when I could enrol for my studies. It made me terrified.

I hated knowing I was just a fuck machine for him. That I was a convenience to have, with nothing special attached. Tomorrow, he could just as easily find a different convenience. It made me feel worthless.

I hated the person I was with him when these feelings took over. I hated lying awake wondering if he was faithful to me, even knowing there really was no reason he should for a scam of a marriage on a piece of paper, with money, a dowry with an end date.

I hated the person I was who had googled his ex-wife and spent hours going through every image I could find, torturing myself. There were pictures of them together. He had probably loved her at one time to make a baby together. They made a handsome couple. She was perfection in beauty.

Image after image showed a sexy blonde with tousled hair, big blue eyes, and plump, red lips. Any man would but fall on his knees for her. Even I might if I were to play for the other team.

My hopes that the ex-wife would be some dark and deformed devil were lost, proving again how naïve I had been to even hope for that.

This man catching onto the Cora Express and swinging her up in the air could easily pose as some sculptured Roman god. I was nothing but a spectator watching this show unfold in front of my eyes.

He turned his gaze on me. Heat pulsed between us as he walked over to me, looking for all the world as if he were coming for his reward, me being the trophy.

His eyes dropped to my breasts and darkened immediately. He took his time to travel to my eyes, stopping on the way to devour me. Fire burned in my veins.

His tongue slipped out to give a soft lick to the side of his lips before letting his dark and smooth voice fall on my prickled skin.

"You are looking exceptionally beautiful today, *mia cara*." His gaze ran through the length of my body, putting me on the stage next to Cleopatra. "More than yesterday and...." He gulped down whatever he was going to say and came back for my eyes. "Is this dress new?"

I wanted to say so many things. But my voice caught in my throat. I dropped my eyes, unable to hold his dark gaze.

"It's something I made a long time ago."

He put his hands out and tilted my chin up, making me meet his gaze again and said, "I love it," sucking me back to the spiral of a love phase.

We fell into the room, arms and legs tangled up, lips fused together after a few days apart. My travelling husband was back home and in a hurry to bury himself in between my legs.

Lifting me up, he walked briskly to our bed and dropped me on it. His glazed eyes moved away from me and cleared for a minute, focusing on the colourful cushions on the bed.

"What's this?"

"I... found them when I was out shopping with Lakshmi." I moved away from him towards the headboard and grabbed a cushion protectively, putting it in front of my naked chest. I hadn't thought he would even notice, but apparently, he had. "It just reminded me of home," I said weakly. "I will put it away if you don't—"

"*Ridicolo.*" He silenced me with a finger to his lips. His eyes swirled again as he watched me while he dropped his dress pants and boxer shorts in one go. Need lit up my body. Crawling onto the bed, he dragged me under him. Grabbing hold of the cushion in my arms, he threw it away.

"I don't mind, m*ia cara*. You can do whatever you want to change things in the house," he rasped, brushing his stubble on my naked breasts, making them swell and go red.

"Really?"

He lifted his head, a frown between his eyes.

"Of course. Whatever makes you happy."

I watched him. I didn't believe he would be okay with whatever change I would make to his impeccably beautifully designed home.

"Is there anything else you want?" he asked me softly.

I smiled, shaking my head, distracted by the thickness between my legs.

"No. Just you," I croaked.

That was all the invitation he needed.

As he came inside me, all thought filtered out. Except I thought it was a good thing that I was on the pill. Because Antonio was lousy at remembering to put on a condom.

———

I was window shopping with Cora in her stroller. We conversed among ourselves, making strangers smile at our baby talking. I stopped in front of a furniture store. It was beautifully designed with heaps of colours in it.

"That sofa has my name on it, *Kutti*," I said to Cora as I eyed the terracotta sofa screaming for me. I glanced at

Cora munching on her rabbit's feet like it was her next meal. I didn't think she liked the sofa. The phone in the stroller started vibrating. I fumbled through the blankets.

Why was it that it was never the first thing I touched?

My hands felt around and finally found it next to Cora's giraffe. I put it next to my ears without bothering to check the caller ID.

"Hi, baby," Adam's voice rang out.

My hands turned cold. How did he manage to find me every time?

I turned back to eye Mario and Franco a few meters behind me. They were watching the window of the store and not paying any attention to me.

"What do you want, Adam? I told you to stop calling me," I hissed.

"You know what I want, baby. I want you." He said the same thing every time. I didn't know how to make him stop. He was like a blood-sucking leech.

"I told you I am not coming back. I am married now." I turned around and found Franco watching me. I didn't want them to report back to Antonio. Something told me he wasn't going to be pleased.

"Baby, I know you are making it up. Stop playing hard to get."

"I am not."

"Fine, then tell me where you are with your so-called husband. I'll come visit you, and I might believe you then."

"I am not going to tell you that, Adam." I shifted uncomfortably on my feet. *Why can't I get rid of him?*

"I told you I know the stock market. I've had a great

victory. I'll take you shopping. You can buy yourself a nice designer dress."

His gloating on the line worked on my agitated nerves. "I don't need a designer dress." Franco started walking towards me. "I have plenty of designer dresses back at the mansion, thank you."

Adam's laugh rang out loud enough to annoy my eardrums. "Really, baby? Which rundown neighbourhood is this, then?"

"Really, we live on Beacon Street, right opposite a big green park, and it's in no way run down," I snapped and cut the line right before Franco reached me. I smiled at him and pushed the stroller inside the store. I hoped that would be the end of it. I wanted to show Adam I had moved on, but I didn't know how.

He found me in our room, propped up against my new cushions, staring at my new purchase. I had bought the beautiful sofa.

I hadn't dared to buy it without asking him, but when I had texted him to ask if I could buy something for the house, he hadn't even bothered to ask what before answering yes.

Now, though, uneasiness was in the air. His scowl, directed at the new beauty in the room, made regret pool inside me.

He moved into the room, standing in between the sofa and the bed. He held his body tight, and it told me to run. His face was dark, and his jaw taut, a muscle twitching.

"This is what you bought today?" His attempt to control the displeasure in his tone was weak.

My happiness at my purchase dropped like concrete rocks to the bottom of the Thames.

"You don't like it?"

He turned to me. "*Why* did you buy it?"

"I loved the colour."

He moved away to the chest of drawers, uncuffed his shirt sleeves, and dropped the cufflinks, watching me shrewdly in the mirror.

"And...?" he prompted.

I shrugged. "I liked the shape too."

He dropped his shirt onto the chair and turned around with a scowl. Displeasure rolled off him.

"Anything else?"

I shook my head.

Without a word, he moved to the bathroom. I heard the shower turning on.

I didn't dare tell him I had been in a bad mood after the call from Adam. The sofa had instantly cheered me up and made me forget arrogant Adam.

The sound of flowing water stopped, sending a tingle of fear up my spine. Sometimes, I just didn't know what way was up with him. I was horny, nervous, and frightened all at once. Confusion crawled in my head.

He appeared at the doorway, droplets of water dripping down to his towel-wrapped bottom half.

"I just felt happy when I saw it and bought it. That's all," I blurted out.

He came to stand in front of the bed, looking down at me, making me regret my choice of sexy lingerie.

"Nothing else?" he hissed.

"No."

He crawled onto the bed, coming to hang on top of me, legs on either side of me. I didn't even know what we were discussing anymore.

He nodded towards the sofa. "Will you be sleeping there now?"

That's what this is about?

Relief washed over me. I wrapped my hand around his neck and drew him closer for a kiss. "Of course not," I whispered before letting my tongue drift into his mouth.

He seemed unsatisfied as he drew away from me.

"Anything else happen today, m*ia cara*?" he asked me, his shoulders tense, watching me closely.

My breath hitched. I drew back. Could he know about the call? I didn't think Franco heard me.

I shook my head. "Nothing interesting to report."

His face darkened with the threat of a fight. I, on the other hand, was not in the mood for one. I was going after what I wanted, and what I wanted was him.

I sneaked my hand in between us and tugged the towel, freeing his erection. I let my hands cup his thickness and brought it closer to me. My back arched, and my ass pushed to his heat.

He ran his hand roughly on my cheek. The pad of his thumb, rough, on my soft skin. His mood wasn't relaxed, but the lust burning in his eyes told me that whatever his internal battle was, he was ready to put it to rest.

He whispered words to me in between kisses. I loved

his language. It sounded magical, although today it sounded harsh. It was probably because of the mood I was in, desperate to get him inside me and hold him tight.

Adam's call brought with it the realisation of how much more my enthrallment was with my husband. My relationship with Adam was immature compared to what I had with Antonio, one-sided as it was. I just desperately wanted to hang on to it a bit longer before he finally decided to break it off. Even though I realised buying a sofa would not help to make a claim on him. The sofa would stay. One day I would have to leave.

CHAPTER TWENTY-NINE

ANTONIO

I t was a strange type of man who tried to steal another man's woman. But a man who tried to steal *my woman* was neither strange nor a man.

Acid filled my throat as I watched the story unfold before my eyes. When bloody fucking Harris leaned over to give my wife a kiss on her cheek, a vein burst somewhere in my body. I didn't miss the fact that he did it in my own living room. Nor that she didn't bother to push him away. But when, instead of staying in the living room where Rosa was, they moved to the garden, venom swirled inside my brain. It was a fucking joke. Coming from me, who was supposed to be the diplomat. But she was mine, and Harris was in the way.

Without a hitch, I switched to the surveillance camera of the garden. When Armando had called to request permission to allow fucking Harris into my home, I should have refused. But like the masochist that I clearly was, I had granted it, wanting to see what would happen.

I didn't care for what was happening.

They were standing too fucking close. From this angle, I could only see Harris's face. I wondered if Divya's was flushed like it was with me. Were her pupils dilated, the greens in her eyes hidden, like when she was turned on?

There was no doubt that it was a passionate conversation, given the body language, while passion should be nowhere around these two. Why had my fucking wife not kicked out this *deficienti* immediately?

Isabella walked in through the door, book in hand.

"Not now," I snarled, making her startle and scurry back out.

I didn't have any fucking time for anything else. Like a man waiting for his verdict, I watched the two. Harris sat down on the sun lounger and dragged my wife along, their knees touching. The same sun lounger where I had fucked her a few days ago. She was obviously not thinking about that now. The fucker had his arms around her, and he was pulling her close. A rage I hadn't known I possessed flushed through me like a red-hot bolt when he stuck his lips to hers. This was no friendly peck. The dumb son of a bitch had his tongue down her throat, and my wife was not pushing him away. The kiss lasted a full damn minute. I slammed my screen, hoping it had frozen, but no, the image was fine. My wife's brain not so much.

Eventually, she shot away from him, words spilling out of her, none of which I could fathom. Harris rose, reaching for her, and she moved away.

Too fucking late.

I watched them go back inside, following the images through every room till he was out of the house.

A fool. A man who tried to steal *my woman* was clearly a fucking fool who didn't care for his own life.

Releasing my clenched fist, I punched in the number for Marco.

"Get the car ready tonight."

I LOUNGED in the back with Marco and Remo in the front. The tight muscles on my thighs made a mockery out of my laid-back attitude.

The bar door opened to reveal the noise and light from inside and spewed out a stumbling Harris. I gave a nod to Marco and watched him exit the car and approach Harris. At this time of the night, only drunks lined the street. Satisfaction hummed in my body when Marco delivered a welcome punch to Harris and dragged him to the side alley.

Taking my time, I slid out of the car and followed in their footsteps. One heavy, the other dragged. When I arrived, Harris had earned himself several more hits to his gut.

Walking over, I stood in front of him. I let my eyes run over him, the fool who kissed my wife.

"Who the fuck are you?" Harris sputtered out.

As an introduction, I punched his face right in the middle, breaking his nose with a loud crack and taking one eye socket with me, my wedding ring leaving a sharp cut across his face. I wanted him deformed for the rest of his life.

I gave him time to reel back from my punch and stop his pitiful groaning before I leaned over, putting my voice in front of his mouth. "She's *mine*, you fucker."

"That bitch," he yelled into my face, earning him another punch in his eye socket. I didn't like the words coming out of his mouth. But then again, there really was no surprise there.

Harris groaned, grabbing hold of his eye but continued, alcohol making him brave or born a moron.

"Is this why she doesn't want to come back? My money not enough for the bitch? But apparently, you have more."

I rocked on my feet. There wasn't a shred of will in my body that bothered to answer him.

"She's only with you for the money," Harris hissed.

If that was what kept her with me, I would shower her with it. As. Long. As. She. Stayed. With. Me.

"Because we all know I can fuck her way better than you," Harris sniggered, looking gleefully from me to my men.

Something I didn't recognise detonated inside of me and blasted its way out, my body burning my oesophagus, my chest, my throat. My hand, which had been itching for my gun, let loose, relentlessly slamming into his face, trying to erase any memory of this man anywhere near my wife. I only stopped when even the whimpers stopped coming, and the jackass was a heaping mess on the ground. I looked at the fool lying on the tarred street and gave him an additional kick to his balls. Crouching down, I lifted his head close to mine.

"I am the one she fucks. I am the one she waits for at home. I am the one she married. And you..." I pin my gaze on his one open eye, "Will be the one six feet under if you come anywhere near her again." I dropped him down and stood up.

"Don't kill him... yet," I told Marco.

I didn't know why I would want him to live. Fucking woman was turning me into a pussy. I looked back at the heap lying on the ground. "Bleed him more."

I ignored Marco's odd look.

Yes. I knew I never fucking did this type of shit.
But he came for my wife. My wife.
No one fucked with what was mine.

I walked away. It was time to go home and find out who my wife thought was the best fuck.

———

SITTING ON HER NEW SOFA, I watched her sleep in our bed, the fury inside me eating me up and making me clench the glass in my hands while my wife slept on peacefully. Not a care in this world.

A fucking seductress. Even asleep, her body was burning a path to my cock, trying to tug it out of my briefs. Not yet.

I can fuck her far better than you.

The glass shattered, the alcohol providing disinfectant to my bleeding hand, blood and alcohol seeping down onto the sofa.

Good. Her fucking sofa will have a stain now.

Her gasp made my eyes shoot up to the bed to find my dishevelled wife sitting on it, looking at my hand in horror. I wondered how she would react if she saw Harris now.

She scrambled to the foot end on her hands and knees.

"Oh my god! What happened?" She made a move to get up, only to be pushed down with the end of my foot. Getting up, I approached the bed.

"Let me up, Antonio, to get some ice and bandages for you. What happened? Were you in a fight or something?"

I pushed her back onto the bed and crawled over, dirtying the linen sheets with my blood.

"Blood all over—"

"Shut up," I snarled, silencing her immediately. "You think I care?" I said tightly, nailing her with my eyes, taking a wicked pleasure in the power I had over her.

At least she was more scared of me.

"What I am interested in is..." I whispered dangerously close to her, watching her eyes flicker nervously, "your visitor today, who came into my house."

I watched her chew her lips nervously. She was going to fucking dent something that belonged to me.

"Please... do tell me what fucking Harris wanted," I sneered.

She tried to move away, and I pounced on her. Pinning her hands on top of her head, I watched her breasts jut out.

My breasts.

"I suggest you don't test my patience today, m*ia cara*," I said stonily.

"He just wanted to offer the money back from my inheritance," she said softly.

"Just like that? No conditions?" I taunted.

She dropped her eyes from mine.

Coward!

"Fucking look at me or I swear to god..."

Her eyes crashed into mine. "What did the swine want?" I growled.

"He wanted to get back together," she muttered.

"Ah... and what did you tell him, m*ia cara*?"

"I told him no... of course," she faltered.

"Of course. Because that is what you should have done immediately. *Sì*? As you are my wife now, *sì*?"

She nodded frantically.

"Was this before or after you kissed him?"

She jerked away, scurrying towards the headboard, a rippled V in between her eyes. "How did you..."

I could almost see the wheels inside her head turning. My wife was no idiot although sometimes she goaded danger like she was. I knew the moment the realisation hit her. A gasp escaped, and her eyes turned round like the big saucers in the kitchen.

"You watched us. You have cameras in the garden." She dared to accuse me.

I yanked her down again, trapping her with my hands.

"Be careful of what you accuse me of, m*ia cara*, when you have done far worse. Do tell me all about this lover's kiss you shared," I hissed through my teeth.

"Why?" she snapped. "Didn't you see everything?"

A growl hit my belly and left my throat. I swear this woman would goad me to kill. Grabbing hold of her mouth, I shoved my tongue in, letting loose my anger, and leaving no victims behind.

My mouth.

I bit her lips harshly. I wanted my fucking mark pasted on her to last a week.

My mark.

Her whimper made me pause, and I lifted my head.

"Don't fucking test my patience today," I gritted.

"I am not going back to him," she whimpered.

"Of course not," I snapped. "Not that there is much to go back to." I should have told Marco to kill him. I should have put a bullet in his goddamn head.

Why had I kept him alive?

I looked at the hand that had slammed into the fool. Divya followed my gaze with horror.

"Oh my god. What did you do to him?" she shrieked.

"Shh... don't worry, m*ia cara*. I didn't kill him... yet. Let's just say he will not come knocking on our door again... unless he doesn't value his life anymore, hmmm."

"You are a beast. I just kissed him to feel what it was like, okay?"

"Did you, now?" I said calmly, catching hold of her

flailing and kicking arms. "What did you find out, huh? Do you like kissing him more? Was he a better fuck?" I taunted her, moving her negligee out of the way with my teeth, latching on to her nipple and pulling hard, punishing her for kissing another man.

"No," she whimpered, the fight going out of her. "I felt nothing, okay?"

"You better hope so, m*ia cara*."

Sitting up, I jerked out of my briefs and bunched up her negligee with one fist.

"You are my wife," I spat out. "Why do I have to fucking remind you all the time?" I pushed my dick inside her without any build-up but found her still wet and dripping for me. I withdrew again to drive deep.

"Who fucks you the best, m*ia cara*?"

"You do," she whimpered.

Grabbing her hair in my hands, I yanked her head closer to punish her with a kiss.

"Whose kisses do you like?" I rasped, my voice broken.

"Yours. Yours, okay."

The urge to bury my hurt crawled all over me. Even as I pounded inside her, the image of Harris's face popped up in between. I should have never kept him alive. Red filled my view.

"Please?" she whimpered.

I shook off the red haze around me to see her again. "Please what?"

"Please make it stop. Make me come. Please?"

"That's fucking better." I slammed harder in and

out, punishing her with my rhythm, punishing me even more for ever meeting this woman who bewitched me and took my control. I wanted to shackle her to the bed and impregnate her. Spilling my seed inside her was the only release I could get of this pain in my chest that I would just lose her one day.

CHAPTER THIRTY

ANTONIO

"That's a dumb idea. It's a train wreck waiting to happen."

I scowled. Angelo was a fucking nuisance. Today more than any other day. "I'm not asking for your opinion, and nothing's going to be wrecked."

"Well, I agree with him," Marco interjected, grabbing onto the chair next to Angelo's and trying to puzzle his big, long body into it.

"Piss off... I never asked for your opinion either," I snapped.

"You're getting it, anyway. Hiding things from your wife is a bad idea on so many counts, and you should know this given your hmm... past mistakes."

I was glad my interior designer chose chairs with arms for my office. There was a certain pleasure to take in watching Marco's discomfort, trying to fit his ass into one.

"Right. How long did you have to butter her up the last time?" Angelo mocked me, false innocence sprayed all over his face.

Too long. But I wasn't going to budge. I wasn't ready yet. Besides, everything was still so fucking raw. Just like it always was in our marriage. We were either fucking like rabbits or on other sides of an imaginary ocean fighting a cold war. However, this time, it was one of my choosing. I needed the distance to think and come up with an action plan before I put a bullet through someone's head. I hadn't even recovered from Harris before I received this blow. My marriage held more tension than the fucking cables on a suspension bridge.

I stalked over to the window and looked down at the ongoing traffic below me. Away from the two idiots behind me forming a team against me. They were nothing but my wife's pawns.

Fuck! I wanted to go back to a few nights ago. Before Harris. Before all of this. Even though I got monstrous pleasure from punching the life out of the swine. I lifted my cracked knuckles, fist clenching and unclenching.

So worth it.

"How did you explain that?" I turned to find Marco nodding to my fist.

I didn't. "She should be happy I let him live."

"You're such an idiot when it comes to Divya."

I scowled at Marco. He was annoying the hell out of me. "You seem to have forgotten that I'm the *consigliere*."

"*Consigliere,* yes, but still an idiot around her."

"Don't forget your fucking place. I wouldn't like to find you with a hole in your head," I warned.

Marco grinned, ignoring my dark words. "Someone's got to tell you when you are a twat."

"You are that," Angelo agreed.

"I'm not a...." I reined in my anger. The woman was going to send me early to my grave, I was sure of it. I always thought it would be *Cosa Nostra,* but turned out it was going to be my own wife. "She's a fucking seductress."

"That she is," Marco agreed.

My eyes shot to Marco. Was he jerking off to my wife? Was he eyeing her ass and imagining his dick in it? Bloody men and their dicks. Something was brewing inside of me.

"That," Marco pointed to me, "Is exactly what I mean."

"Get to the point," I snarled.

"Twat," Angelo muttered, earning him a death glare. He just grinned and slouched further in his chair. My brother never seemed to know how to sit straight in a damn chair.

"All women around you are fucking seductresses. Nothing new there. Yuliya was one of them. But Angelo," Marco looked at his brother with confusion, "Did he beat Yuliya's lover up?"

Angelo sat up and went into his exaggerated thinker pose. "I believe he didn't. In fact... he didn't even pay the dickhead a visit while she *was* fucking him. What was it Divya did anyway with this Harris?"

"Ah." Marco shot him a grin. "Just a kiss."

Just a kiss.

"That can't be it. I mean, my brother, who has punched no one for quite some time, took to his fists for just a kiss—"

"Are you calling me a pussy?" I growled.

"Nah. But you are the fucking *consigliere*. Aren't you advocating for diplomacy? Since when do you go around punching people ...unless... of course... it was personal." Marco sniggered.

"It is fucking personal," I growled. "He came after my wife."

"Contract wife. She's more like an employee."

"She's my fucking wife," I roared. Some days I could easily put my fist through bloody Marco's face. Today was one of those days.

Marco and Angelo exchanged a look I wasn't privy to. I didn't fucking like the dynamics these two had going. I didn't fucking like anything. I didn't like constantly being on edge, waiting for the other shoe to drop. I didn't like the distance with my wife. I didn't like the bruises I had left on her the night I had fucked her all night long to stake my claim. I didn't like the man I was around her. She was changing me, doing things to me.

"Oh man, she had you by your balls the day she walked in." Angelo chuckled.

Like fuck she did. She didn't have me by anything. I was in control. Which is exactly why I would decide when to tell her, if I did at all.

"I am fucking tired of you two giving me marital advice. When was the last time you were in a relationship?"

"I am swearing off women," Angelo declared, kicking himself up out of his chair. "If I see the way Divya has you twisted and tied up, I want no part of it."

"What am I? Some kind of rope to be twisted and tied up?"

"I am waiting for Divya to be free. I'll take her any day," Marco sniggered.

A flash of rage sparked inside me. I clenched my fists. It was going to be one of those days.

Marco laughed, glancing at Angelo. "He's never going to give in. That wreck is going to happen soon."

If I wasn't knocking him down, then I was going to cancel that order for new chairs.

"Get the hell out of my office," I growled. "I am sick of your fucking metaphors."

"Yeah, that must be the reason." Marco stood up and walked to the door to join Angelo. "I want it noted, though, that both Angelo and I are against it." Angelo high-fived him at the door.

"Piss the fuck off. My marriage. My rules. Just keep your fucking mouths shut."

"Yeah, yeah. We'll just have to be here to glue the pieces together," Marco told Angelo.

"Story of our lives." Angelo let out an exaggerated sigh. He opened the door to let them out. "Such a twat," he muttered under his breath.

My head shot up. "I heard that," I yelled through the closing door.

A SILENT HOUSE GREETED ME. It bothered me more than I liked to admit that she wasn't downstairs waiting to have dinner. She took away the pleasure of dining alone from me. I found Rosa setting the table for one.

"*Dov'è* Divya?"

Rosa shot me an angry look. "Did you fight with her again?"

"Why?" Worry crept into my body.

Things had been awkward, but we weren't really fighting, were we?

"Because she was sad the whole day," Rosa snapped. "You must have done something. You make that girl sad all the time. She went off to bed without even eating."

I dropped my bag onto the table. "Put the food away," I said as I made my way to the stairs.

"Ah, now what? *Mamma Mia!* What is with you two? I make all this food, and it is in vain now."

I let her lament and sprinted up the stairs and into our room to find her sleeping, the lights still on in the room. I listened to her breathing. She wasn't sleeping.

"*Mia cara?*" I whispered.

Silence.

So she wanted to play this game. She was a whirlwind of emotions, and sometimes she drove me mad trying to figure out which end of the stick I had. I had left this morning before she was up, but last night she had been fine. Not sad, for sure. But today, she was upset about something.

I kicked off my clothes and crept into bed. A sniff escaped her.

Was she sick?

I scooted closer to her and wrapped my body around her. My dick went on high alert.

Fuck!

I caught a silent tear sliding off her cheek.

She was crying.

"What's the matter?"

"Nothing," she muttered.

At least we were out of the pretend sleep phase.

"What happened? Did someone hurt you?" I demanded.

"No."

"Then what?"

"It's just...." A hiccup escaped her. "It's my father's birthday today."

My breath snuck out, leaving me wanting.

Fuck! Why had I asked?

I didn't know what to say. I didn't know how to deal with this. I wasn't great with emotion, and I didn't know how to start now. My mother never showed anything except anger, and even my father rarely indulged in it. Now I had to console my wife out of the grief she felt for someone she had obviously deeply loved and missed.

"I don't know what to say," I muttered.

"Nothing. There is nothing to say. You didn't know them."

There was a small part of me that was jealous of these two people I had never met but had somehow been the centre of her world. It had been the three of them against everyone, and I wasn't part of it.

Like hell. I wasn't about to let her push me out.

I flipped her around and tilted her tear-stained face to

me. "Tell me then. Tell me what I don't know about them."

"Like you'd care," she snapped, trying to scamper away.

I swear she was a test to my patience. I held on to her tight. "Try me anyway."

She eyed me suspiciously. "All right. What do you want to know?"

"Whatever you want to tell me."

"I am not sure he would have liked you," she mused.

No surprise there. I wouldn't give my own daughter to me. "Tell me what he would have said."

"He wouldn't have trusted your motives. He was very protective of me, you know," she chided.

"Rightly so." I tucked the loose strand of hair behind her ear. "My motives are as dirty as they get." I dropped my eyes suggestively to her breasts, getting a flush out of her skin. "What else?"

"He would have still supported my decision, though.... He was that kind of dad. Same as my mum. Even if they didn't agree with me, they would still support me."

"Goals to live up to," I murmured, tucking her closer to me.

I listened to her talk of them with so much love in her voice. Something crawled under my skin because I didn't know how to help her with this pain she carried.

They were good people. I discovered her more through them. Two people who had given me this gift tucked into my arms.

What did Marco and Angelo know anyway about the

intricacies of marriage? Especially one like mine with a contract and an end date on it. I knew what was right, and not telling her now was it. What I needed was time and a plan of action. So when I finally told her, she would forgive me and not let go.

CHAPTER THIRTY-ONE

DIVYA

Cora crept on top of me while I lay down on her thick rubber play mat. Using her dimpled hands, she grabbed my blouse and pulled herself up onto my body, settling in when her drool-covered face was hanging above mine.

There really was no dress code with this one. My crushed cotton blouse and naked waist were evidence of that.

Saliva dripped down as she latched onto my face and launched into an intense conversation of, well...blah blah.

I loved this little bundle of joy. She was pure in her innocence and uncomplicated.

Unlike her father.

There was no practised ruthlessness hidden behind her cheeky grins. There was no beast waiting to be unleashed. There definitely was no distance between us because, seriously, how much closer can you get than her dribble painting my face?

We were in the midst of an important conversation when my nerves picked up the tension wafting into the room. He moved quietly with the grace of a predatory animal, and he filled the room instantly with an intangible, sizzling fury.

When he finally came into view, standing close to us, eyes hooded, hiding his thoughts, I knew he wasn't his usual self. I regretted the moment I decided to kiss Adam back. I don't know why I thought to do it when I'd spent days trying to throw him off. But somewhere in me, there was a desperation that wanted to find out if this love for Antonio was an exaggeration in my damn mind. It wasn't. That's what I found out. And that the jealousy spiking up in my husband had no end to it. Days had passed. Still, the static electricity ebbing off him was enough to put me on fire.

"We are leaving for India for a few weeks," he said, his tone flat, his eyes on my exposed belly.

"Oh." I tried to loosen the pudgy fist entangled in my hair. A few weeks was a long time.

"Make sure you are packed by tomorrow morning." He turned to leave.

"Wait." I snatched Cora and flipped her next to me on her back so I could see him clearly. "Where am I going?"

"To India, of course."

"What?" I shot upright. "I don't get it."

"What is there to get?" He moved his eyes to my face. "You are my wife; you and Cora go where I go."

He didn't look happy about it. His stance growled and roared while he remained silent. "I don't have to," I said.

"Why not?" The growl spilt out.

Because I wasn't really his wife.

I couldn't have this conversation sitting down while he towered over me. Standing up, I faced him, keeping Cora in my peripheral view crawling after her rabbit.

"You don't look happy about it. If I am bothering you with your work or something, I can stay back." Plus, I was really not his wife in the proper sense. But I didn't dare voice that in his dark mode.

"*Ridicolo.*" He stepped closer, letting his lust-filled eyes drop on my body. "You'll be my entertainment."

That was that, then.

JUST LIKE THAT, we were off to India. I didn't know what type of work he had there to warrant a work visit. I didn't dare to ask, and he didn't bother to tell me. I hardly saw him at work, though, except for a few hours on his laptop each day. Instead, we travelled. From the south to the north.

It was strange. Strange but beautiful to be in my father's homeland. Everything he had told me, described in vivid detail, came to life before my eyes. Déjà vu. It was like watching a movie from a book I had read. I began seeing it, this country, as he would have wanted me to see it.

You either loved or hated India. I loved it. The good and the bad.

The smell was so specific for the country, the humidity almost unbearable, but all things you took in stride with the vibrance of life.

The landscapes were breathtaking, including everything from mountain ranges to coasts, deserts to plateaus. India had it all.

Colours, everywhere, anywhere. Women attired in rich sarees and shalwars, men in sarongs. Even in the cities with Western clothing, everything was so much more colourful. Even the buildings exuded vibrancy.

The spices, the aromatic smell of them, the variety of dishes, so different from the south to the north.

The many languages and the incredible beauty of each of them in written form. It was pure art, the letters comprising lines and curves.

The music. It haunted me, tingling my nerves with familiarity, dragging me back to a living room in Portsmouth. The same beats, yet different. Everywhere. From the rickshaws to the posh restaurants to our bedroom.

I dived into everything head first, enjoying and leaving the regrets for later. I had left my head back in Boston and packed only my heart for India. My heart loved what it saw. My lub-dubs beat wildly above the chaos and noise of the horns going *toot toot* in India.

Joy. Joy. Joy.

I didn't have the hands of my parents holding mine. I didn't have Antonio's either. He let me lead. Seemingly content to follow me anywhere I went. And I went everywhere that I could.

I found myself falling in love again and again. Every day I found myself with something new to love. New to discover. I dug deep and found myself. Me. Divya. Part of my roots.

In all this, Antonio kept following me, silent. He looked so casual in his linen trousers, crisp white Kurta tops and open-toed leather sandals that I could almost forget his background. *Oh, who am I kidding?* He could be donned in nothing, and his dark vibes would still pull me in like black on white. But sometimes there was a softness to his dark edges, and he looked like he'd lost something. I didn't dare to ask what.

All I knew was that he shared my relish of beautiful Indian craftsmanship and went tirelessly with me in the streets of Jaipur, looking for traditional Indian jewellery. He surprised me by placing a set on my prickled skin in one particular shop. A gorgeous, heavy, traditional necklace with matching dangling earrings and bangles. Tears clogged in my throat till he whispered gruffly in my ears, "Promise me you'll wear them tonight." What had I expected? I kept my promise and rode him in the night, wearing nothing but the new jewels. Now I had earned my keep.

He made no secret that he found sarees sexy. When we were roaming around on the banks of the river Ganga, he bought me a few of them in Banaras, one of the oldest cities in India. Later on, in the privacy of our room, I showed him how I could drape the nine-yard-long fabric on me without a stitch underneath, only for him to show me how quickly he could undress me with a tug and a twist.

He seemed to take to the country as much as I did. He watched me with a glint in his eyes, listening to the beautiful music. I didn't need to understand the language to appreciate the beauty of the flowing words. It seemed neither did he.

He joined me in any street side stall I would spring into, trying out all the different types of *dosas, paratas,* and *kottus*. Only Cora never got to taste the deliciousness of the local delicacies except for a dry *rotti*. At least that's what I thought until I caught Antonio sneaking food into her cute little mouth time after time. I should have known when those small greedy eyes followed the trail of food to my mouth that she'd had a taste before. I let it go. I just loved that she could experience this with me, even though she would never remember it.

There were so many things to try. The little girl in me was awake with all the stories I had ever heard from my dad, but it was the woman I was now that touched, tasted, and enjoyed the India I experienced, even more so with the man at my side and the baby in my arms.

The only true disappointment was that I never truly fit into India, either. In England, I was not fully English, and it turned out that in India, I was not fully Indian, with many people not recognising me as part Indian and, on some rare occasions, when some simply refused to acknowledge me as Indian at all.

I tried to take comfort in Antonio's words. *You're too special to fit into just one country, mia cara.*

I knew that. I knew I was special to not have just one

but two cultures in my skin. But I still had a hard time accepting it even though it was the opinion of a few. My father's family disowning my father and not acknowledging me and my mum had cut deep, leaving sharp wounds. The feeling of never being good enough for anyone except for my parents was something I had a tough time living with.

I WOKE up early to the hum of the ceiling fan. A heavy humidity hung in the room, rudely sticking to my skin and sucking the air out of my lungs.

I crept out of his arms and got dressed in a short linen dungaree dress. I didn't bother to add a bra underneath. The maid, who came in the morning to this house in Goa we rented, wasn't due for another hour, but the heat in the air had me wanting another one of those delicious mango juices to cool me off.

I made my way in our one-floor bungalow towards the kitchen, my bare feet silent on the terracotta floor. It was small and cosy, just the way I liked it. Full of wood, white, and colourful details, like the bright blue coloured shutters on every window. I peeped in on Cora, lying on her belly, naked except for a Pamper. She slept soundly under a mosquito net, hugging her rabbit. This baby could sleep through a storm. I paused at the living room window, looking out towards the beach. Dark clouds were gathering with impending rain, which would explain the suffocating heat floating over the house like a blanket of doom.

Hot. More than usual. My feet stuck to the floor when I pattered to the kitchen. I smacked to a stop. Sneha, our maid, stood in the middle. She was early and already finishing up preparing the meals.

A flush hit my face. I wasn't decent without a bra.

She looked up. "Good morning, madam," she said cheerfully.

"Good morning." I blushed. "How are you today?"

She did a wobble with her head that most Indians did. It was neither a yes nor a no, but more a dance of your head that could mean anything from a yes, no, good, maybe, or anything in between.

"I come early, madam, for rain. I make mango juice, and I go," she said sweetly in her simple English. "You want try?" she asked, holding up a mango.

Why not?

I always had a tough time cutting one of them, and it was time I learned it before we left back home in a few days' time.

CHAPTER THIRTY-TWO

ANTONIO

The emptiness of the bed woke me up. Even though it was hot enough to be a fucking oven, a shiver penetrated my body. The corner of my eye caught Divya sneaking out of the room. I resisted the urge to pull her back into bed.

They were rare, the times she was out of bed before me. I liked to keep it that way. Waking up in an empty bed was not something I wanted to familiarise myself with, even though I had spent years doing nothing other than enjoying it. Women were good to fuck, but not to share my bed with. Their long hair in my mouth and cuddle-demanding closeness pissed me off. Another thing she had taken from me.

With a groan, I rolled onto my back, giving up on sleep now that she wasn't near me. I didn't understand this constant need for her. What a fool I had been to think having her would resolve everything. She was an addiction in my blood. The more I had her, the more I wanted her. If I couldn't have her, I wanted her near me in my line of sight.

She pulled me to her with her swaying body and magical eyes. She radiated pure innocence when she was lying on the floor playing with my baby, unaware of her naked belly and visible cleavage. Then she would change into a hot siren riding me wildly, wearing only pieces of jewellery that did nothing to outshine her body.

She was fucking gorgeous. A man's wet dream. She was mine. Which is exactly why I hadn't told her. I hadn't wanted to tell her when I came home a few weeks ago to find her playing with Cora, distracting me with her naked skin and innocent looks. Instead, I had packed them all up and rushed off to India.

What a brilliant idea it had been. This had to have been the best three weeks of my life. It wasn't my first visit to India. Yet somehow, it was so much more interesting to experience the country through her eyes. Everything was so much more. More life, more joy, more beauty.

Definitely more sex. My number one favourite activity with her. If it wasn't for Cora, I would never let this woman out of my room.

I shifted in my bed. My dick needed some serious attention, and she was missing to give it some.

Yanking on my boxer shorts, I strode through the house. I knew she loved the house. I had already contacted the owners with an offer to buy it. Investing in a property here seemed like a good idea. We could spend some time each year here till Cora started schooling.

I followed the sound of her giggles floating from the kitchen. The scene was worth a movie. The maid, whose name I had forgotten, was showing Divya how to cut a mango neatly and make juice out of it. Loads and loads of cut mangoes piled on the worktop next to the window, ready to be put in the juicer. There was also a shitload of mango splattered all over my wife and her sweet boobs. Did she not know that her breasts were clearly visible under the scrap of fabric she was wearing? The fucking maid probably did.

The maid noticed me first, her "good morning" dying on her lips as she looked away, embarrassed at my semi-nudity. Did she really think I would have eyes for her when the key to my cock was sitting on that work-top? Divya looked up, her giggle dying on her lips.

"Oh, good morning," she breathed, a flush rushing up her skin.

She is parading herself half-naked in front of the maid, and now she's shy in front of me?

"I go, madam?" Both of us looked at the maid, who looked like I was the big bad wolf who might gulp her down. Couldn't the woman not see that I had eyes only for the jutting tits begging for the suction of my lips?

"Go," I said, tightly watching her scurry out of the house.

"You're so rude," Divya admonished me.

"Am I?" I went to stand between her legs, the maid already out of my mind. I had other important things to ponder about, like how to unbuckle this thing she was wearing. "You were rude to leave me alone in bed."

"I was thirsty," she grabbed a half-cut mango in her hand. "For some mango juice."

"Hmmm." I loosened the two buckles on her shoulder, making the top part of her dress fall open to reveal two perfect boobs standing proud and upright. Why does this woman have to taunt me like this by running around practically naked all the time?

An idea sparked inside me. I could say she brought out the wickedness in me. But I was never nice to begin with. Watching her watch me, I caught the mango from her hand and rubbed it on her nipple to her gasp. The juice slithered all over her breast, leaving it sticky and hot. I had made a fucking mess, and now I had to clean up. I ducked my head and took one delicious, mango-soaked nipple in my mouth. I sucked, and I licked, and I bit amidst her groans. Mango juice off a boob. This could easily replace the best espresso in Italy. I came up for air. "I was thirsty too." I watched the juice tickle south over her belly. "For mango juice."

Reaching behind her, I took another cut mango, all bright yellow and squashy in my hand. I rubbed it on her other breast. She watched me, her teeth on her bottom lip.

"I think this one was feeling lonely. *Sì?*" I asked her, hovering over her juice-dripping breast.

"Yes," she whimpered.

I smothered my grin on her breast and devoured it just like I had her other one. I moved my juice-dripping hand to her twin and squeezed it, pinching her nipple sharply.

Good thing the maid left. Her groan was so loud it

was a miracle Cora didn't wake up. I let my hands roam her body, painting her with sticky yellow juice till I reached her face, where I pulled her head and stuck my tongue inside, cooling her warm mouth with mine.

She shoved her needy body closer, rubbing herself against my dick.

I yanked my mouth off hers and caught her deranged eyes. "More?"

She nodded wildly.

"Words, Divya, I need words."

"Yes," she groaned. "More. Much more."

"Good girl." I shoved her back against the wall and followed the pattern of the flowing juice with my mouth. I couldn't decide whether I should lift her dress up or remove it completely. She didn't have the patience for my debate and shimmered out of her dress, dropping it on the floor. She lay in front of me in nothing but a sheer yellow panty, matching the mangoes.

I sighed. "Haven't we learned any lessons, *mia cara*? If you don't want your underwear torn, don't wear any." I confirmed my words by tearing off yet another piece of her wardrobe.

My eyes scorched her skin, burning her like a trail of hot wax. My caramel-coloured sex goddess, wrapped in yellow. I ignored my pulsing dick, pushing me to make haste. I wanted to enjoy this moment, take a picture, and store it in my memory forever. How did this woman become more beautiful day by day?

I grabbed hold of another mango and squeezed the juice out onto her naked pussy. She jerked as drips of juice hit her and tried to move my hand away.

"Tsk." I swatted her hand away. "My mouth is dying for some of that juice." Grasping hold of her knees, I spread them wide and pinned them to the countertop. I ducked my head and let my tongue slide along her thick lips, making my way to her clit. She bucked right off the worktop with a loud groan. I pushed her down again and continued my assault. Fucking nirvana. The taste of mango mixed with the essence of her.

I lapped up the juices, both of them, while I ran a hand to grab a sticky boob. I sucked her clit into my mouth, nipping it gently with my teeth before letting the flat of my tongue slide over it.

Taking two digits, I thrust them inside her wet and moist cave while I lapped her pussy like a man dying of thirst.

"Oh god," she groaned, putting on a strong attempt to yank my hair off my skull.

"So close," she whimpered, rocking her hips in time to my thrusts. I lapped faster, my fingers slick with all the juice.

Yes. She was close. She was a fine violin, and I was fucking playing her. I read the signs. The sweat beading on her forehead, the flush heating her skin, the tightness in her thigh muscles... before she launched and started to clench. With a loud groan, she came, shaking and sputtering all over.

Withdrawing my fingers, I stood up. I licked my fingers with a hum of pleasure. "Best mango juice I've ever had," I said unabashedly.

Pushing herself up, she grabbed a piece of mango

with her other hand. She jerked my boxers down, my cock springing free, precum leaking.

"Fuck," I hissed when she leant forward and rubbed the mango over my dick while fisting me tightly in her hand. Cold juices on my hot rod. All the blood in my body rushed to one point. My vision hazed.

"What?" she asked, fluttering her eyes innocently. "I want the best juice too."

I groaned loudly, pushing her back against the wall, grabbing hold of one leg and lifting it on top of my shoulder. "Inside, NOW." Taking hold of her hips, I jerked her closer to me while I pushed inside in one go. Our simultaneous groans echoed in the empty kitchen. With her leg on my shoulder, the angle was so much deeper.

Absolute heaven. I wanted to make this last longer. I really did. I withdrew slowly to launch myself into her again and again. Only the sight of her naked, wanton, emitting husky groans tested my fucking patience. I loved the croak in her voice. Except it wasn't fucking helping that I could smell her cum and feel her spasming around me already.

Fucking temptress.

A groan spilt out of my lungs. I needed to last longer and not come like a teenager. I withdrew, and lifting her, I spun her around. Spreading her legs wide, she pushed her ass up while she leaned over the counter. I slammed into her again, pushing her shoulders to the cold marble countertop.

Reaching back with her hands, she grabbed my ass,

her nails digging into my skin, leaving scratches for sure, like I would give a damn.

The noise of skin slapping against skin, accompanied by our moans was enough to test any man's patience. I needed to make her come again before I could. One hand grabbed her hip, the other on her shoulder. I pumped into her like a madman, withdrawing and thrusting deeper, again and again, till I finally felt her shake uncontrollably, crying out her orgasm. With a groan, I let go, shooting my juices inside her warm body, letting them flow inside her. My legs suddenly let go. I let my weight drop onto her, skin to skin, the sweat and juices in between us sticking us together.

She took another thing from me. I was never going to be able to look at a mango again without picturing her like this.

CHAPTER THIRTY-THREE

DIVYA

The doorbell ringing shook the drowsiness out of the jet-legged haze I was in. I didn't know why it was ringing and why no one was answering.

Ding-dong

The house was swimming with men in black on any day, and now no one was around?

Ding-dong

I sat up on the sofa, trying to orient myself. Boston was just so different from India. So quiet.

Ding-dong

With a groan, I put foot before foot towards the door. Where were Armando and Rosa...?

Crap!

They had gone on another errand for Mrs Capizzi. I hoped it wasn't history repeating itself. I wasn't in the mood to have Antonio's mother on the doorstep with a shitload of opinions and a canon ready to fire.

Relief fuelled me to smile when I found a smartly dressed, young, blonde woman reaching for the doorbell.

"Oh, sorry I didn't want to disturb you."

So you rang the bell four times?

She was pretty, in an obvious way. Her blonde hair curling at the ends unnaturally, her lips a shade of crimson, her ample bosom spilling over her tight top.

"I am looking for Antonio... I mean Mr Capizzi," she said with a private smile, hinting at an intimate acquaintance with my husband.

An uneasiness beyond the jet leg I was feeling sent a cold tingle up my spine. "He's not home."

"I am from Mr Popolizio's office, his lawyer," she said, giving me information I didn't ask for.

I frowned, my glance slipping beyond the woman's shoulder to find two of Antonio's men watching the interaction from the street. Is that how she got past them? I sighed impatiently. "Why are you here? If you are from Roberto's office, you should meet downtown."

"Oh...." The woman faltered at my sharp tone. "I was told to hand over this file...." She tried to shove the thin file she was holding onto me.

I took a step back, wanting nothing to do with whatever this woman wanted. At the same time, she purposefully loosened her grip on the thin file, feigning surprise. The contents of it, the few pieces of paper came loose and scattered onto the floor.

"What are you doing?" I dropped to my knees, flustered,

helping the girl pick the papers up. My movements were choppy, but I wasn't blind. An unusually large font glared back at me for what appeared to be documentation about the custody case. Before my sense gave word to my brain, I snatched the papers away from the girl, taking a closer look.

Shit.

I didn't understand this legal jargon. It was a whole lot of black lettering, but Cora's name sprang out together with Antonio's and the address in Boston. It was signed a month ago.

"What is this?" I asked quietly, trying to figure out what it was saying, but the pounding in my head and trembling in my hands wouldn't allow me to see the sense right in front of me.

"The signed custody, of course, for the baby. You must be happy that the mother signed off all her rights so quickly."

So quickly...

"When?" I croaked.

"Oh, you see the date here...." She pointed towards the date a month ago. "We are already working on the divorce for Antonio now." She didn't even bother to correct herself in addressing him properly this time. "Oh!" She let her hands fly to her mouth, feigning shock. "I shouldn't have told you that."

But she wanted to tell me that. I was no fool. This woman turned up at my doorstep with the sole purpose of informing me. At least that was clear.

I let the woman grab the papers from me, eyeing the approaching men nervously.

"I will just bring this to his office," she whispered, turning to leave.

"Yes. You do that," I said, watching the woman hurry out, her sway so obvious that even David, one of the men, stopped to follow her ass before approaching me.

"*Signora* Capizzi?"

Yes. There was no doubt that she was behind this plan.

"*Signora* Capizzi?" I blinked. He meant me, of course.

"Who was that woman?"

Who was that woman? Was she really who she said she was?

"A salesgirl," I lied easily. Swallowing the lump in my throat, I elaborated, "She was very persistent."

I wasn't going to jump to conclusions. I was definitely not going to inform these men about what had happened so they could tell my husband. I was going to wait calmly for him to tell me the truth, like he should. I was sure he would do that. He would not let me down. Again.

————

"How was your day?"

Great. I found out that my husband was not only lying but also planning for a divorce when he could have just fucking asked me.

"Good." I watched him having his dinner, one hand holding mine, his rough thumb burning a path on my palm. "How about you?"

Tell me.

"Good. Same old." Dropping his fork, he turned sideways, straddling the bench. He drew me closer to nestle in between his thighs.

Shit. Don't touch me.

"I am leaving early tomorrow for Italy for two weeks." He nuzzled my neck with his scruff, leaving behind goosebumps on its trail. "I have some work for *Cosa Nostra*," he said quietly, the words almost lost on my skin.

Funny. This was the first time he actually gave me some kind of information. Guess I was getting more now that we were a done deal.

Leaving soft bite marks, he reached my ear and sucked on my earlobe. It must have had a direct route to my core because I felt a pulse beating madly down there. I just couldn't allow him to wrap me around his thumb anymore. He used sex to get what he wanted all the time. *Not this time, buddy.* I jerked away and stood up on wobbling legs.

"I am tired. Jet leg and all...." I trailed off, watching his frowning face. I cleared my throat to get the rasp out. "I am off to bed."

He grabbed hold of my hand before I could move away. "I am gone for two weeks, m*ia cara*," he impelled.

"I know." I tried to shake his hand off.

His grip tightened. "I wish you would tell me what you are thinking in that pretty head of yours."

"As if you do," I snapped.

"What do you want to know? What I am thinking now? Huh? I am thinking I want to bury my dick deep inside you all night long before I can survive two weeks without you," he murmured, eyes turning dark.

"Typical." I shook his hand off. "Have a nice trip." I hurried off but stopped and turned near the door to find him watching me, confusion and disappointment clear on his face.

"I do want to know something." At his encouraging nod, I continued, "Do you know anything more about the case?" I pushed through, ignoring his darkening face. "I want to see if I can enrol for my studies."

"You can enrol for your studies anytime. No one's stopping you," he said tightly.

"No." I shook my head, adamant. "I can't do two jobs. I am paid to look after Cora and..." I faltered. Unable to hold his gaze, I let mine drop to the floor. "This arrangement. I can't do my studies with it as well."

Uneasiness crawled into the room. Silence joined in. I swear I heard the clock ticking in his office. I peeked up to see him watching me, his lips in a tight line, a muscle ticking madly on his jaw.

I thought he might not answer. He turned back to the table and rubbed his eyes with his hands. With his shoulders slumped, he looked tired.

Well, so am I.

"Roberto is working on it," he said in a low, tight voice just when I was going to move away. "We'll know more when I am back."

Nodding, I scurried off to our room, fighting back my tears. I couldn't cry now and have him see how badly I had fallen for him. Tomorrow. Tomorrow, when he wasn't around, I could let go.

Later on that night, I put on my best performance, pretending to be asleep when the bed dipped next to me. Subtly, I moved further away, but surprisingly, he didn't drag me back to him like he did most nights. It truly was the end of our scam of a marriage.

THE NEXT DAY, I woke up to that feeling of emptiness. Someone had snuck in during the night and jerked my heart out, leaving me empty. Just when I thought I was finally over it, it was back, the feeling hitting me right in the gut, there, as if it had never really left me at all.

I knew he had left early. I had heard him move around and felt his soft kiss on my forehead. Had he known I had been awake the whole night, running our story on a reel, trying to find where it had gone wrong or if it had ever been right? Did he know when he softly closed the door to our room behind him, it had felt like he was closing the door to our life together?

He wouldn't call. I knew that. I knew his routine now. If he was travelling for his banking work, he called. But if it was for "the family," as they liked to call it, he never called.

The family. Seemed like everyone was part of his family. His mother, Rosa, Armando, Cora, of course, except for me. I was his to marry and to divorce at his will.

I couldn't really blame him. He had promised nothing else. The only person to blame for the whole thing was me. I was the idiot who had brought in the feelings and fallen in love. He didn't need emotion to have sex. I did, and that was the grave I had dug myself. Had he fucked that woman on my doorstep? *His doorstep.* Nothing was mine. He wasn't mine. Rosa was not part of my family nor Armando, and, most importantly, Cora wasn't mine. No matter how close I thought that sweet munchkin was to me, I had no right to her.

CHAPTER THIRTY-FOUR

DIVYA

I played with Cora and made meals with Rosa, all while I covertly went through everything in my mind. I replayed the slides of my life after I met Antonio. Step by step. But I couldn't figure it out.

Why would he not tell me that the case was settled? Why would he not tell me he was arranging for our divorce? Was he scared, just like his mother, that I would ask for more? More money? Was it because of that stupid prenuptial? But I've seen many moods of his, and scared wasn't one of them. I had a feeling nothing scared my husband much.

So no matter how many times I reeled my life back in, only one solid explanation stayed. Antonio Capizzi didn't care. He was just not into me.

I finally understood his win-win deal now. He got what he wanted. Full custody of Cora and a fuck buddy for as long as he wanted. I got what I wanted. I could finally enrol in my studies and pay off the mortgage of my parents' home. This was the deal.

I just hadn't realised that somewhere along the line, my studies had taken a backseat to Cora and Antonio, and I wanted something more than a house in Portsmouth.

Stupid, stupid Divya.

What had I thought? That he would drop everything for me, and we would ride off to the sunset to live happily ever after?

How could I be mad at him when the fault was mine? I had changed my priorities along the line. He had stuck to his. Somewhere in the weeks and months we had spent together, I had pinned all my hopes and dreams on him. The woman who wanted to enrol in her studies and achieve her dreams was nowhere to be found. Instead, I was left with a girl pining for a man who clearly neither wanted nor needed her anymore.

By the eighth day on my own without Antonio, I decided I had to focus on the good things this situation had given me, pick up my pieces, and go.

In my utter selfishness, I had forgotten one of the most important things my parents had taught me. Gratefulness.

I was grateful that he had somehow got full custody of Cora. That bundle of joy deserved nothing but the best, and I was sure he would give her nothing but that. It didn't matter that it broke my heart to leave her behind. He might not care for me, but he was pure magic with his girl.

Even without my studies, the most important thing

for me was that I could keep my childhood home full of memories of my parents, right? This was good too.

When he was back, we would have to have the talk. I can give him time to find someone to look after Cora, and after that, I could leave. Start my life again. That I would have to glue the pieces of my shattered heart was no one's problem but mine.

A FEW DAYS LATER, when I was going to put Cora for her nap, I passed Armando on a ladder. I halted, watching him clean the camera screens.

"Everything alright?"

He looked down at me, smiling. "Yes, *Signora* Capizzi, it is just too high for Rosa, so I am helping with the cleaning."

I nodded as doubt sneaked in.

Was anything my husband had told me true?

"Armando...." He turned around, "Who can see these images? Can, huh... someone from outside access these images?"

Understanding crept into his kind eyes. "Don't worry, *Signora* Capizzi. No one can access these cameras. This has the highest security. Only *Signor* Capizzi has access to it, and if he wants, the security team, but only on his orders."

"No one can... like, hack into these cameras?"

"That is impossible. *Signor* Capizzi has taken strict measures. Don't worry. He will never allow anything to happen to *la piccola* Cora or you," he said, misunderstanding my worry.

Another day, another lie. My steps slowed down as I walked to Cora's room. Something heavy was pulling me down.

———

"You are marvellous with Cora."

"You are comfortable in my home."

"We can scratch that itch we both have..."

"Win for me because I get custody, and, of course, you are not bad to look at..."

"Win for you because you will get a handsome reward and me."

I woke up with a shout, sitting up in the empty bed.

But I didn't get him. I was supposed to get him at the end of this.

What was the point of a reward when it didn't include him?

I made a mental note in my head to transfer it right back to wherever it came from, the very day it landed on my bank account. I didn't want it anymore.

Rosa had changed the sheets. Now even his smell was fading. The clock told me it was six in the morning. Frustration ebbed at me as I sat up on the bed. Too early to get up. But I didn't want to be pulled back to my dreams. I grabbed my phone, ready to scroll aimlessly through social media when a new message chimed in.

It wasn't a number in my contacts. I saw it was a

video. I wouldn't have clicked on it, except the frozen image was of Antonio in our bedroom.

Even though dread infiltrated my body, I clicked mindlessly on a video that my head screamed not to watch.

He was in our room. Antonio stood at the dressing table, removing his cufflinks just like he did every night. His shirt hung loose and unbuttoned.

A woman came into the picture, approaching him from behind. My breath hitched, dread lodging in my throat. His ex-wife. The reflection of the mirror showed the face that matched my crazy Google image searches.

No. This had to be an old video.

But the date on the bottom right corner was recent. This was from six weeks ago.

Where had I been?

I couldn't think above the pounding in my skull.

She was whispering in his ears, and he was allowing it. He turned around, watching her the whole time while she spoke. Then she took a step back and started removing her clothes. She was like some kind of professional stripper when she did a beautiful, exquisite striptease for him. She had so much confidence in her body. A jolt of jealousy rushed through me.

Look away.

He watched her the whole time, unmoving but not averting his gaze either. Butt naked, she slithered over to him and touched him. Unbuttoned his trousers, dragging his pants and boxers down in one go. She was amazing. A woman born to seduce a man. Going down on her knees, she took his erection in her mouth, sucking him like it was the most natural thing in the world.

Bile shot up my throat out of nowhere.

Walk away.

He did anything but that. His expression was one I'd seen so many times on him when he was inside me and about to explode.

Except now he was balls deep in his ex-wife. He was married *to me*. Why would he do this?

My throat constricted.

Stop.

He pulled her away. Only to put on a condom and drag her onto him, pumping into her.

The sounds of moaning grated on my teeth. It was louder than the pounding of my heart. I couldn't see her face anymore, but I could fucking see him as he jerked inside her just before the video stopped.

The guttural sound of my anger spilt out of my lungs in a scream in the quiet room.

My lungs hurt from the fist that had slammed into me, and the wheezing sound in the room must have been the air being pulled in. I rocked my shaking body back and forth, back and forth, clutching my phone to my chest.

The bile in my mouth left an aftertaste enough for a lifetime.

I tasted salt on my lips. How could I be crying when my eyes hurt from being dry?

"Mum." Just a whisper in the room. An ache for someone who wasn't there so I could creep onto her lap and seek solace.

I DIDN'T KNOW for how long I sat like that, but it must have been a long time because Rosa came looking for me. Detached, I watched a scene unfold before my eyes. I saw Rosa come over, worry lining her forehead, her words, which I had no understanding of, falling out of her mouth.

She must have known. Armando must have known. When had she come in? When had I not been home? Countless times I had gone out with Lakshmi shopping or to the park. Where had I been six weeks ago?

I glanced around the room. When my eyes caught that dressing table, the bile in my stomach pumped up. Pushing past Rosa, I hurtled to the bathroom, hugging the toilet as I emptied the contents inside me.

If only I could heave out the pain inside me. I want it gone. Gone out of my wretched body.

Commotion surrounded me when I came back to the room. Rosa running around like a headless chicken with Armando in tow. He avoided my gaze, embarrassed to see me in my nightdress. I couldn't care less.

I snatched my bag from the wardrobe. I had to get out. If I stayed here for one more day, he would kill me. He might not take a gun to me like I would expect from The Mafia. But he would with his words and actions. My legs wobbled. All the blows he threw at me, I had still been able to get up every time. But this time, it was one too many. No fucking man was worth this. I deserved better. Better than him.

Even though my heart hammered in my chest, I

fought through. Filling my small overnight bag, I veered around Rosa and Armando.

I had to change.

I grasped some clothes and took them with me to the bathroom. Haphazardly, I threw some clothes on myself. Gone. Gone was the inner stylist who meticulously chose what I wore every day. I didn't give a damn anymore.

I just needed to get out first. I would not fall apart. Here. In front of his family. I concentrated on mundane tasks.

Putting one foot in front of the other.

Brushing my teeth.

Upper left side, middle, and right side.

Lower left side, middle, and right side.

Spit.

Brush tongue.

Rinse.

Floss.

Rinse.

Rinse face, cleanser, tonic, eye cream, and face cream.

I caught my face in the mirror.

Do I even care about fucking face cream?

When I opened the door, my phone was ringing. I crossed to the bed to see Antonio's number. A boost of fury rushed through my body. It spread all over till all I saw was red. Picking up the phone, I smashed it across the room, the splintering metal the only pleasure I could get when the man behind it wasn't in the room.

"*Signora*..." Rosa's voice trembled with emotion.

I didn't want to hurt her feelings. "I'm sorry," my

voice croaked, breaking the awkwardness of the uncomfortable behaviour in the room.

Silent tears fell out against my wishes. Brushing them angrily away, I looked up at Armando "Please... I cannot be here anymore... I—" my breath hitched.

Cora. I didn't want to leave. That bundle of joy who was probably sitting up in her cot, rocking on her bum, waiting for me. But I couldn't. If I had seen her, I might not have left. I might have stayed. I might have put myself down again for a man. I might have given up everything for him. I might have let him walk all over me. Again.

"*Signora* Capizzi, please wait till *Signor* Capizzi gets home. Whatever it is, it can be resolved—" Armando urged me. He looked like a worried father, except he wasn't.

"No," I cut him off. "If I stay, I will lose myself. I will not allow the girl my parents brought up... to be lost."

I picked up my bag. "Please..." I implored with my eyes to Armando, who was blocking the door. "Give me the respect I deserve."

Maybe he *was* like a father to me. With a reluctant sigh, he stepped to the side, and I rushed past him. My rapid steps lost the conviction behind them in the hallway and came to a complete halt outside Cora's room. Something heavy landed in the pit of my stomach. I rested my forehead on the door, the bag falling out of my hand. Silent tears slid down my cheeks. I could hear her bubbling voice crooning. I wanted nothing more than to rush in and take part in her blabbering conversation.

I can't do this.

My resolve wavered.

I should stay. In a few weeks, Cora will turn one. Her first birthday. I've been planning how to celebrate.

I turned my head to find Rosa and Armando. But all I saw were the images of the damn video playing like it had never stopped. I was sick of not being good enough. I wasn't good enough to be informed. Wasn't good enough to be a proper wife. If I wasn't good enough for him, then I would rather spend my days alone than with a lying, cheating bastard.

"I can't." I looked at Rosa and tried for a smile, but it fell just like my life. I had grown to love this woman even though we hardly understood each other. "She'll walk soon." My voice shook. "You'll have to childproof."

The only relief in all of this was that Cora was too small to remember me. Only I would. Remember the joy she had brought every day to my life.

CHAPTER THIRTY-FIVE

ANTONIO

I didn't know how long I stood there in that rundown warehouse in Palermo, clenching my phone to my ears, trying frantically to reach my wife.

The only thing I knew was in that time, what felt like hours, I wanted nothing more than to rewind to two weeks ago when I was back home. I had known she was upset, but I hadn't pushed to find out why. I didn't do feelings, and I had difficulty keeping up with hers. Now it was back to bite me with regret.

I had left in my bed a happy wife, and by night, she was distant, visibly putting barriers in between us, getting ready for the cold war she was so fucking good at. Except this time my gut feeling had told me it was much more. I had known her to be mad and throw a fit, as well as be cold and distant. But this time, it felt like she had just given up. Still, I had left. *Cosa Nostra* always came first.

But here I was now, doing the unthinkable, handing the reins over to a shocked Marco and catching the first flight back. Carlo could put a hole in my head for all I cared. I was going home.

Why had Armando not stopped her? He could have easily called in my men and locked her up in our room. No one fucking left the family. She should have known that.

On the flight home, I mulled over my frantic calls to Rosa and Armando, neither of whom seemed to know what the problem was. Only that Rosa had found her crying and she had immediately packed up and left. Just like that. Not even a goodbye to Cora. *Or to me*.

Anger boiled inside me, sending acid to my stomach. It was that easy for her to put an end to our life together.

But I wasn't going to make it easy for her. I would find her wherever she thought she was going to hide. I would find her, and I would drag her back and lock her in my room if that's what it took to keep her there.

The eleven-hour flight with a stopover stretched my patience. But it was not all in vain because I had results at the end of it. Going through the security images had delivered a hint of information. I had watched an exchange between Divya and a woman I didn't recognise. But a quick search had resolved that.

By the time the flight landed, I had a massive headache from clenching my teeth for most of the day.

I needed to find her. Angelo had already gone over to her apartment and found it empty and uninhabited. I didn't know where to look. I called him as I strode to the car.

"He hasn't seen her since the last time," Angelo said.

"I don't care. Keep him with you till I get there."

"Antonio—"

I hung up on him. I didn't care to hear his opinion. I was fucking done sharing. I would put a bullet through Harris's head just because he had once fucked my wife.

I felt like a man split in two, in excruciating pain and lost without my other half.

Hopping onto the car, I made Remo drive me to Roberto's offices, where I was shown into a private room with the bitch with the death wish, as I had requested. Roberto, though, was a nuisance I didn't want to deal with. He inserted himself into the room.

"I am not trusting you alone with her," Roberto muttered.

I ignored my cousin. He shouldn't. I had never thought I would have to hurt a woman, but I was not sure I was beyond it.

I watched the girl on the chair wilting under my stare. Charging over to her, I put myself in her face, put my hands on the armrest, and confined her.

"Who sent you to my wife?" I asked softly, my voice in complete control in comparison to the boiling anger burning inside me like a scalding iron.

She tried to drop her gaze, which was the wrong move as far as I was concerned.

I snatched her face tightly with my hands and turned her towards me. "Who *fucking* sent you to my wife," I yelled in her face. *It better not be my mother.*

"Your mother... sir." Her voice quivered.

"What did you show her?"

"The fi—files for the custody case…"

"What else?" I bellowed, making her jerk away, her eyes wide with fright.

"She told me to tell her… that you are… working… on your di—divorce."

I shot up straight, shocked at even my own mother's tricks.

"What did you get from this deal? Money?"

I watched her squirm in the chair, her short skirt riding up. Realisation dawned.

Leaning forward, I put my mouth on her ear and whispered, "Were you going to get me?" Her reddening skin gave her away even as she shook her head.

I stood up, a laugh bursting out of me. "What was she going to do, wrap you up like the cheap trash you are and leave you at my doorstep?"

Growling, I stepped back and kicked her chair, making the chair and the girl in it skid across the floor and crash against the wall with a loud thud, plaster falling off the wall.

"Antonio." Roberto rushed to hold me back. I shook him off easily, looking at the trembling woman in the corner with disgust.

"What you nor my mother seem to understand is what an amazing woman my wife is. You're fucking shit beneath her shoe."

I NEEDED HER. This feeling in my chest that something was about to detonate would only heal when she was next to me. I was sure of it.

This was why she had left.

Fuck!

I should have told her when the case was dropped. I should have listened to fucking Marco and Angelo. It had been pretty easy. Just the threat of Yuliya's grandparents cutting her off was more than enough for her to sign all her rights away.

But I hadn't wanted to tell her. If I had, she would have rushed off to her studies, dropping Cora and me like a hot sack of potatoes. Instead, I came up with a different plan. What harm would it do if I held on to this bombshell for just a bit longer and we took off to India for a month?

Only I wanted more. I wasn't happy with a month while I wanted a lifetime of waking up next to her, inhaling her smell, listening to her hum her strange songs.

I struggled to sit still in the moving car while my mind raced ahead. I wanted to fucking kill my mother, but I wanted to find my wife first. Then, at least, this pounding in my head would be gone.

The moment Armando opened the door, I felt the loss expand. I didn't recognise the house anymore. It was just full of space. Empty. No playing Divya on the floor. Instead, I found Rosa with an agitated Cora in her arms, screaming like a banshee gone mad.

Just when I thought things couldn't feel worse. Seeing your child in pain is so much more. Briskly, I lifted her into my arms. "*So bambina, so bambina,*" I whispered soothingly, even though my hands trembled, and my body jittered with sickness. I tried to hum one of those strange songs Divya hummed but came up empty. Nothing worked anymore.

I paced the floor, with Cora howling in my arms, while I tried to listen to Armando and Rosa. What bothered me was the timing. She hadn't left straight away. That fucking woman had been on our doorstep before I left for Italy, which explained her apathetic response, but it didn't explain why she waited almost two weeks.

I stopped short at Armando's words.

"Come again?"

"*Signora* Capizzi was worried about the security system, *Signor.*"

"How?" I snapped, setting off Cora into another shrieking parade.

Armando winced. "She was asking if it could be hacked from outside. Who could look at the images..."

"*Cazzo!*"

"But I reassured her, *Signor.* I told her there was no way that could ever happen."

"Fucking hell."

They stared at me in confusion. "Did I say something wrong, *Signor*?"

"No," I sighed, sitting down. My legs felt like two wooden beams left out in the rain, the strength that they once had, fading away slowly. It was my own fucking fault.

The simple lie had slipped out so easily so many

weeks ago. I would have said anything to fuck her, and now I had to face the consequences.

"Why didn't you just stop her?" My voice broke.

The pained expression on Armando's face spoke of more volumes than my words had intended to. "*Mi dispiace—*"

I gruffly waved his words off. "Not your fault."

This wasn't me. Fucking blaming my people for a fault of mine. I was exhausted. The pitiful looks from my staff told me I was no help to anyone when I couldn't think clearly.

Taking Cora, whose cries had finally melted down to hiccupping sniffles, I walked over to our room.

Empty.

Not that I expected anything else. The frame with her parents' picture was missing, of course. If only I had thought to put a GPS tracker in that frame because wherever she went, she took it with her. I noticed her smashed phone, which Armando had recovered from the floor.

It was still working. I was, for once, happy with my wife's lack of interest in new technology because my team could easily crack the passcode to her phone.

I scrolled through her recent phone calls and messages and came across a video in her messages.

The pounding in my head only increased when I watched it. I finally knew why she had picked up so suddenly and left. I had heaped lie upon lie on her, and when she was lying injured on the floor, this video had given her the last kick.

I had lost my wife.

CHAPTER THIRTY-SIX

ANTONIO

I forgot. For a goddamn few minutes, I forgot. Till the absence of a familiar floral scent of lotus and lilies brought with it a sickening reality. With a harsh groan, I let myself drown again in the memories of yesterday, reliving my past and my wretched mistakes.

A strong man learned from his mistakes. It was only an imbecile who repeated them.

I flipped Cora a glance before I pulled myself to the bathroom. I had thrown Divya's rules out the window and put her to sleep next to me. She was missing her as much as I did, through no fault of hers. She lay there now, her thighs and arms spread wide apart, swaddled by pillows and her favourite rabbit. It made me crave my favourite cuddle too.

When I came back to the room, my phone was lighting up.

"Yeah."

Marco's voice filled my ears. "We tracked the number. It's new, under fucking Igor's name."

"Igor as in—"

"Yuliya's fuck buddy," Marco cut me off.

"*Che cazzo* Marco," I roared. Even I shocked myself with my lack of control. Rearing back, I swiftly glanced at a stirring Cora. I waited for a few seconds for her to settle down before stalking away. Thank fuck my girl could sleep through a blast.

"Why is this not a surprise?" A sigh escaped me as I ran my agitated hands through my hair. "Pick him up—"

"Done," Marco said, proving again his worth as my right-hand man. "Got our story out of him after some persuasion."

I didn't bother asking what methods they had used. They might as well cut his dick off, as far as I was concerned.

"He was in an apartment below Divya."

"What?"

"He was the one who gave Divya the suggestion to apply for a job."

"I didn't know this."

"Yeah... Let's face it. You don't think with your head when it comes to her. Well... at least the one on top."

I let the comment fly. He was right, anyway. Had I really not bothered to find out how she came to apply for the job?

"She didn't know, of course," Marco said. "She probably thought he was being helpful. They wanted her to get in and hoped you would fall for her. Yuliya knows your type, it seems..."

"No-brainer. Just the opposite of her," I muttered.

"They wanted a scandal, you fucking the nanny, for the case... but you just skipped a few steps and went straight to a marriage, of course."

"So the film... *merda*..." I whispered. "She wanted her revenge."

"Bingo. Apparently, she wasn't happy at being financially controlled by you through her parents and now grandparents."

"Fuck!" I hissed. I had underestimated a woman scorned.

"I don't know how you stayed married to that woman."

"Patience, lots and lots of it."

"Well, something tells me she wasn't so bad in the sack either," he quipped. Only Marco would make a comment like that and get away with it.

I couldn't be bothered to think about that fucking episode. I should have known she would use the film. The rage boiling inside me plotted the slow death of her. My fists clenched and unclenched slowly as I mulled over the idea of sticking my claws into her and shredding her to pieces. The satisfaction alone would be immeasurable. She had it coming a long way off. If only she weren't Vladislav's daughter. What a crap idea that had been to join the two forces.

"Can we bring her in?" Marco broke the silence, giving word to my conniving thoughts.

Frustration leaked out of me. "You know we can't. I'll call Vladislav."

I was connecting the dots to a scheme to keep me away from what was mine. "What's my mother's involvement in this?"

"Fucking Igor didn't have a clue, and I believe him. Given the state he is in, he wouldn't dare lie. But that doesn't mean Yuliya isn't involved with Maria."

I thought about it. The two couldn't stand each other when I was married to her. Now it felt like a bad joke that those two were teaming up against me. Fucking women in my life. The only good one had to run away to god knows where.

"I need her found, Marco."

"I'll collect Maria—"

"No, I need my wife found, Marco. Get the men on it. I don't care what they have to do. What kind of resources you have to pull. Find her."

Didn't he understand? I needed her to breathe, to find relief from the fucking bulldozer parked on my chest. The only way that would work was if she was back near me, under me, on top of... anywhere. I might even allow the separate room thing if I could just have her near me. Be able to smell her, hear her voice breaking for me...

This is exactly why I didn't do feelings. I didn't like the bitter taste of it, nor the bruise on my fucking lungs. I would gladly take any day without emotion over this heaviness in my chest. Fucking feelings.

I needed to have a calm conversation with Vladislav. I paced the room while my shaking hands dialled his number.

Fucking hands. Letting me down as well.

"Antonio."

"Get her out of my fucking life," I growled.

Merda!

"Calm down, Antonio—"

"Get your daughter out of my fucking dry," I cut him off. "She's messing with my life, my wife."

"What has she done now? I thought the custody..."

"She sent a sex tape to my wife, Vladislav. Now my wife is missing. I can't find her." My voice broke.

Everything was fucking breaking in my body. I needed to find her soon so she could glue me back together.

"I didn't know this," Vladislav said quietly.

"I know, but I need you to deal with this. If you don't, I will, and you won't fucking like it," I hissed.

"Of course," the other man said quietly. "I will take care of this."

"Good."

"She got to you, huh?"

"She didn't get to me. She got to my wife."

"I don't mean Yuliya. I meant your wife. The nanny, yes?"

"What about her?" I asked. What business was it of his if she had been the nanny or not? She was my wife now. That was all that should matter to anyone, including her. Instead, she just picked her bag up and fucking ran.

"Nothing. Nothing." The other man laughed.

"What's so fucking funny now?" I snapped.

"Welcome to the other side, my boy."

"What side is that?"

"Love, of course. It will make you do crazy things."

Love. I scoffed. I just needed her back.

"It's nothing of that sort." I gritted through my teeth.

"Of course." Vladislav chuckled again. I didn't get the joke. "I will take care of things on my side. You just go find her."

Hanging up on a man I respected very much, without a certain future between us, left me irate. I only hoped this damage was not irreversible.

The whiff of her clothes, when I opened the wardrobe to take mine, clenched at my lungs. This. This was why I didn't do feelings. It was too damn restrictive. I buried my face in between her clothes, breathing her scent in and filling something inside.

Why are her clothes here?

I opened door after door and every drawer I could find. Full. I looked around. The only thing missing was the frame of her parents and now that I thought about it, one of Cora, which had stood right next to it. But the one with the both of us at our wedding reception still stood there screaming words I didn't want to hear.

Stalking over to the little jewellery box on the chest of drawers, I opened it to find the garish wedding ring of my mother's lying in it, neatly tucked in with the rest. Of course, she would leave that behind. I had never liked the gaudy thing, and it certainly didn't fit with her fabulous style. I should have...

I didn't think she had taken anything at all. Didn't

she want the rest of the money I promised her? How was she going to survive? The woman was a damn fool.

Sinking down onto the bed with the box, I touched the necklace I had got for her in Jaipur. My rough hands felt strange on it. She had looked gorgeous riding me that night, her caramel skin glowing even more than the jewels on her skin. That hot, humid night, she had moaned out my name, trailing a blaze to my dick as she came. That broken voice of hers could drench my skin anytime.

Where are you?

I should have put a fucking tracker on her. I should have kept her tied to my bed. Then I would know where she was. I wished I knew her well enough to know where she would go, except...

I did!

My head jerked up. I did know her well.

Fucking hell.

Getting up, I raced to get ready, calling out to Rosa to be with Cora. I didn't trust her not to take a dive off the bed when she woke up, and when I brought Divya home, which I would, she would give me hell for that.

Hurling down, I passed the open-plan living space and barged into Armando, coming to find me.

"*Signor* Capizzi, *Signora* Capizzi is at the door..."

The breath left my lungs with a whoosh, and everything else stalled.

"I meant your mother, *Signor*," Armando said, his eyes not meeting mine.

Right. Of course. Why would it be otherwise?

"Send her in. No," I said, stopping Armando's progress to the front door. "I'll open the door."

Storming to the door, I yanked it open to find the woman intent on ruining my life. Was it not enough that she ruined my father's?

"Oh, Antonio, I heard that gold-digging bitch just picked up and left you and the baby."

I didn't yield from the doorway. I wasn't sure if I had enough self-restraint to let her survive this. There was an awful itch on my trigger finger.

She frowned. "Really, Antonio, let me in..."

"No."

She jerked her head back, uncertainty lining her face. "Just because you are angry at her—"

"I am not angry at her, *Maria*. You are in the way of me leaving, so I can bring her back home. So I can make many, many beautiful brown babies with her."

She gasped, disgust ageing her face.

"You are thinking with your dick again—"

"Shut up," I snapped. "How I think is no business of yours. It is definitely no business of yours to send some bitch over here with false information."

"I was only trying to look out for you, *figlio mio.*" She tried to grab hold of my hand, which I swatted away.

"You have never looked out for me or Angelo just like you never did for Papà. He might have had a shitload of patience with you, but this stops here for me."

Any colour she had on her face shrank away to leave an empty palette of nothing with crimson paint. *A fucking joker.*

"Do you think I don't know the shit you pulled on him? Binding him to you?"

I stepped off the doorway, getting in her face, and hissed between my teeth. "This is your final warning. If you do anything, anything at all, to my wife or my daughter, I will put you in a fucking box."

She gasped, her hands flying to her chest. "Antonio, you wouldn't."

"Go ahead and try me." Walking back, I slammed the door in her face. I needed to go get my wife now.

CHAPTER THIRTY-SEVEN

DIVYA

Silence. That's all I heard in here.

When I woke up in the morning, there were no welcoming squeals of Cora, no *Buongiorno* from Rosa. There was no Angelo popping in for breakfast or a friendly hello from Armando. There was especially, especially no Antonio, whispering soft musical words in my ears, giving me kisses of satin with velvet touches.

Silence. The hole where my heart used to be hurt. It hurt too much to breathe. My breath hitched every time I tried.

Silence. My eyes hurt from holding in unshed tears. It hurt from the burden of knowledge of a viewed video. It hurt knowing I could never unsee it.

Silence. I was sick of it. I hated it. But the walls in this place I used to call home refused to repeat the words of my parents, and the floors refused to echo the sound of their footsteps.

Hold me one more time, Mum.

My jaw hurt, and my lips trembled from holding back my tears. But I wouldn't let go.

Silence. I couldn't bear it anymore, following me around like a shadow I couldn't catch.

Silence. I gave up on it. Finding my father's old records, I put them on. Sitting by the window, I watched the cobblestone street. I let the music wash over me, just like the memories and the tears, finally free, flow down my cheeks.

Silence finally broken. There was a strange sound I could hear above the music. Long and loud, a high-pitched cry. I realised it was coming from me.

I was home, finally, but I had never felt so alone.

I CALLED my father's phone and listened to his warm voice, telling me he would call me right back if I left a message.

I did.

Help me, Dad. I don't know. How to live.

He never did call me back.

I WANDERED AIMLESSLY through the house. The comfort I had hoped for was not to be found here. This home, it had been one of laughter, warmth, respect.... The only place I had ever been accepted just as I was. Where I had been loved unconditionally, as only a parent could a child.

Now it was just a house, with a musty smell of desertion. In spite of the weekly cleaning, the soul of the house was disappearing, being sucked out, leaving it cold and damp and empty.

I had to let go. There was an iron fist in my heart that refused to. I had to let go of my parents and move on. Remember them, keep them in my memories, and move on. I knew that.

What a silly idea it had been to come here to look for solutions. How could they, who were gone, help me forget a man they had never met, who I did not understand?

I had to let go of everything and simply start over.

Everything.

I LET DAYS PASS BY. I didn't know when one ended and the other began.

I dreaded going to bed, but I dreaded waking up as well. So I tried to keep awake till my eyes hurt, my head pounded, and my body collapsed into a sleep full of awful dreams. Till I woke up in a sweat-soaked scream and I walked off to the next day.

I WALKED BACK from the beach, my feet swallowing one cobblestone at a time, the chill in the air wrapped around my heart in amity. Even the sun had tired of my depression and left off to another land. Nearing home, I looked up to find an Italian stallion crowding the doorway of my parents' brightly painted blue door.

Lying, cheating, Italian stallion.

He stood there leaning against the door, his cold grey linen suit in sharp contrast to the door. His white shirt breathed free of a tie. Again.

My breath hitched. Like I'd rushed up a lift to the twenty-fifth floor and left my lungs on the ground floor. My body jerked. My movements became unsteady. He wasn't even close, yet he was already working me like a puppet. I lurched to a halt in front of him, pulling my lips into a stubborn straight line. I didn't like that I couldn't get inside without him moving. He was in the way of everything, but the air sizzled between us like a spark in a thunderstorm.

"*Buona sera, mia cara,*" he whispered, his face showing something I didn't understand.

"This's private property. If you're looking for a bed and breakfast, there's one at the end of the street."

"I am looking for my wife."

"Was that when you were fucking your other wife?" I barked.

"Ex-wife," he corrected.

"Whatever." I rummaged in my bag, like I had a tornado behind me, looking for my stupid keys and dropping things in the process. I was going to cry.

Shit!

I was *not* going to cry before this lying, cheating bastard.

"Let me explain, *tesoro*."

His voice was like warm honey. Looking for a crack to slide in. Lucky for me, I was airtight.

"No!"

With relief, I looked up, my stupid keys in hand. "Move!"

He didn't budge from the doorway.

"Please," my voice wobbled.

My tone must have implored him because he took a side step. I opened the door, hurled inside, and slammed it shut on his shocked face.

Ha! He didn't see that coming.

I yelled from inside, "Go away and leave me the fuck alone."

"Let me in, *tesoro*."

I ignored him, just like I did the consistent tapping and ringing of the bell. I didn't care to hang around and hear him speak through the door, so I scurried up to my bedroom. Sitting up in my bed, I rocked myself, humming to calm me down.

Tomorrow I am buying myself one of those noise-cancelling headphones. I want my silence back.

Fifteen minutes on the dot, I gave up. I could still hear his voice, and the bell was on the way to breaking down with all the wear and tear he was giving it.

I strode out to the balcony and looked down.

"Go away," I hissed.

He looked up, something bright in his eyes. "Let me explain."

There was no way I was letting him in. I didn't care what the neighbours thought. "Will you go after that?"

He nodded.

"Promise me."

Something crossed his face, closer to anger than a promise. "I promise."

A memory of him kicking down a different door filtered in. "Fine."

I was mad. Mad to trust him. Still, I didn't want to repair a broken door. So I walked down, opened it, and let him in. The air shifted the moment he walked in. Coldness snuck out and let the warmth in. I didn't like it one bit. I led the way to the second-floor living room.

I skirted away to the far end of the room and left him in the doorway. I imagined a ten-foot pole between us. He looked tired, like he'd survived a train wreck. But he'd still come out beautifully. His hair was rough, and the scruff was thicker, but damn, did he look good enough to eat.

I watched him take in the house. "Nice place."

"Yeah, yeah, it's no designer house," I snapped.

"It doesn't have to be a designer house to be beautiful, m*ia cara*. There is a lot of love here and... family, I can see that."

He made me feel callow. In our time together, and in India, he had never been snobbish, appreciating everything, especially authenticity. I didn't have to be a bitch, I knew that, but I just needed him to leave. He was crowding in on me, sucking the air out of the room.

"Why are you even here? Do I have to sign something for the divorce? I am sure Roberto can send it to me."

"And how can he send it to you if he doesn't know where you are?"

"Fine. Now you know," I snapped. *He didn't even deny the divorce.* "He can send it to me, and *you* can leave."

"I don't want a divorce," he said softly, looking extremely out of place in my parents' cluttered interior.

"Yeah, right."

He ran his hands through his hair, messing it up even more. But all I saw were sparks calling out for me to wrap around.

I'm not going to give in.

"Can I sit down?" He nodded towards the chocolate brown sofa.

I shrugged.

His soft linen and cotton clothes conflicted with the fake leather of the sofa.

"Come sit next to me." He patted the place next to him.

No way am I going to sit next to him.

"*Sì?*"

"Fine," I muttered, sitting down but keeping a space in between. "If you dare touch me, I am tossing you out." I ignored his dark look.

He muttered something in Italian.

"Huh... English please."

He sighed. "You are not going to make this easy for me, are you?"

I stared at him, my mouth firmly closed.

"I don't know where to start... I should have told you about the case. We got Yuliya's grandparents to stop financing her. She lost interest in the case immediately and signed off all her rights to me. I was going to tell you, but I just didn't know how to."

"'Hey, I got full custody,' would have done it," I said bitterly.

He let out a frustrated growl. Leaning over, he caught me by surprise and latched on to my hand, dragging me closer to him.

"Let me go," I yelled in his face.

"I won't do anything else, I promise. Let me just hold you," he rasped.

This close, he looked exhausted. Like he survived the wreck and hadn't slept in a week, just like me.

Stupid illusions.

I let him hold me, though. It was purely because I didn't have the energy to put up a fight.

"The rest was all lies." Now he was pissing me off. I yanked to pull free, but his bruising hold refused to let me go.

"Fuck's sake! My mother sent that fucking woman to you. Divorce was the last thing on my mind."

Was.

"Did your mother also send your ex-wife so you could fuck her?" I asked sweetly.

"No," he admitted.

The punch to my heart bruised me for a lifetime.

He leaned towards me, and I tilted sharply away. But it was only for him to grab my phone from his back pocket. I didn't know if I was relieved or disappointed.

I had to be relieved.

It was strange to see my phone in his rough hands. Opening my messages, he switched on the video again.

This time, I broke free, kicking away to the other side of the sofa. "What is wrong with you? I am not watching that crap again."

"I am so sorry, m*ia cara*, but I need to show you something." He scooted towards me, playing the video.

I snapped my eyes closed. He must have put it on silent because I heard nothing. I didn't think I could live through hearing all the groans and moans that would haunt me till I was buried six feet under.

"Open your eyes," he said tightly.

I squinted them tighter.

"Fine. I'll just have to fuck you then."

My eyes flew open.

"So fucking predictable," he muttered, playing the video. Thankfully, he paused it almost at the very beginning.

"Look at the image. Notice anything?"

"Other than your sexy ex-wife in our room?" I asked sweetly, earning myself a dark look.

"Where are your colourful cushions on the bed?" he asked, pointing towards the bed, which was clearly visible in the video.

I looked closely. "You probably moved them away."

He inhaled deeply. "What about your sofa, then? And before you say I moved that away, do I really look like a man who is going to go to all that effort for a quick fuck?" I gasped at his crudeness. I eyed the video closely. The man had a point.

"Look at the date. It was after you bought the sofa. Can you remember? The video was altered."

I studied him, scepticism overriding my feelings.

"This is an old video, m*ia cara*. I stopped fucking Yuliya long before our divorce went through. This was one of the rare times I did. She fooled me into believing she was going to stop with her addiction, and I fell for it. I knew she liked to video things, and I let her once in a while. But this is an old film. I can show you the original if you want..."

"No." I jumped off the sofa. "It doesn't matter anymore. I don't know why you are here. But this," I pointed to him and me, "won't work anymore."

CHAPTER THIRTY-EIGHT

DIVYA

"Why the fuck not?" If looks could kill, his just stabbed a knife right through me.

"Win-win situation, right?" I said tightly. "You got what you wanted. Full custody and sex with me while it lasted. And I got..." I swallowed the spiked wrecking ball in my throat, blocking the way to my air pipes, "money. I'll give Roberto the details to transfer it."

"That's all you want?"

He stood up, swallowing the distance between us, threatening me with the heat of his body. The ache to reach up and run my hand through his rough scruff was too heavy. So I took a few steps back. "Yes..." I faltered, averting my gaze and looking down at the hardwood flooring. There was a patch with a stain. "I would like to see Cora if you allow it..."

He closed the distance between us again. "Is that really all you want?"

"Yes."

He glanced away, looking out through the windows on the side, his jaw stretched tight, a muscle ticking angrily. He was angry now. I knew that. That was the only emotion he ever showed me.

He caught me with his gaze again. Determination flashed on his face. "Why end it when the sex was good...." He advanced towards me, forcing me to entrap myself between the wall and... him. "It was beyond good." He nuzzled his lips on my shoulder, giving a soft nip where my neck began, just the way I liked it. A shiver of a tingle spread up the back of my neck. "I would even say...it's the best sex I ever had."

Why does he have to make everything so damn difficult?

I closed my eyes, tilting my head away from him. All I saw was a filter of images of him with Yuliya. "I can't," I whispered brokenly.

"I can give you an extra allowance, you can start your studies, you don't even have to look after Cora, just..."

"No!" I yelled, breaking away. "Just *fuck* you, and I get paid."

He latched onto my hand and yanked me back to the wall, pinning me between him. "Just. Stay. With. Me," he hissed.

"No. I want out."

"Why not? Am I not good enough for you?"

Love is insanity. The unbearable urge to hurt him flowed into my body till that was all I could think of.

"No, you're not."

"What is it? Harris still on your mind?" Bitterness laced his voice.

I broke free of him. It was easier for me to hurt him when I didn't have to look at him. "I loved Adam."

He spun me around and jerked me back to pin me in between, his voice ragged. "Only man who should be in your fucking mind is me."

He crushed his mouth to mine, holding my head fixed with his hands. Without an invitation, he barged into my mouth, taking over and sucking the life out of me. He bit my lip, punishing me for the words I had dropped so carelessly.

I tried to fight him off. I did. Honest to god. Even though I didn't thrash my arms, even though I hoisted myself and wrapped my legs around him, I tried. But he had such a way with me. As always, there was no way I could ever win. He put me in a fucking trance, with his hands and mouth and crazy stream of Italian words.

Yanking his mouth away from mine, he tore my blouse open in the middle. "Now you decide to wear a bra?" Frustration ebbed his voice as he tried to remove it without letting me go.

I pushed him away, unhooked my bright yellow lace bra and dropped it onto the floor with my torn beige blouse. His eyes went dark. He grabbed me again, diving onto a nipple, sucking it into his mouth while pinching the other one. Our simultaneous groans echoed in the room.

He wasn't gentle. It was anger that was biting my

nipple, pulling it tightly in between his teeth to let go and repeat. Pain and pleasure washed over me.

Later, I will kick him out. Later, I promised. But now I just wanted him for one final time, to lock this in my memory, to keep it safe with no videos around.

I jerked my hand in between us, unzipping his trousers and grabbing his erection inside his boxers. God, he was so hard.

I shoved the devil on my shoulder, who reminded me he had been hard for Yuliya as well. I whimpered, running my hand up and down his shaft, aching to have him inside me. "Please... please fuck me."

He dropped me. He kicked off his shoes and socks, then sent his trousers and boxers flying. He dropped his jacket and tore his shirt open.

He hauled me over to the sofa, bunching my denim skirt painfully high and tearing my knickers. Dropping to his knees, he lurched me forward, pushing my legs wide and holding them high. A cruel smile fell on his lips when he looked at my core. "Fucking mine," he hissed before diving into me, lapping away like a thirsty dog. He took my nub into his mouth, sucking and rolling his tongue round and round. He let the flat of his tongue roll on my lips, drinking all the wetness that was pooling out. Jerking my hips, I rocked against him, drawing his head closer with my hands in his hair. I whimpered, vaguely aware that the thin Victorian walls were not doing me any favours, and I might have some explaining to do to Mrs Smith next door. Tomorrow. Today, I was going to let him fuck me senseless. Enough for a lifetime.

Shit!

I felt the build-up approaching, climbing up that mountain. My core clenched rapidly, wanting to let go. When he took my clit in his mouth again, I let go, screaming out my pleasure, my body shaking uncontrollably. I wasn't even done riding my orgasm when he stood up and thrust himself in so deep that his balls slapped against me. Pulling me half off the sofa, he pounded into me over and over again. "Mine," he growled, sweat collecting on his forehead. His lust-filled eyes ravished me as he thrust in and out of me. "This, forever," he muttered, almost to himself.

Shit!

His gaze on me was so intense, sending sparks that made my toes curl. I clenched around him, whimpering out my pleasure, and somehow, I was climbing again. He thrust into me harder, faster, hitting my head back and forth against the back of the sofa.

Recipe for a headache. I don't care.

My muscles spasmed again, sending me into another fall. His throat spanned, eyes rolling to the back, and with a growl, he shot his seed inside me.

Our heavy breathing in the silent room sizzled with intangible feelings. His eyes darkened, watching my naked breasts rise and fall.

Shit!

If I wasn't careful, we were going to move seamlessly to round two. I tried to pull my ankle away from his firm grasp. He ignored me and, bending down, scooped me into his arms. Dropping his shirt down on the sofa, he sat down with me on his lap, his thickness inside me, already stirring for the next round.

"Let me go," I whimpered, the unabashedness of a few minutes ago deserting me like sand in a capsule.

"Never." He gathered me closer. "Tell me what you want. Whatever you want, I'll give you, *mia cara*," he said, his tone low.

"This will never work, Antonio. I am never going to be good enough for you." It was better to end this now.

"You are enough. You are so much more." He let out a frustrated growl. "I don't know how to show you. I don't want a life without you. Tell me what to do. Just don't ever leave me again."

Something ignited in my body and sent sparks into every waiting vein. I reared back, shock making my mouth hang open inelegantly.

"What?" A frown foamed in between his eyes. "What did I say wrong?"

"Do you... *love*... me?" I croaked. I didn't even believe the words spilling out of my own mouth. Then why should he?

"Love you?... I don't know... I don't do feelings... What is love? Is it wanting a fucking lifetime of this? Is it wanting to be with you all the time? I want to pick you up and put you in here." He patted his heart. "Is that love?"

I nodded slowly, tears collecting in my eyes.

"Then I fucking love you." He growled with such conviction that even my dream breathed reality. Taking my hand in his, he placed it above his heart. "You are in here. I will do anything to have you with me. You might grow to love me too. Try, at least?"

"I might grow to love you?" I questioned, testing out the ridiculous words falling out of his mouth.

"I know I am not Harris. There isn't a shred of good in me. I have done so many cruel things and will do so much more, but I promise you—"

"Shhh..." I silenced him with my fingers on his lips. "That can never happen..." I rushed on as his face darkened heavier than any thunderstorm I'd ever seen. "How can I love you more than I already do?"

He looked up with a frown.

"I left because I couldn't bear not to be loved back when I loved you so much. I left because I thought I wasn't good enough. I left because it hurt so much to see you with another woman. I left—"

He crashed his mouth to mine, building down from a harsh kiss to end with soft nibbles. "You love me," he rasped in a voice that sent tingles down south.

"And you love me," I mumbled, scooting closer to him and grinding my hips on his erection. He shoved me hurriedly off his lap, his hard-on bouncing out angrily.

"Get dressed."

"What?" I leant back, jiggled out of my skirt, and spread my legs wide. I must not have heard him right.

"I don't want to do this naked," he growled while putting on his trousers sans boxers.

"Do what naked?" I wasn't in the mood to get dressed. I was only in the mood for him. All of him. This Roman fucking god loved me.

He let a frustrated growl at my lack of haste as he dug into his back pocket and knelt in front of me, presenting me with a box. I snapped my legs shut, sitting up on my knees. I knew this box. It was from the jeweller's in Jaipur.

With a pounding in my heart far greater than what I could stand, I watched him open it to reveal the most beautiful and uniquely designed ring. It had five gemstones of different colours. One in the middle and four around.

"I had this designed for you... and it arrived a few days ago. If you don't like it, we can exc—"

"I love it," I silenced him.

"They are all birthstones. Yours is in the middle. I put Cora's, your parents, and mine around... I thought... we could get married again ..." he trailed off nervously, watching my silent tears and shaking head.

"No need.... This is perfect.... All I want is here," I pointed to the ring, "and here," I pointed to my heart, "and here." I pointed to him.

I let him put it on me, his trembling hands showing the emotion behind his actions. He had given me something no one other than my parents ever had. He gave me love and acceptance of who I was.

I drew him in, in between my legs, my gaze blurred, emotion deep, a big, fat lump in my throat. I drew him in for a soft, meaningful kiss. Letting him feel all that I felt for this man and for love.

I drew him in further, showing him that there really was no need to don trousers for this, that, in fact they were a mere hindrance.

EPILOGUE
A YEAR LATER ...

ANTONIO

Goa's bright sun shone on Cora, who was wobbling off on her pudgy legs, hanging onto the maid's hand. Her face hidden under the huge sunhat and wearing shiny pink kiddy sunglasses. I watched the four of them, an odd group. Two huge men wearing black, carrying plastic buckets and spades, the colourfully dressed Indian maid, and the toddler in her pink swimming Pamper with little mermaids printed on it.

It had been a mission to get the four out of the house, especially Cora, who was almost permanently attached to Divya's legs, *mama* a constant sound ebbing off her sweet lips.

Even though she had never told me this, I knew Divya felt insecure knowing she had no claims to her. Something I had put right when she officially adopted Cora last month as her mother.

I had taken my time getting the paperwork done, giving respect to Vladislav after his daughter's death. I didn't know if Yuliya and her lover being found dead of an overdose in their apartment was her father's doing.

I wasn't sure when I had called Vladislav if I had insinuated it. I didn't think I had. But I was sure in my knowledge that the man did nothing without true conviction.

It was unfortunate. The death of the biological mother of my child. But no one would argue that she was ever going to be a mother to her. One day, when she was old enough, we would have that strange talk with our daughter about her heritage. This was something Divya strongly desired, never wanting to diminish Cora's Russian roots. It was also because of her, mainly, that Vladislav, his wife, and their sons were a part of our life and of Cora's. My wife had enough charm in her to wrap even the *Bratva* around her sexy little pinkie.

The only person I knew who didn't fall for her charms was my mother, with whom I neither had contact nor wanted to. She was better off out of our life, a choice she herself had made.

I watched the foursome disappear beyond the coconut trees and walk towards the beach. I cared for the life we lived in Goa in this small terracotta-coloured beach house with blue wooden shutters. Divya wanted to come here three times a year, and I gladly allowed it. Although I equally enjoyed the time we spent in Portsmouth, Milan, or Palermo. I honestly doubted if location mattered to me as long as my wife and child...

children were near me. But I was glad I didn't have to live in Boston anymore.

When they were almost a speck on the beach, I closed the door. They would be back soon enough, even though I had given strict instructions to my men. I wanted to use the time to maximum advantage.

I stalked through the living room and skidded to a stop in the kitchen, letting my eyes fall on the beautiful sight that met me. Barefoot and pregnant in a dress the colour of the sun, she was the creation of all God's talents, exuding hotness.

Moving from the sink to the blender, she carried in her hands a bunch of ripe mangoes, bringing back memories of another time. Her face lifted when her line of sight fell on me.

Her face was a bit rounder than six months ago, but what I didn't like was the frown that fell on it.

"I know that look, and the answer is no."

I sauntered over to her and stood on the opposite side of the island, lazily watching her drop one cut mango after another in the blender, her hands the colour of her dress.

"What look?" I emanated innocence.

"It's the middle of the day, mister."

"Since when has that ever stopped me?"

"Am I just a fuck machine to you?"

"And more," I said, my voice catching on the more.

So much more.

Shaking her head, she grabbed the lid of the blender. Leaning forward, I latched on to her wrist, stopping her from closing off the blender.

"Antonio." She let out a frustrated sigh, "Cora and Sneha..."

"Are at the beach for at least a few hours," I finished for her.

The change was instant. The lid fell out of her hand. Lust rushed into her eyes. I tugged her closer and guided her around the island. I knew her so well. She was horny as hell throughout her pregnancy, and, well, I wasn't complaining.

When she was close enough, I hitched her up onto the marble slab, bunched her dress up, and found her naked underneath. Any blood I had up north rushed down immediately.

"Really, *mia cara*. We have staff running around," I croaked.

"As if that has ever stopped you," she quipped. "Besides, I am so tired of you tearing all my underwear."

"With good reason, *tesoro*, paradise waits for no one," I rasped, running my hands on her thighs and spreading them wide. Rough hands. Soft skin. Sandpaper on velvet. I could smell her cream already. She was always on edge, a single touch was sometimes enough to set her off. I imagined it would be the same with the next pregnancy, even though I knew I had to give her time off to continue her studies.

I stopped the path my hands were on just before her pussy, earning a frustrated growl from her.

"Patience is a virtue you seem to miss these days." Moving my hands away, I slid them to her back and unzipped her dress, sliding it down to her waist and finding, to my disappointment, a bra hiding what I sought.

"Pfff.... Why do you bother with these?" I muttered, unhooking the fragile lace thing and letting it drop on the floor.

"Because they are twice the size now, and I can't have them bouncing around freely."

"Why not? If it was up to me, you wouldn't be wearing a stitch." I caught the skin behind her ear. "Just my dick inside you... All. Through. The. Day."

She bit her lower lip, her pupils enlarged. "You and your words," she murmured huskily, "If only we didn't have staff...."

"Let's get rid of them," I offered.

"As if you would." She laughed.

My heart clenched, a feeling I hadn't known before sneaking up on me. Watching her laugh was beautiful as much as it was frightening because I never wanted her to stop laughing. Always mine. Always happy.

"What?" she whispered.

"You are so beautiful today, so much more than yesterday...." I croaked, a heaviness in me carrying emotion. I ran my rough thumb over her soft cheeks.

"A.k.a fat, ugly, and—"

I shushed her by slamming my palm on her mouth.

"Beautiful. Breathtakingly gorgeous.... Although," I murmured, "something tells me you will outshine this tomorrow."

Letting go of her mouth, I grabbed hold of her face, pinning her with my eyes. "You are me, I am you. We are one. *Ti amo, mia cara*," I whispered.

She lifted her head to the ceiling. "And the man says he's not good with words." She grinned when she picked my expression up. "*Ti amo,* my darling," she whispered back.

I loved the Italian falling off her lips. She had the hottest accent I've ever heard. I sank onto her breast, big, swollen with nipples twice the size because she carried my child inside.

The day I hadn't bothered with a condom was probably the moment I fell in love with her. This woman took me and my child and turned us into a family.

To this day, I kept the business of *Cosa Nostra* apart from her. I couldn't bear the darkness overriding her innocence nor that of my daughters. The goodness in her I never wanted to see being reduced.

"Antonio." Her broken voice, heavy with lust, revived me out of my thoughts. Taking two fingers, I thrust inside her, finding her oozing with thick cream coating my fingers. I had a plan. Involving some mangoes. But the sight of my wife distracted me again. *Next time*, I promised myself, feeling her body shudder in between her breasts. She jerked her hips, keeping pace with my thrusting fingers, her nails digging painfully into my back.

"Arggh.... Don't stop, don't stop.... Arggh." She shook in my arms as she screamed out her release.

I dropped my shorts hurriedly. She wasn't the only one who had been going commando. Even before she came down off her climax, I thrust inside, a groan escaping me. I gave her a shove, pushing her to rest her back on the island. She put her hands behind her and held onto the other side as I pounded inside her, thrusting deep and hard. How did she make me feel like a teenager fucking for the first time? Every time. "Fuck," I hissed, gritting my teeth as I tried to hold on. I swear she took my control and chucked it out the window. Every single time.

I grabbed onto a full breast and squeezed firmly. So fucking sexy, this woman, mine, only mine.

I withdrew and went in and out so deep my balls brushed against her pussy, giving her just the right amount of sensitivity to send her screaming to her second orgasm.

Her muscles clenched around me, dragging me in, spurting batch after batch of cum inside her as I came growling.

I heaved and tried to get my breath under control again. She smiled a private smile only I knew too well. Slowly, painstakingly taking deep breaths, I watched the rise and fall of her heavy breasts, my cock stirring.

There were no secrets between us. It was quite obvious she held the strings to my heart, with a smile driving me to do whatever she wanted.

I might be the *consigliere*. But with her, I was just a man bowing to my woman.

WANT MORE FORCED MARRIAGE, enemies to lovers, Mafia romance? Pre-order Princess of the Mafia today.

AFTERWORD

Shhh...

Do you hear that music in the background?
That's me doing a little jingle because you took a chance
on my writing and read my book.
Thank you for your time and your trust.
As gratitude, I would love to show you how Divya and
Antonio's life continues.
Please **subscribe to my newsletter and receive a
bonus epilogue.**
P.S: Time is the one thing we can never earn back. I will
appreciate yours and promise not to spam you.

If you enjoyed my book nothing would make me happier
than a review. If you could just help one reader find their
way to a new book, that's one story being read.
I would appreciate you leaving a review.

ACKNOWLEDGMENTS

It took me a year from that first inkling of the idea of writing a book to publishing it. If anything, this book picked me up when I was down, set me upright, and brought me joy. It opened the window to let the sunshine in and allow me to enjoy the things I love to do.

But putting those words onto paper wouldn't have been possible without my husband and daughter, who allowed me to be who I am, all the time, even when I was crazy, and even when they didn't fully understand me. On those rare periods that I got crazier than even they could handle, I always had my nephew, my brother from another mother. He listened to me rant and rave with a patience no one else could possibly possess. Thank you.

A nanny is so much more in the world of a child. My own nanny passed away a month short of this book coming out. She was my warm blanket on cold nights. She was my world, and I loved her dearly.

I am blessed to have many people supporting me and pushing me when I need it the most. But through my book, I met strangers who became an integral part of my book. Strangers who helped me out of the kindness of their hearts expecting nothing back in return. Thank you, Sienna Zini and Katie Awdas.

ABOUT THE AUTHOR

Sophia crossed continents for love. She was born and raised in South-East Asia and now lives in Europe with her husband and daughter and has rediscovered her passion for writing.

She has a soft spot for her jealous, possessive heroes who place the heroine at the centre of their world. Her books will always have a happily ever after, just because she cannot stand it otherwise. She would even go as far as to say that she's allergic to sad endings and does her best to avoid them at all costs. That includes reading the last page of a book and checking out the synopsis of a movie before she sits down to enjoy either! Feel free to reach out to Sophia.

Printed in Great Britain
by Amazon

44404237R00219